A LITTLE BIT OF

SPICE

GEORGIA BEERS

A LITTLE BIT OF SPICE

© 2015 BY GEORGIA BEERS

THIS TRADE PAPERBACK ORIGINAL IS PUBLISHED BY BRISK PRESS, BRIELLE
NEW JERSEY, 08730

EDITED BY HEATHER FLOURNOY
COVER DESIGN BY STEFF OBKIRCHNER

FIRST PRINTING: JULY 2015

ISBN-13: 978-098998959-6

By Georgia Beers

Novels

Finding Home
Mine
Fresh Tracks
Too Close to Touch
Thy Neighbor's Wife
Turning the Page
Starting From Scratch
96 Hours
Slices of Life
Snow Globe
Olive Oil and White Bread
Zero Visibility
A Little Bit of Spice

Anthologies

Outsiders

Georgia Beers
www.georgiabeers.com

Acknowledgements

I have never been a beer drinker. I don't really like the taste of beer (which I tried to "acquire" while in college...like every other college student). It just doesn't appeal to me. So I resigned myself to living my life as a Person Who Does Not Like Beer and accepting the looks of pity or the expressions of sadness from those who do (which seems to be most everybody else). It's been fine being slightly outcast among my friends. I have survived.

Cut to me deciding to write *A Little Bit of Spice*, a book about two women...and some craft beer. I realized in order to write it authentically, I was going to have to rethink some things, mainly how I looked at beer. So I began to research. Articles, blogs, websites...I visited many. Mind you, my wife is a beer lover of epic proportions, so this research sent her into a realm of happiness which I rarely see. I explained things I had learned to her. We visited local breweries. We tasted lots of beer. *Lots* of beer. And lo and behold, I actually found a few that I like (bless you, Blue Moon and Shock Top for making beer I enjoy drinking). I knew my work was complete when Bonnie came home one day and said the following words: "Um, why is there more beer for you in the refrigerator than there is for me?" Yes, unlike most of the research I've done in the past, this was fun. And any mistakes or flubs are mine and mine alone.

Thank you to my wife, Bonnie, for taking this (and every) journey of the past twenty-one years with me and for your unending support, brainstorming, enthusiasm and encouragement. I am ridiculously lucky to have you in my corner always, in writing and in life. (And no worries; you can keep your IPAs. I will not be drinking them. Blech.) Heart.

To Steff Obkirchner, cover artist, webmistress, photo-graffer, and friend extraordinaire. You make me look good just because you want to and I can't thank you enough. I hope you know how much you mean to me.

Speaking of making me look good, thanks to my editor, Heather Flournoy. This is a better book because of your sharp eyes, gentle hand, and crazy smart brain. Thank you for your guidance and hard work.

To the Triumvirate, Nicole Little and Melissa Brayden (aka The Comic Relief and The Writing Soul Mate). I like to think I'm a pretty good friend, but there are times when I can also be childish, insecure, and needy. You know that and love me anyway. Thanks for making me laugh and keeping me on track.

To Carrie and Susan at Brisk Press, thank you from the bottom of my heart for taking such good care of me. Every writer should have it so easy when it comes to publishing. You guys rock.

And last but never, ever least, thank you to you, my readers. I'm so happy to be able to share my work with you, and I'm even happier when you tell me how much you enjoyed it. Keep the correspondence coming. It means more than you know.

CHAPTER ONE

"Are you *fucking* kidding me?" Andrea Blake threw up her arms in angry exasperation. "Come on!"

Kendall Foster did her best to ignore the comment, just as she had the three previous, similar comments from Andrea, and held her arm out to the right, indicating which team had the serve: not Andrea's. The gym had become stiflingly hot with three full courts hosting volleyball games, and she felt a bead of sweat trickle uncomfortably down the back of her neck. The heat, combined with the echoing sound as if she was standing in an enormous tin can, did its best to jump-start a raging headache at the base of Kendall's skull.

"Unbelievable." Still Andrea. Still the same snotty, disgusted tone.

Whistle gripped tightly in her teeth and feeling her anger bubbling up from the pit of her stomach, Kendall reluctantly spared a glance at her. Strands of wild auburn curls escaped the ponytail, refusing to be tamed, full lips slightly parted, and deep color on high cheekbones. Kendall's gaze flicked up to meet those flashing green eyes, and that direct contact was all it took; they were off to the races.

"This is ridiculous," Andrea snapped at her, jabbing a finger at her as she took a step in her direction. "You're calling nothing. *Nothing.* That last set was a carry. Do you know what a carry is?" She was on a roll now, and Kendall could feel the heat of embarrassment slowly crawling up her own neck to color her cheeks, adding to the already uncomfortable temperature, making her stomach roll. "Do you? Have you ever even *played* volleyball before? Because you'd never know it."

It was a verbal slap in the face, and Kendall took it as such, as they'd played against each other for five years during school. Her face was flaming hot, and a dozen nasty responses flew through her head even as Andrea's teammates hauled her to a corner in an attempt to cool her down. One of the teammates, who actually seemed to look somewhat apologetic, signaled to Kendall for a time-out. Kendall happily granted it and then let her whistle fall to her chest as she gripped the bar in front of her on the referee stand, and dropped her head between her shoulders. She rocked forward and back, forward and back, willing herself to calm down, willing the anger to dissipate, trying her best not to flash back to high school.

Twelve years later, Andrea Blake didn't look a whole lot different; time had been very kind to her—not that Kendall had noticed or anything. Still in lean, athletic shape, she was a year older than Kendall, but the wild hair, the striking green eyes, the confidently blistering attitude: all the same. True, this was only a recreational league, the players ranging anywhere from early twenties to upwards of fifty, but Andrea obviously took the game just as seriously now as she had in high school and, Kendall imagined, college. She'd been one of the best players in the region back then, and she'd argued calls just as vehemently, though with less cursing and slightly more respect for the officials. Teams had dreaded playing against her. That much confidence in a teenager was intimidating, and Kendall could easily recall the feelings of frustrated incompetence she'd felt the majority of the time she'd played on the opposite side of the net and tried to spike the ball, only to have it stuffed back down in her face by Andrea Blake and her goddamned perfect timing.

Inhaling a steadying breath, Kendall called for an end to the time-out and thanked the universe that the game was almost over. *I do not get paid enough to deal with this shit.* She blew her whistle to signal the serve. Thankfully, the last three points went by quickly and they were finished, the win going to Andrea's team. Of course. Kendall climbed down the ladder, got quick signatures from the team captains, grabbed her stuff, and booked off the court as fast as she could. She had no desire to face the wrath of Andrea Blake and get an earful about what a terrible ref she was. It was exactly the way she'd responded to being beaten by Andrea and her team in high school: run off the court and into the locker room as quickly as possible. Avoid any and all contact. Don't let her see the frustrated wetness in your eyes. This occurred to her as she was hurrying toward the door, and it annoyed her. She was not seventeen any more. She was thirty. A grown woman. One who had no reason to be the least bit intimidated by somebody like Andrea Blake. She was being ridiculous.

Get a grip, Kendall. Stop being a baby and pull it together. You're not a kid anymore.

She slowed her pace, stopped at the half-bleachers that were pulled out on rec nights, and pointedly set her stuff down. She bent to retrieve her gloves from her bag when she heard the familiar voice.

"You should report that bitch. They can ban her from the league, you know." Liz Sheridan plopped herself down next to Kendall's bag and glared across the gym in Andrea's general direction as she ran a hand through her short dark hair. "We could hear her bitching from two courts over."

3

"Nothing new there," Kendall said with a shrug.

"Yeah, some things never change." Liz looked up at Kendall. "Still. You don't have to take that shit, you know. Tell John."

Kendall made a face and shook her head. "Nah. It's okay. I'm a big girl." There was no way she was going to the head of the league to whine about one player getting a little...nasty. The last thing she wanted was a reputation as a tattletale.

"Well, if that's the case and you don't mind, how about *I* pay you thirty bucks and get to verbally abuse you for an hour or so? Same diff, no?"

Kendall couldn't hide her grin. "Okay, okay. I get your point. Still..." She let the sentence hang, hoping it was clear to her best friend that this would go no further. Liz let a beat go by, then blew out a breath and slapped her hands against her thighs as she stood.

"Fine. At least have a beer with us."

"That, I can do." Kendall gathered her things, stuffed her gloves back into her bag, and followed Liz through the gym's door and into the other half of the building.

Spikes was a unique establishment in town. Owned by two young businessmen, it was part gym, part sand courts, part bar and grill, and hosted volleyball leagues all year round. Women's leagues, co-ed leagues, men's leagues all gathered at different times on different days. Some played on the regular gym courts. Others preferred the sand courts, which also boasted two-on-two tournaments on weekends. Teams of all shapes, sizes, and skill levels played at Spikes. Everybody complained about the exorbitant league fees, but nobody left because there were very few alternatives for playing volleyball in the dead of winter in upstate New York. And more often than not, a game ended with a beer and wings in the bar and grill section of the enormous warehouse-like building, so there was that.

The rest of Liz's team was already at the bar, passing around a pitcher of some light beer Kendall wouldn't serve to her worst enemy. Catching the eye of Rhonda, the bartender, she said, "Could I get the Treehouse Lager, please?" Rhonda gave her a wink, grabbed a glass, and pulled the tap.

"Kendall's going all beer snob on us again," one of the girls said with a chuckle.

"Maybe we should listen to her," said another, Gina, as she raised a glass filled with what looked a lot like the same beer Kendall now had. "To real beer," she said.

"I'll drink to that," Kendall replied, and stretched across the bar to touch glasses with Gina. Over her shoulder and several feet down the bar, Kendall saw Andrea Blake, whose gaze locked with hers for what felt like several long seconds before she blinked slowly and Kendall could have sworn one corner of her mouth quirked up in an almost-smile. But she shifted her attention back to the teammate speaking to her and Kendall was left with nothing but a weird flutter in the pit of her stomach.

"Hey." Gina was suddenly next to her, startling Kendall.

"Hey yourself," she replied.

Gina held up her beer. "This is really good stuff."

"Yeah?" Kendall smiled proudly. "Glad you like it." She gestured toward the bartender with her chin. "Rhonda's been great about letting me put some of our beers in here. This one's fairly new, but has been selling well."

Gina sidled up closer, resting her forearms on the bar so that from elbow to shoulder, she was touching Kendall. She was tall with dark blond hair cut in a shaggy style that wasn't exactly a mullet, but probably used to be. And probably not that long ago.

5

Kendall noticed how long her fingers were as they held her beer. "So, is that what you do? Sell the beer?" Her voice had dropped slightly in volume, and her brown eyes were focused on Kendall's face.

"Yes, to a certain extent. I'm also marketing, but I do have contact with a lot of the bars, stores, and distributors." She shifted just enough to subtly move her arm so they weren't touching. Gina was nice enough, but she didn't need to be so close. "In fact, Hagan's is looking to add some more local brew to their inventory." Hagan's was the largest grocery store in upstate New York, most of the Northeast really, and was slowly spreading west and south. They had a sterling reputation, and if Kendall could get her beer on the shelves at Hagan's, the sales bump would be significant. "There's a big meeting tomorrow with their head of beer distribution."

"That's got to be exciting."

"It is. It really, really is." Kendall couldn't keep the proud smile off her face.

"And your family owns the brewery."

Kendall nodded. "Yup. My brothers and I."

"What a cool job."

"It is." Kendall knew she'd repeated herself, but Gina leaned in just enough to once again press her arm against Kendall's.

"Maybe you can take me on a tour some time." The tone of her voice conveyed exactly what kind of a tour she meant, and it had little to do with beer.

Kendall cleared her throat. "Well, we have regular tours set up every weekend and also on Wednesdays. My brother Adam is a wealth of information." When she turned to look in the opposite direction of Gina's too-close face, Liz was looking at her in amusement from three people down. Kendall widened her eyes in the hopes of telegraphing the need for rescue.

Liz left her hanging for nearly another five minutes before finally calling, "Hey, Kendall. Come here. I've got a beer question."

Thank God. Kendall tossed an apologetic smile to Gina, then slid off her barstool and tried not to run to Liz.

"Took your sweet time," she muttered in Liz's ear.

"Gina's nice. You should give her a chance."

"Not my type."

Liz shook her head. "Yeah, nobody's your type, apparently."

Kendall feigned offense. "You wound me."

Liz bumped her shoulder. "Shut up."

After skillfully avoiding yet another discussion about her non-existent love life, the evening went better. Gina hung around the circle Kendall was in, but seemed to have gotten the hint and backed off. Infuriatingly, Kendall kept finding her gaze pulled in the direction of Andrea Blake. Two more times, they made eye contact, and the last time, Kendall made sure to be the first to break it. She was irritated with herself for continuing to let her eyes roam in that direction. Andrea was not somebody she cared to give the time of day to.

Looking at her, on the other hand...

⁓

The next morning, Kendall steered her SUV into the parking lot of Hagan's corporate buildings, pulling in between a tiny Honda Civic and an enormous Lincoln Navigator. The thought of filling the behemoth's gas tank made her shudder, and she figured her cost of fuel probably fell neatly right in between the two vehicles just as evenly as she parked.

She gave her blond hair one last glance in the rearview mirror, tucked a little bit behind an ear. She normally wore it off her face in some way—ponytail, French braid, baseball hat—because it was more practical. But when she was making a business call of any kind, she liked to soften up. Hair down. Nicer clothes and shoes. A little makeup. Sexist as it was, feminine softness went a long way in selling product. Especially beer. And Kendall Foster was no dummy; she used that fact to her advantage whenever she could.

The biting February air hit her like a slap when she stepped out of her car, and seemed to reach right in and pull the air from her lungs. Shouldering her bag, she hurried across the lot, entering the front doors with a gust of wind so strong, it was as if she had simply been blown through the entrance. She stomped the excess snow off her dress boots and smiled at the sixtyish receptionist sitting behind a horseshoe-shaped front desk. Large, potted ferns gave the lobby a bit of a tropical feel and the leather couches for waiting actually looked almost inviting.

"Hi there. Kendall Foster from Old Red Barn Brewcrafters. I'm here for the distributor meeting."

The woman nodded and turned a binder around so Kendall could read it. "Just fill out this visitors' log, and I'll have somebody escort you."

Kendall was writing her name when the doors opened again and hit her with an icy blast that sent a quick shiver through her body. She looked over her shoulder to see Matt Stark and Jeff O'Hanlon—competitors and friends—stomping their feet on the black industrial mat stretched out from the doorway.

"Kenny!" Matt knew Kendall hated the nickname, and therefore used it every chance he got. He was as bad as her brothers that way. "Nice to see you, sweetheart." He was a very

8

large man with hands the size of small hams and a thick, dark beard and moustache that framed surprisingly red lips. He gave her a one-armed hug as he told the receptionist his name.

"Hi, Matty," Kendall responded, returning the hug. Then she opened her arms to Jeff, who hugged her so tightly he lifted her off the ground, his usual M.O. He had sandy colored hair that was always just a bit too long, and he habitually tossed his head to the right to shake it out of his constantly smiling blue eyes. He smelled like pine trees and rosemary, and Kendall inhaled while her nose was pressed against the shoulder of his coat. "It's good to see you guys," she said and meant it. "I feel like it's been ages."

"It was before the holidays," Matt said. "McBannon's retirement party?" He referred to a colleague of theirs from another brewery who'd finally decided to retire at the age of eighty-three.

Kendall nodded. "I think you're right. When was that? October? Wow."

Their conversation was interrupted by a tall man in a suit jacket, a walkie-talkie attached to his belt. The receptionist pointed to him. "You can follow Bert. He'll lead you to the conference room." Bert turned and began walking back the way he came.

"People still use walkie-talkies?" Matt asked in a stage whisper.

Jeff snorted a laugh and Kendall smacked his arm. She adored these guys.

The conference room was sizable and already held representatives from six other breweries that Kendall recognized, as well as four she didn't. A long table ran the length of the space and two large platters of donuts and bagels were there for the taking, along with a large coffee urn and another labeled Hot

Water. Matt and Jeff wasted no time on small talk and went right for the pastries, making Kendall shake her head with a grin. It was like hanging out with her big brothers all over again.

The room was functionally plain, but pleasant. Hagan's was a multi-million dollar company, but they didn't get that way by spending money on frivolous things. The chairs surrounding the table looked practical and comfortable. A small wooden podium stood angled in a corner, the green Hagan's logo painted on the front. Three large windows looked out onto the gray of the morning, and the slight buzz of the overhead fluorescent lights took Kendall back to high school.

After helping herself to a plain donut and filling a small cardboard cup with coffee and creamer, she made small talk with a couple of the reps she knew and watched as four more people arrived before the round, industrial wall clock read ten o'clock sharp. A small man Kendall recognized as Brady Kerner stepped quickly into the room. He was part of the Hagan's marketing department, and Kendall always got the impression he was moving one speed faster than everybody else. His steps were quick. His speech was clipped. He wasted no breath or movement, and today was no exception. He stepped up to the podium and introduced himself.

"As you know, Hagan's has been slowly adding craft brewers to the stock in our stores across the Northeast. Little by little, we're increasing our inventory from store to store. Our last influx of new breweries was six months ago, and we believe we're ready to add more. To talk to you about the details, I introduce you to the person who, along with her staff, will be making the final decisions, our new head of beer distribution, Andrea Blake."

Kendall thought she'd heard wrong until she saw all that curly auburn hair and Andrea Blake walked into the room.

"Oh, you have *got* to be kidding me," Kendall breathed out, closing her eyes against the onslaught of her bad luck. It actually crossed her mind to just stand up and leave, since she probably wouldn't have a prayer of getting Old Red Barn's beers into Hagan's—ever—if this was the gatekeeper, but politeness won out, and she kept her butt in her seat.

Andrea was stunning. There was no denying that, no matter how frustratingly angry Kendall was at the situation. Her navy blue pantsuit seemed expertly tailored to fit her lean body, the pants hugging the slight roundness of her hips. The short, matching jacket was open, a white blouse underneath showing just enough cleavage to warrant a second glance, but not enough to make eyes bug out in shock. The heels made her seem more intimidating and in command than her five-foot-nine-inch frame normally did. Her green eyes were already the most striking feature on her face, but highlighted with subtle eyeliner and dark mascara, they were like jewels, hypnotizing anybody who looked in them.

Looking around the room, Kendall realized the effect Andrea instantly had on the men. They were riveted.

"Good morning, everybody," Andrea said, and Kendall could have sworn she'd heard the tiniest of tremors in the low, sultry voice. "I'm so glad you could all make it." She reiterated the things Brady had said about Hagan's expanding their selection of local brews, and then continued about some other details Kendall zoned out on. The combination of irritation and arousal she was dealing with pissed her off, and she blew out an annoyed breath just as Matt posed a question out loud, much to the surprise of Ms. Blake, but not to anybody else.

"What's your favorite beer?" Chuckles went around the room. Anybody who knew Matt, and most of those in attendance did, knew he liked to make formal gatherings casual, lighten the mood. He was a favorite at trade shows and beer festivals for his jovial personality and laid-back attitude. Matt was the sweet, fun frat brother who never grew up. He was often infuriatingly immature, but never mean-spirited and always fun.

Kendall glanced from Matt's face, wide with a playful smile, to Andrea's, which was the antithesis of Matt's. All the color had drained from her skin and she looked like the proverbial deer caught in the headlights. She glanced down at the podium, then back up at Matt. "Um...well..."

"It's okay," he assured her with a casual wave. "You don't have to name a brand. That would be tipping your hand. But how about a style? What style do you like best?"

Andrea blinked at him, wet her lips, and glanced down at the podium again. Her fingers gripped the sides tightly. Too tightly.

Kendall could see her throat move with a swallow. She glanced from Andrea back to Matt, and she suddenly had a flash of the volleyball game the night before. Curling her lip a little, feeling maybe Karma had entered the room, she muttered under her breath, "Has she ever even *had* a beer?"

Before she realized she'd said it loud enough to be heard, Jeff repeated the question.

To the entire room.

"Have you ever even *had* a beer, Ms. Blake? Do you like beer?"

Kendall's head snapped up as a rumble went through the room, chuckles mixed with surprised gasps mixed with sounds of annoyance. When Kendall looked back at Andrea, those green eyes were boring into her like lasers. Kendall felt her face heat up and she dropped her gaze to her lap.

12

Brady Kerner, ever the consummate professional, must have acknowledged Andrea was losing control of the meeting because he jumped up to the podium, smoothly moving her aside, calmed everybody down, and detailed the procedure Hagan's used for meeting with potential vendors. The brewers continued to grumble a little bit, but for the most part, settled down. Brady reminded everybody to make sure he had their contact info, and said Andrea would be in touch via e-mail to set up appointments with each brewery. Then he thanked everybody for their time, grasped Andrea by the elbow, and steered her out of the room before any more damage could be done.

Only then did Kendall fully release her breath. Lifting her eyes to Jeff, she snapped, "Why did you do that?"

"Do what?" he asked with a detectable flinch.

"Why did you embarrass her like that?"

Jeff shrugged. "I just asked a question. The same question *you* asked, let me point out."

"But not so *she* could hear it. You took care of that."

"I did. You're welcome." He turned and began to chat with Matt, and Kendall was baffled—not for the first time—at how easily men could just be done with something. Kendall was mortified that Andrea had been made a fool of. Not because she liked Andrea, but because she knew how it felt. Again, she thought about the previous night, how small and worthless Andrea had made her feel, in front of an entire court full of players. And if she was being honest, she had to admit to the tiny part of her the felt a little bit of satisfaction over Andrea getting a taste of her own medicine just now. At the same time, she felt sick that she'd caused somebody else to feel the way she had last night. She was not the kind of person who believed in an eye for an eye and she knew immediately she had to find a way to fix this.

But how?

CHAPTER TWO

The day had gone from bad to worse. Andrea looked at the clock on the wall in her office. 2:45. Too early to go home, though she wanted nothing more. Home, back to bed, start the day fresh from the beginning again. Or maybe not. Maybe she should just skip this day altogether, because the truth was, nothing would change if she started over. She would still be as uninformed as she was the first time she stood in front of that crowd. There was no way around it.

It wasn't her fault.

That was the God's honest truth, not that anybody would care. It was the way they did things at Hagan's. The company was huge, dizzyingly successful, and beloved. If you wanted to manage your own store at some point, which Andrea did, you had to make your way through each of the departments. It didn't matter if you knew anything about, say, pasta when they put you in charge of the Italian foods department. Or cakes and donuts when you were to run the bakery department. Or shrimp, salmon, and tilapia when you headed up the seafood department. You weren't there for the products so much as you were there for the people. Andrea's new job was to take care of the Hagan's staff that made up the beer distribution department, not to be the walking Wikipedia entry for all things that had to do with beer. Today was her very first day. Her very. First. Day. And that goddamned Brady Kerner had thrown her to the wolves.

"Have you ever even had a beer?" Andrea sneered in a whiny voice, doing her best to mimic the blond hippy asshole who'd asked the question that had ripped control of the meeting right out of her hands with frightening ease.

"How could he have known?" she asked quietly to the empty office. A growl emanated from the back of her throat. "Because I panicked. That's how. I couldn't just name a beer, for Christ's sake? Pretend?" She shook her head and then dropped it into her hands and stayed that way for a long moment.

A vision of piercing blue eyes popped into her brain, and she jerked her head up. Kendall Foster had started it, Andrea was sure. What other reason would she have had to look so ridiculously guilty when Andrea had regarded her?

A short, sarcastic laugh burst from her lips then. Payback. That's what it was. Payback for last night. Andrea flashed back, remembered the things she'd shouted at Kendall as she stood up in the official's box calling absolutely nothing. She deserved to get chewed out. She knew the rules; she'd been a decent player in school. The looseness of her refereeing made Andrea's teeth grind, and speaking her mind had never been a problem.

She pushed off her desk so she flopped backward into her chair. "I embarrass her at a recreational activity, so she embarrasses me at work?" she asked aloud. "Not cool. Not cool at all." She turned her head and stared out the window at the swirling snow, guessing the wind from this morning had yet to die down.

Andrea hated February in upstate New York. Thank God it was the shortest month because it made her cranky and irritable. Too far from Christmas to allow you to hold onto residual holiday cheer, yet also too far from spring, when the cold would release its grip, the snow would finally melt, and Andrea would

16

be warm again. She'd grown up here; you'd think she'd be used to the winters. But February made her prickly.

A knock on her doorjamb interrupted her thoughts, and she looked up to see Brady Kerner standing there. Wanting nothing more than to jump across the desk and throttle him, she instead pasted on a very phony smile and stared at him.

He knew. She could tell by the expression on his face and his nervous stance that he knew he should have pushed this morning's meeting out a week or two, that he'd tossed her headfirst into the deep end and expected her to swim. She kept her eyes riveted on him, something she'd learned over the years made a person squirm like a trapped mouse. Brady Kerner was no exception.

Finally, she spoke. "Hey, thanks for this morning, Brady. That was awesome." She held out two thumbs-up, the phony smile still in place.

He had the good sense to at least look a bit ashamed. "Yeah, I'm sorry about that."

"I told you I needed more time. I looked like a fool."

"In my defense, Andrea, the meeting was set by Greg a long time ago." He said it with a bit of an edge. "Rescheduling nearly twenty people would have been impossible. As it is, it took me nearly a month to round them all up. Beer people are all over the damn place."

Andrea sighed. "I know that." She wanted to say more, wanted to impress upon him that it wasn't up to Hagan's to meet their schedule. If the beer people, as he called them, wanted in, they'd find a way to make the meeting, whenever it was. And now, instead of having the upper hand, she was the one with ground to make up.

17

As if reading her thoughts, he added, "You're still the one in control here. You make the cuts. Doesn't matter what they think of you. You're the decision maker." With a nod, he turned and left.

He was right. Andrea knew it. This wasn't her first rodeo with Hagan's. She'd been working for the store since she was sixteen years old. She'd worked the cash register all through high school, and kept it up on a very part-time basis during college whenever she was home for holidays or weekends. Once her business degree was in her hot little hands, she went to HR and applied for a management position. She'd never looked back.

Beer distribution wasn't her first new department. She'd known virtually nothing about dairy when she'd started there. Same thing with the deli. But she read like crazy, took courses, picked the brains of her department staffs until she was knowledgeable in the field and comfortable enough with that knowledge to talk to vendors and customers alike. But in most other cases, she'd had time before she started. She had a couple weeks, sometimes a month, to read up and get herself educated on what she was about to enter. That hadn't happened this time because her predecessor in beer had taken a new job with a competitor at the very last possible minute. Andrea was being groomed to replace him anyway, but that schedule was stepped up by nearly two months. She went in totally blind.

As evidenced by this morning's meeting.

The worst part was almost laughable: Andrea didn't really care for beer. Therefore, she rarely drank it. Ergo, she knew very little about it. Had she had time to do some research before this morning's meeting, she'd have been able to fake her way through and nobody would have had any idea.

Kendall Foster had taken care of that.

And now the beer people were probably laughing it up at her expense, downing their bitter concoctions and doing impressions of her stuttering.

There really was only one way to get ahead of this.

She adjusted herself in her seat, turned to her computer, and Googled "craft beer for beginners." Then she blinked in shock at the enormity of the list that popped up. She scrolled, clicked to the next page, scrolled some more. There were articles and blogs and websites and chat rooms. With her elbows on the arms of her chair, she steepled her fingers and rested her mouth on the tips, willing herself not to be overwhelmed. She was a highly intelligent woman. She could work through this. She was just about to click on the blog of a microbrewer when her phone rang. Without looking, she snatched it up.

"Andrea Blake."

"Um, hi, Ms. Blake. This is Kendall Foster."

Andrea blinked, wondering if she'd heard correctly.

"From volleyball?" Kendall went on, obviously concerned Andrea didn't know who she was. "And this morning?" she added, her voice going smaller.

"Ms. Foster." Andrea purposely kept her voice flat, disinterested. "What can I do for you?"

"Well." Kendall seemed to search for words. "I needed to... I wanted to apologize for this morning. I had no idea Jeff would ask that question out loud. It hadn't been meant to be asked out loud. It sort of popped into my head and I said it and he heard me and..." Her voice trailed off and Andrea waited her out. "Anyway. I just wanted to say I'm sorry."

Intentionally letting the silence hang, Andrea finally said, "And you figured if you apologized, there'd be a better chance of you getting your beer into my store." It wasn't Kendall's beer and it wasn't Andrea's store, and they both knew that, but neither cared. "This is damage control."

Kendall was obviously smart enough not to deny it. "I guess it is a little bit. Yes."

She had a nice voice. Andrea surprised herself with that thought. It was a gentle voice. Feminine, yet with a firmness to it. She may be coming to Andrea now with her tail tucked between her legs, but Andrea would bet Kendall Foster was no pushover. Scanning her computer monitor as she let more silence hang, a thought suddenly struck Andrea, and she couldn't keep the grin off her face. "Tell you what," she said. "How about you make it up to me?"

Several beats went by, and Andrea imagined Kendall was trying to figure out her angle. Finally, she said slowly, "What do you mean?"

"I will completely forget this morning ever happened if you do one thing for me."

"Okay…" Kendall drew the word out, obviously waiting for the other shoe to drop.

"Teach me." *Boom*, Andrea thought with glee.

"Teach you? Teach you what?"

"Beer. Teach me all about beer. That way, I won't be embarrassed again, and I promise to hold no grudges when making my decisions on which vendors to welcome into Hagan's."

"So…you're blackmailing me?" There seemed to be a small tinge of amusement in Kendall's voice, but Andrea couldn't be sure.

"Of course not. You did something detrimental to your business and this is how you can fix it. Simple." It was hard not to let any laughter leak out, but Andrea managed to keep her lips pressed tightly closed. Any minute now, Kendall would hang up in anger and Andrea would feel better.

"Teach you." Kendall was quiet for a moment, and Andrea was tense with anticipation, waiting anxiously for the insulted click of the line going dead, when Kendall responded, "Okay. Deal."

"What?" It came out as a choked sound, but Andrea covered it with a cough.

"I said okay. I'll teach you. When do you want to start?"

Andrea dropped her head into her palm. It was icing on the cake of her horrible day to have even a little joke backfire on her. How could she possibly get out of this now without looking like even more of a jackass than she had this morning? With a quiet sigh, she lifted her head and glanced at the monitor in front of her. The bottom of the screen told her there were six hundred forty seven pages of things to choose from regarding "craft beer for beginners," and all of a sudden, she felt completely, utterly overwhelmed.

"How about tomorrow?" The words were out before she even realized she was about to say them. *Jesus Christ. What am I doing?*

"All right. I can come there if you'd like." Kendall's voice was crisp now. Businesslike, as if she'd totally shifted gears. "We can talk about what you know, what you need to know, that kind of thing. Then I'll be able to figure out where to start, how best to proceed." Andrea got the impression Kendall had taught this exact thing before or had at least thought about it, and she found herself nodding.

"Okay. That sounds good." She clicked off the internet and back to her schedule. "I'm open at ten tomorrow morning. That work?"

"I can do ten. I'll see you then. Bye."

Andrea pulled the receiver from her ear and looked at it, finding it both odd and interesting that Kendall had hung up so quickly. She replaced the handset, then reached for her keyboard and typed "Kendall Foster" into the ten o'clock spot on her calendar for tomorrow. It took until that very moment, the actual typing of the letters, for Andrea to close her eyes and shake her head in self-disgust. Tomorrow, she had to spend time with a woman who hated her, a woman of whom Andrea herself was no fan. This was not going to be fun and it was her own damn fault.

Still shaking her head, she muttered a curse, reached into her bag in the bottom drawer of her desk, and pulled out a Snickers bar. She was still scowling when she took the first bite.

❧

Kendall stood in her tiny office and stared at the cell phone in her hand. She narrowed her eyes at it, thinking maybe if she glared hard enough, the phone call she'd just had would be magically erased and she could go about her day without a care. After several beats, she realized this was not about to happen, so she slid the phone into the back pocket of her jeans and stepped into the hall, only to collide with her brother.

"Whoa," he blurted in surprise as he grabbed her upper arms to keep her from toppling. "Gotta look both ways before you enter the flow of traffic, Ken-Doll. Haven't you learned that by now?" Kendall nodded absently, and Adam ducked his head so he could catch her eye. "Hey. What's up? You okay?"

She looked at eyes exactly the same blue as her own. Adam was taller and older, but they looked so much alike people often mistook them for twins. His sandy hair needed a trim and his face was rough with two days of stubble, but women swooned over him. "Yeah. I'm fine. I just…I did something stupid." She spilled the entire story to him, starting with the volleyball game and ending with the phone call and the subsequent meeting the next morning. "How the hell do I get out of that?"

"Get out of it?" Adam's eyes went wide. "Why would you want to get out of it? This is great. It'll be good for business. Do you know how much our profits will increase if we can get into Hagan's? They've got, what? Thirty stores?"

Kendall scratched her eyebrow. "Something like that."

"This is good. This is *really* good." She could see the wheels turning in Adam's head already, and part of her knew he was right. Still, she felt uneasy.

"You realize she's blackmailing me, right?"

"I guess that's technically true. But so what? It's *Hagan's*."

"Who's to say she won't deny us a spot anyway, no matter what I teach her?"

Adam simply shrugged and gave her a dimpled grin. "Have some faith, little sister of mine. This could turn out to be the best thing that ever happened to you. To us." With that, he pinched her cheek like he used to do when they were kids specifically to annoy her, and went on his way, down the hall away from the offices and into the heart of Old Red Barn where all the tanks and vats were housed. She stood in the same spot as the door swung shut behind him. Then she turned and went back into her office.

Kendall loved her little space. It really was the size of a large storage room, but it was hers and she was proud of it. She'd worked hard to make herself relevant, to show her big brothers that she was ready to take on the marketing and sales side of the business. She'd come back from four years of college with a business degree and a boatload of ideas for marketing what was then a tiny, backyard brewery. Old Red Barn's size and profit had quadrupled since that year, and it was in large part due to

Kendall's hard work and tireless efforts to make the brand known all around upstate New York. Her brothers had hired her full time two years ago and had made her a partner six months later.

She flopped into her expensive desk chair: her one big splurge when she furnished her office. She had back issues that stemmed from a slipped disk during recreational volleyball the summer after she graduated high school. She'd recovered from it with minimal effort, but it still acted up if she overdid things. It's the reason she gave up playing volleyball and refereed instead. And when furnishing her office, she promised herself if she was going to be spending an inordinate amount of time in one chair, it was going to be a nice, comfortable one.

Kendall spun her chair slowly a few times, her head resting against the back of it, eyes glued to the ceiling. Tomorrow, she had to teach Andrea Blake all about beer.

Andrea Blake.

Kendall's brain conveniently tossed her an image of Andrea this morning, that smart suit, all that hair, the flashing eyes. Kendall swallowed hard, closed her eyes, wet her lips. But then the image changed; Andrea's expression changed. It went from confident and in control to embarrassed, ashamed. Kendall's eyes popped open.

I have to do this, she thought. *That meeting mess was my fault. I owe this to her.* She pushed herself out of her chair and woke up her computer. A few clicks later, the printer was whirring and she was pretty sure the direction she would take things tomorrow. She wasn't just going to teach Andrea. She was going to *educate* her.

That night was family dinner night—which was really almost every night at the Foster farm. Adam and their older brother, Rick, each had their own houses, but spent so much time at the brewery that they ate in their mother's dining room more often than in their own homes. Kendall had an apartment above one of the old barns that now served as a garage. It was a good two hundred yards from the main house and three hundred from the brewery, so she felt like she had her own space even though the property was all one.

"Ken-Doll has a private meeting with the head of beer distribution at Hagan's tomorrow," Adam said to the table.

"Adam," Kendall whined and threw a roll at him.

"Hey," Cathy Foster scolded her two youngest. "Enough of that. You'd think you two were eleven and thirteen instead of in your thirties."

"What do you mean a private meeting?" Rick asked.

"Oh, right. You weren't there when she told me." Adam cleared his throat. "So, Ken-Doll was officiating volleyball last night and one of the players got mouthy with her."

Kendall shoved a forkful of peas into her mouth and nodded.

"Like, really mouthy. Like, nasty. So she gets past it, whatever. This morning, she goes to the big Hagan's meeting for all the local brewers and who is presented as the brand new head of beer distribution? The mouthy volleyball player."

"Andrea Blake," Kendall supplied, holding a hand in front of her mouth as she spoke. "Remember her from school, Mom?"

Cathy narrowed her eyes. They popped open with a memory. "Was she the one with all that auburn hair?"

Kendall nodded just as Adam threw up his hands in recognition. "Oh, *Andrea Blake*," he said, as if her name was suddenly different than earlier. "I remember her. She was *smokin'* hot."

Kendall rolled her eyes.

"She was a good player, wasn't she?" Cathy asked.

Kendall nodded again. "She was. Very good. I could never spike against her. Drove me crazy. I hated her."

"Well, I wouldn't lead with that tomorrow," Rick commented with a wink.

Kendall laughed. "I think that ship has sailed, big brother of mine. She's basically blackmailing me." She told Rick and her parents how tomorrow's meeting had come about, ending with, "I have no idea what will happen after I teach her what she needs to know, but…" She shrugged. "I just feel like I have to. It's my fault she was ridiculed this morning. I really want to fix that."

"Explain something to me." Jim Foster spoke for the first time since they'd all sat down. Everybody turned to him as he pointed at Kendall with his fork. "How the hell does somebody who doesn't know a thing about beer get put in charge of beer distribution?"

Kendall shook her head. "I'm not sure. Though Liz's brother has worked at Hagan's for years and apparently, that's how they do things. They move you from department to department so things don't get stale."

"That's the stupidest thing I've ever heard," Jim muttered under his breath and went back to his pork chop.

When Kendall glanced across the table, Rick was looking at her. "You got this?" he asked. He was much more business savvy than Adam, and the fate of Old Red Barn Brewcrafters meant everything to him.

She gave him one firm nod. "I got this."

CHAPTER THREE

Kendall's knee bounced up and down as she sat in the lobby of Hagan's corporate offices and waited. She'd arrived at 9:50. It was now 10:10 and she was letting her nerves get the better of her. Andrea was probably making her wait on purpose as a show of dominance; Kendall was sure that was something she'd do. She'd been a bit of a control freak in school, bossing her teammates around, intimidating the line judges who were just members of the J.V. team.

"Is it weird that I remember so much about her when we were in high school?" Kendall had asked Liz on the phone the previous night.

"Considering that was, what? Twelve years ago? Yeah. It is. Totally weird." That was Liz's response, and Kendall had suddenly not wanted to delve any further into it, so she'd changed the subject.

Well, she wasn't going to let this annoy her. She could wait just as long as Andrea wanted her to. Tired of looking out the enormous windows at the gray sky and flurrying snow, Kendall slipped a folder out of her briefcase and studied the printout of the PowerPoint presentation she'd made. She'd gone over it last night several times and had most of it memorized, but she gave it one more read-through. Why not? She obviously had the time.

Halfway through the entire presentation, she heard the click of heels on the tile floor and glanced up.

Andrea was dressed a bit more casually than yesterday, but still looked incredibly classy and put-together. Black pants hugged her long, slim legs. An emerald green sweater with subtle gold stripes brought out the green of her eyes in a way that was impossible for Kendall to ignore. Her expression was blank. Not welcoming, not off-putting. Completely neutral. She held out a hand as she approached. Kendall stood.

"Ms. Foster."

Kendall grasped Andrea's hand firmly, the soft warmth of it in complete contrast to the cool demeanor that was emanating from her. "Kendall. Please. I think we've known each other long enough for you to use my first name."

Andrea inclined her head once, conceding the point. Without further chatter, she turned on her heel and ordered, "Follow me."

Kendall scrambled to gather her things and almost had to jog to catch up with Andrea, who was apparently not going to wait. Not for the first time, Kendall wondered why she'd chosen to come here and do this rather than tell Andrea Blake she could stick her distribution deal right up her ass.

And a very shapely ass it is. The thought startled her, and she literally gave her head a gentle shake to dislodge it. A complication she absolutely did not need, thank you very much.

They passed several people as they walked, some moving along, some standing, all of them either nodded or said hello to Andrea. She said hello back and actually smiled more than once. Kendall's eyebrows raised at this newfound information. The corners of Andrea Blake's mouth actually could turn upward. Who knew?

A quick left and Andrea was through a doorway. Gesturing to an empty chair, she said, "Have a seat," and took the chair behind the desk. Then she folded her hands on the desk in front of her and simply waited.

So this is how we're going to play it. Okay. Fine.

Kendall was used to dealing with assholes. It was a harsh way to put things, but it was true. As a woman—an attractive one—in the world of beer and bars, she dealt with more than her share of sexism and people thinking she didn't know her shit, couldn't possibly know her shit. Well, she wasn't going to take it from Andrea, just as she didn't take it from the men with whom she did business. The only way to win their respect and wipe that sheen of doubt off their faces was to show them that she did, in fact, know her shit. Inside and out.

"Okay," she said, hefting her bag up onto the chair and sliding out her laptop as she glanced around the nicely appointed, very tidy office. She'd been telling Rick for the past six months that a tablet would be so much easier for this type of thing, and she was pretty sure she was wearing him down. But for now, the laptop would have to do. "If you check your e-mail, you'll see that I sent you the presentation I'll be using so you can look at it later if you want." Her eyes fell on the small, round table in the corner with four chairs around it. "You can follow along on your own computer or," she jerked her head toward the table, "we can sit there and just look at mine."

Andrea seemed torn for a split second, as if she hadn't expected to actually have to make a decision in this meeting. With a clear of her throat, she stood. "The table will be fine."

"Great."

Kendall moved her laptop to the table, pulled two chairs close together, and waited for Andrea to come around and take a seat. Then Kendall sat next to her and tried desperately not to inhale deeply when the spiciness of Andrea's perfume hit her nostrils. God, she smelled good. *Seriously? Can I not have a break today?* Giving herself a mental shake, she forced her brain into business mode.

"All right. I decided to begin at the beginning, to assume that you know little to nothing about beer and the brewing process in general. Stop me if I'm covering old ground, okay?" At Andrea's nod, she called up the first page of the presentation. "I won't go into minute detail because you don't really need to know all that, but here's the basic process of how beer is made." She went through each of the steps, telling Andrea a little bit about mashing and sparging and boiling the wort, then moving on if it seemed like it was becoming boring or a bit much. Andrea wasn't completely in the dark. She knew that barley malt and hops were big ingredients, and she surprised Kendall by also getting that boiling the grains releases sugar, that sugar is necessary for fermentation because it produces alcohol.

"I bet you did really well in chemistry class," Kendall commented with a grin.

"I did all right," was Andrea's reply, and she smiled. It was a really, really nice smile.

"So. After fermentation is the last step before packaging: carbonation."

"Oh." Andrea furrowed her brow. "That doesn't happen naturally? I assumed it did, from the yeast and sugars and stuff."

"Common misconception," Kendall said, holding up a finger. "No, if we drank beer as-is after the fermentation process, it'd be flat and gross. Carbonation takes care of that. There are different ways to carbonate, but you don't really need to know all that."

They went on to the next slide.

Half an hour had gone by when they finished up. Andrea had been leaning on her forearms on the table, watching closely as each slide appeared, taking in all the information Kendall gave her, even asking questions. She'd been an impressively rapt student and Kendall was shocked to admit she'd actually enjoyed teaching her.

"End of lesson number one," Kendall said as she closed the application.

Andrea blinked at her. "Lesson one?"

"Oh, yeah. There's more to learn." Kendall's grin was wide. Andrea held her gaze for a moment and something passed between them. "Sizzle" was the only word Kendall could come up with to describe it. She pulled her eyes away and cleared her throat as she busied herself shutting down her computer. "You need to learn the different kinds of beer. That's actually much more important than the brewing process, but I thought you should at least know the basics if you're going to be picking who gets distributed." She was babbling and she knew it, but couldn't seem to stop herself. "And then, after we go through different kinds of beer, you'll taste them so you can understand the differences. Otherwise—." She blinked at Andrea's palm held up.

"I have to taste them?"

Kendall scoffed. "Well, yeah. It's important."

"Why?"

Biting on her bottom lip, Kendall tried not to snap when she spoke. "Because it is. You're in charge. You should know what you're buying and putting in your stores. Don't you think?" She could tell by the slight hardening of the expression on Andrea's face that she may have overstepped, that maybe she could have used a different tone. Andrea's gentle grin slid away and the green of her eyes cooled noticeably. *Yeah, telling the distributor she's not very good at her job? Probably not the smartest of moves.* But what did she think? That Kendall was going to give her a quick-

31

and-dirty rundown of how to make beer and then be done? That she would half-ass it? If she expected a fair shake when it came to being chosen, she was sure as hell going to give the woman a thorough education. She watched as Andrea stood and went behind her desk, put a hand on her mouse. Assuming she'd been dismissed, Kendall sighed quietly and slid her laptop back into its bag. "Um…look, Andrea, I…" Her voice trailed off as she looked in vain for a way to smooth over the bumps she'd stirred up, though once again, she wondered why she should bother. The flash of humanity Andrea had shown her must have been just that: a flash. Before she could say more, Andrea spoke.

"How about Tuesday at eleven?"

"I'm sorry?" Kendall looked up and was immediately snared by those jade green eyes.

"For lesson number two?" Andrea asked, her reddish eyebrows raised. "Does Tuesday work for you?"

"Lesson number two. Right." With a swallow and a half-grin, Kendall pulled out her phone and did a quick check of her schedule. "It does. Eleven, you said?"

Andrea nodded.

"Okay. Got it. I'll see you then." She crossed to the desk and held out her hand. Andrea took it, her hand still just as soft and warm as before, her grip firm.

"Until Tuesday."

∽

"Well. This is inconvenient," Andrea said softly to her empty office. "Very, very inconvenient." She could see some of the parking lot from her window, and she tried to be subtle about watching as Kendall walked across the newly fallen snow and got into a midsize SUV. It was red, and Andrea approved of the color. It suited Kendall somehow. She'd dressed to impress today, something that surprised Andrea. In a good way. The beer people at yesterday's meeting had been far below even business casual, showing up in jeans and T-shirts, sneakers, work boots, unshaven. Brady had told her that's how the beer guys were, that they did their own thing, that that was why they were in the beer business in the first place: so they could be themselves. Many of them had left the business world for just that reason—too stiff, too smothered, too many rules.

Kendall Foster obviously disagreed. She hadn't gone as far as a suit, but her navy pants and navy-and-white striped blouse had been the perfect complement to her light skin tone and sparkling blue eyes. Her shoulder-length blond hair was down, worn straight and tucked behind her ears. Dark lashes highlighted eyes the color of the summer sky in August, and her lips were glossy, full and shiny. Andrea had always thought she was cute when they were rivals in school. But now…she was more than a decade older and no longer a kid. She was a woman. Andrea had noticed.

And then Kendall had told her she sucked at her job.

Okay, she hadn't said that. Not in so many words. But it was implied, wasn't it? That she didn't quite know what she was doing? That she should know more in order to do things right? The worst part about it was that Kendall was right. Andrea *did* need to know more. She *should* know more. It was only fair to the vendors who wanted to sell their goods to her. So, Kendall had been right. That didn't mean Andrea appreciated hearing it.

With a sigh, she turned away from the window and muttered, "That woman hates me."

She'd only been working for a short while when her cell phone dinged, letting her know she had a text. It was her sister,

Julia, confirming their lunch date. With a smile, Andrea sent a text back saying she was looking forward to it.

A short meeting and two phone calls later and Andrea was in her car on her way to Elfie's, an out-of-the-way café she and Julia frequented. The roads were in halfway decent shape as the snow had stopped and the plows had had time to do their thing. The sun was even trying hard to make an appearance, fighting the gray cloud cover that did its best to act as a curtain. Andrea found a parking spot in a shockingly short period of time, pulled her coat tighter around her body, and hurried into the warmth of the café where the smell of fresh bread surrounded her like a hug.

Julia waved from a corner table. Her chestnut brown hair was pulled back from her face, her green eyes smiling as she stood to hug her sister. "Why does it feel like I haven't seen you in forever?" she asked as she let Andrea go and sat back down.

"Because you haven't?" Andrea hung her jacket on the coat rack behind Julia, smoothed her blouse, and sat. "How long has it been? I've seen you since just after New Year's, right?"

Julia sipped from a glass of what Andrea knew was her usual Diet Coke and then shook her head. "No. I don't think so."

"How is that even possible?" Andrea asked in disbelief as the waitress stopped at their table. Neither sister had to look at the menu, as they always got the broccoli and cheese soup, small salads, and a basket of Elfie's homemade bread. Andrea ordered herself a Diet Coke as well. "How do we live in the same city and go for nearly two months without seeing each other? It's ridiculous."

"It is. Your nephew and niece miss you."

There was no accusation in Julia's tone; she wasn't like that. Not like their mother, who could make even the most innocent of sentences feel like a guilt trip. But Andrea felt the weight of guilt just the same. Brittany was seven, Ben only five. This was an important, formative part of their lives. Andrea should spend more time with them. She knew that. She reminded herself often. But knowing it and making it happen seemed to be two very far apart things.

"I miss them, too. Are you around this weekend?"

Julia's eyes brightened. "We are. Want to come over for dinner on Sunday?"

Andrea's brain quickly tossed her a list of all the things she needed to get done, not to mention the party she was invited to, but she heard her own voice before she realized she was speaking. "I'd love to."

Julia looked momentarily surprised, then a big smile split her face. "Great. The kids will be so happy to see you. I'll make stew. That okay?"

"That's perfect. I'll bring the wine."

Their lunch arrived and they fell into comfortable chatter, as they'd always done. "You talked to Dad lately?" Andrea asked.

Julia rolled her eyes. "Last week. He's in Boca with…" Her voice trailed off as she searched for the name. "Laura?" She shook her head. "Lara? I can't keep track."

Andrea spooned some soup into her mouth, swallowed, and said, "Think Laura's older than you?"

"I wouldn't bet on it."

They both laughed, but it was a slightly uncomfortable humor.

"What is this, his fourth girlfriend since the divorce?" Andrea shook her head.

"Might be the fifth."

"And Mom? Talked to her?"

Julia gave her a look. The one that said, *You know, you* could *call her once in a while.*

Andrea grimaced. "I know. I know."

"When you go too long without talking to her, I get to hear all about it." Julia ripped a piece of bread and dunked it in her soup.

"She's so depressing. Such a downer. I hang up from talking to her and I just want to slit my wrists."

Julia's chuckle was warm. "I know. I totally get it. I feel the same way, which is why it'd be nice to share the burden a bit, little sister of mine."

Andrea nodded. "You're right. I'll try to be better about that." They both knew she wouldn't follow through, but they did this dance often enough to know the steps by heart.

"So, are you getting all ready for the new job?" Julia asked, thankfully changing the subject. "You start in a month or so, right?"

Andrea groaned as she stabbed a cherry tomato with her fork. "Yeah, that schedule was tossed right out the window." She told Julia about her predecessor leaving his position early, her being thrown into it, and the disaster of a meeting yesterday.

Julia's brows reached up toward her hairline. "They just pushed you into the role and stood you in front of a bunch of people? Holy crap. Were you freaking?"

"I was actually okay. I thought I had it all under control until somebody made a comment." She told Julia about Kendall's comment, which was then reiterated—loudly—for all to hear, and how it had gone downhill from there. Glossing over the fact that it had started as a joke, she then told her how Kendall had been by this morning to teach her all about beer.

Julia had been rapt with attention during the whole story, chewing slowly, her eyes focused on her sister. Now, she said, "So, this Foster woman is trying to make up for her misstep."

"Or she's trying to get on my good side so I'll choose her beer to go on our shelves."

"Or she thinks you're cute." Julia waggled her eyebrows.

"Or she's trying to get on my good side so I'll choose her beer to go on our shelves."

"Cynic."

They grinned identical smiles at each other, looking very much like siblings in that moment. Then Andrea shook her head good-naturedly. "Nah. I think she's just trying to do what she thinks is right. Probably."

"You don't even like beer."

"I know. But I'm not stupid. I'm completely taking advantage. It's nothing more than that." She flashed to the volleyball game and then the meeting in quick succession. "No. There's no love lost there. The woman hates me."

❧

"That woman hates me," Kendall said to Buster, the black lab mix that technically belonged to Rick. Buster went home with Rick every night, but during the day, he was free to wander the brewery or the farm as he pleased. More often than not, he ended up in Kendall's office. Now, he cocked his head, his warm brown eyes looking concerned and almost human as he seemed to intently listen as Kendall spoke. "Seriously. Between you, me, and this wall over here? Hates me. Cannot stand me. I mean it."

Kendall had left Hagan's corporate offices feeling pretty good about the meeting with Andrea Blake. She'd seemed interested in what Kendall had to say, had to teach her. She paid close attention. Then, of course, Kendall had gotten a little...

snippy and probably shouldn't have. That's when she knew she'd stepped in it and that maybe Andrea was simply using her. Would she do that? Use her for information and then not give her the promised fair shake when it came time to choose vendors? She'd been sitting in her office for nearly two hours rolling the whole thing around and around in her head. It had gotten her exactly nowhere.

"I don't know, Buster." She sat back in her chair and Buster laid his head on her thigh. "Am I making too much out of this?" The dog looked at her, but offered no solution. She scratched his square head. "Big help you are."

Adam popped his head through the door of her office. "Hey. How'd it go this morning?"

Kendall gave a nod. "Okay."

"Yeah? How far'd you get?" Adam was familiar with the presentation Kendall had; she'd used it for trade shows and other meetings in the past, and the two of them had tweaked it together more than once.

"All the way through beer making. I stopped there so I wouldn't overwhelm her."

"And?"

"And I'm going back on Tuesday."

"For beer varieties." At Kendall's nod of affirmation, he grinned. "That's promising. Nice work, baby sister."

He was gone before she could respond.

"Well," she said, looking down at Buster who hadn't moved. "I'm so glad he approves of my job well done. Aren't you?"

Buster licked her hand.

Just as she settled herself back into work mode, her phone rang.

"Kendall Foster."

"Good afternoon, Ms. Kendall Foster. This is your good friend, Ms. Elizabeth Sheridan, and I would like to know if you happen to have an in with Mother Nature. Because I am fucking freezing my ass off."

Kendall laughed. "Let me ask you, Ms. Sheridan. How long have you lived in upstate New York?"

"Um, my whole life. But I don't see how that's relevant."

"I only ask because...well...I'm sort of surprised by your surprise. I mean, it's February. In upstate New York. Where you've lived your whole life. And yet, you expect somebody to bring you an early spring? Presumptuous."

"Why am I even friends with you?" Liz asked with a world-weary sigh.

"A valid question, ma'am."

"What's going on?" Liz asked, as she usually did when she called.

"I have no idea. You called me," Kendall responded, as she usually did when Liz called.

"Right. Well, I'm calling to tell you to dust off your good jeans because we're going to a party tomorrow night."

"A party? Where?" Kendall was all ears. February was a good time for a party. The winter was feeling endless. The cold was annoying people. There were no holidays coming up to give them something to look forward to.

"Over near Park. A couple my cousin knows. Good people from what I hear. Should be a decent time."

"Anybody we know going?"

"Well, I'm going and you know me."

"Very funny."

"I'm sure it will be some of the usual crowd."

The city wasn't all that big; it wasn't unusual to run into a handful of the same people at almost any event. "Okay. Sounds good. What time?" Kendall asked.

"I'll pick you up at eight?"

"Perfect."

They chatted about a few mundane things before Kendall begged off so she could get back to work, but she was surprised to find herself looking forward to the party. For every four lesbians there she knew there might be one or two she didn't, and that was worth getting a little dressed up for. Her thoughts immediately turned to Janet, and a minor panic rolled unpleasantly in her stomach. There was a good chance she'd be at the party, as she knew just about every lesbian in the community. And if she was at the party, chances were even better that she'd be there with the new girlfriend, the one she absolutely *was not* seeing before she left Kendall, claiming Kendall worked too much, but then ended up dating publicly not two weeks later. It had been almost eight months since the breakup. Kendall hadn't been devastated, which was a good sign that breaking up was the right call, but still.

"Don't blame my work schedule when it's glaringly obvious you've got your eye on somebody else," she muttered for the seven hundredth time since it happened. Buster looked up from his spot on the floor as if to say, *Are you talking to me?* When she said no more, he laid his head back down and sighed out a huge breath. "You got that right, Buster. Women are *hard*."

CHAPTER FOUR

"Okay. Deep breath." Andrea brushed some hair off her face and inhaled slowly, then let it out gradually. She was nervous. A little. It had been a while since she'd been to a party alone. More than six months, to be exact. It was time. She glanced down at herself: the new, snug jeans, the high brown boots. She'd gone shopping for the first time in ages and purchased the white Henley she wore under her coat, enjoying the way it fit. The outfit worked. *I hope my social skills still do,* she thought as she rang the doorbell.

The door was pulled open and Andrea was bombarded by light, music, and laughter.

"You made it. I'm so glad!" Kylie O'Brien wrapped Andrea in a tight hug, a big grin spread across her face. "I feel like we haven't seen each other in ages. Here, let me have that." Andrea shed her coat and let Kylie drape it over her own arm. "Come in. Don't worry about taking your boots off. I'm going to run this to the bedroom and I'll be right back. Drinks are in the kitchen." She waved behind her, her blond hair bouncing as she turned her head. "I think Gretchen's in there, too."

Andrea watched her friend leave with her coat, and stomped her boots off on the mat. The party was in full swing, Pink playing from the iPod dock in the corner, pockets of women chatting. Some, she recognized; some she didn't. Again, she thought about it being her first time to a party alone, and then she realized it was her first time at a party *at all* in a very long time. *Okay. This was obviously the right call then,* she thought. Gripping the bottle of Cabernet she'd brought with her, she headed toward the kitchen. Immediately identifying the black curly head of Kylie's wife in a small group of people, Andrea snuck up behind her, pressed her body tight along her back, and whispered, "I brought your favorite wine in all the world."

Gretchen Kaiser was petite—no more than 5'1"—but she was the epitome of big things coming in small packages. She spun around in Andrea's arms, dwarfed by the eight-inch height difference, and threw her own around Andrea's neck. "You made it!" Her voice was surprisingly deep and throaty for a woman of her size.

"That's what Kylie said. You two have very little faith in me, you know."

"With good reason," Kylie interjected as she came into the room. "You like to say you'll show, and you rarely actually do." There was no accusation in the words, mostly because they were factual and Andrea knew it.

"Well, I've decided that should change. Where's your corkscrew?" One appeared out of thin air, and Andrea smiled, grabbed it, and went to work, then poured two glasses. Kylie was already having a beer. Andrea held up her glass, clinked with Gretchen's. A couple in the corner snagged Gretchen's attention, and she held up a finger to Andrea.

"Be right back."

Andrea focused on Kylie. "So what's new with you two?"

Andrea had met Kylie not quite two years ago in the bleachers of a softball game, something they both continually laughed about, as it was "such a lesbian place to meet." They'd begun chatting, hit it off immediately, and had been fast friends ever since. Kylie was smart, funny, and a sweetheart. She and

Gretchen had been together for nearly ten years, and the way they still looked at each other... Andrea shook her head with a smile as she watched Kylie glance at Gretchen over the rim of her glass and Gretchen wink in return. *I want that,* she thought, not for the first time. *I want somebody to look at me that way. And I want other people to look at me and my wife and want what we have.* With a gentle sigh, she pulled herself back to the conversation at hand.

"So, we're not quite sure yet. Jake's getting up there in years and Gretchen thinks we should get a puppy now so when it does come time, we won't be dogless, but I don't know. It feels like we're replacing him already. You know?" Kylie grimaced.

"I completely get it. I was actually thinking I might want... something." Andrea hadn't said this aloud to anybody yet, but Kylie had that effect on her. Andrea wanted to spill her guts whenever her friend was around.

"A dog?" Kylie asked gleefully.

"I think a kitten. My hours might be too crazy for a dog."

"Mmm. Good point. Well, my friend Lisa is around here somewhere and she works at that no-kill shelter, Junebug Farms. I should introduce you guys." She stood on tiptoe and scanned the crowd, then gestured to Andrea to follow her. "Come on." Andrea grinned and shook her head, falling into step behind Kylie. As she cleared the doorway of the kitchen, she ran smack into another body. They collided hard and the red wine in Andrea's glass splashed all over the place, suddenly feeling like a lot more than just a glassful. Arms held out to the sides, she looked down at the giant crimson stain decorating the front of her brand new, very white Henley as the rest of the activity in the kitchen ground to a halt amid gasps and small cries.

"Oh, my God, I'm *so* sorry." The voice was familiar and when Andrea glanced up, she found herself looking into the extremely blue eyes of none other than Kendall Foster.

"You just can't give me a break, can you?" Andrea muttered.

Kendall grabbed a nearby towel, but stopped to blink in obvious surprise at the comment. "Hey, I didn't run into you on purpose. Maybe you should pay more attention to where you're going." She began blotting at Andrea's shirt, none too gently.

Andrea slapped her hands away. "Seriously?"

"I'm trying to help."

Kylie returned in time to keep Andrea from spouting off the snotty comment on the tip of her tongue. "Oh, my God. What happened?"

As if they'd heard a cue, everybody in the kitchen began to move again, and no less than four women were suddenly trying to help Andrea clean off her shirt. She looked up, but Kendall had disappeared. Amid the bustle, Kylie gripped Andrea's arm.

"Come with me. I have something you can put on. We need to get this rinsed and sprayed if we have a prayer of getting that stain out."

"I'm not optimistic," Andrea said with a grimace, suddenly noticing Kendall on her hands and knees mopping up spilled wine.

"Yeah, me neither."

She followed Kylie down a hardwood hallway toward the back of the ranch-style house to the master suite. Decorated in tones of cream and muted burgundy accents, the room was warm and inviting. On a dog bed in the corner, Kylie's Australian Shepherd lazed, but lifted his head when he saw Andrea.

"Hey there, Jake," she whispered, squatting down to pet the dog as Kylie disappeared into a mammoth sized closet. She was out again in less than a minute with a shirt that looked alarmingly like the one Andrea was wearing. Andrea blinked in surprise.

"I know," Kylie laughed. "As soon as you took your coat off, I thought, 'Hey, that looks a lot like the shirt I bought last week.'"

"Lucky for me." Andrea took the shirt and went into the master bath. She sighed as she took her top off. Kylie was right; this stain was never going to come out. *Chalk up another point for Ms. Foster,* she thought with irritation. *The woman is clearly out to get me.* In good news, Andrea must have arched her body, as one does when liquid falls on their front, because her white bra was left unscathed by red wine. She pulled Kylie's shirt over her head, adjusted it in the mirror. It was a tiny bit smaller than she would have liked, but it worked. She finger-combed her hair, and pronounced herself almost as good as when she'd arrived.

"Perfect," Kylie said as Andrea exited the bathroom. Waving a finger around in front of Andrea's torso, she added with a wink, "And mine accentuates the girls a bit more than yours. Maybe you should be buying a smaller size."

"Ha ha." She held up her stained shirt. "I think we're going to just chuck this one. Where do you want it?"

"You sure?" At Andrea's nod, she said, "Kitchen garbage."

Andrea squatted down to give Jake a little more love. "I can't believe he's just hanging out here with all these people in the house."

"He doesn't hear as well now, so it's easier for him to just relax in here. He doesn't seem to mind."

Andrea left the dog with a kiss on the head, then followed Kylie out of the room.

The party had gotten back into full swing. Maroon 5 was now the music and it looked to Andrea like several more people had shown up. The low hum of voices buzzed through the house, punctuated by laughter and occasional raised voices. As Andrea returned to the kitchen, a full glass of wine appeared before her.

"Here you go." Kendall Foster held it out to her. She met Andrea's eyes quickly, then looked away. "I'm very, very sorry for spilling your first glass. Cheers." She clinked her glass of beer very gently against Andrea's wine, then turned and left the kitchen before Andrea could utter a word. Instead, Andrea simply sipped and watched Kendall's departure over the rim of her glass, refusing to admit to herself that she was enjoying the view.

"She's cute," Gretchen said from behind Andrea, causing her to start.

Andrea gave a subtle nod. *You're not lying,* she thought, but said nothing.

Gretchen came around in front of her and leaned her back against the island so she and Andrea were face-to-face. "How goes the dating life?"

"What dating life?"

"That's what I was afraid you'd say."

Andrea shrugged. "My job is nuts, Gretch. I have very little time. Dating just seems like so much work." She acted as if the words weighed her down, her body collapsing on itself just a little as she grinned.

Gretchen laughed. "Oh, I get it. That's exactly how I felt before I met that one." She gestured with her chin across the room to where Kylie stood, laughing with a bunch of women. "You can't be alone forever."

"Can't I?"

"Okay, you can. But do you want to be?"

Andrea pressed her lips together. "No. I really don't."

"That's what I thought. Want me to introduce you to the hottie who drenched you in wine?"

"No," Andrea said, and it came out a bit more adamantly than she'd intended, judging by Gretchen's raised eyebrows. "No," she said again, gentler. "We've met. But thanks." She didn't want to go into detail. She had no idea who Kendall knew here and bashing her wasn't something Andrea wanted to do; it wasn't her style. She simply wanted to…keep her distance. And hopefully, stay dry.

"Well, okay then. How about I get you into a group so you stop standing here alone like a loser?" Gretchen took Andrea by the elbow and steered her over to where Kylie stood, still laughing, then handed her off like a relay baton. Kylie wrapped a warm arm around Andrea's waist, pulled her into the circle, and introduced her to all four women. In no time at all, Andrea was part of the conversation, sipping her wine and laughing.

❧

"Well, if she didn't actually hate me before, she certainly does now." Kendall rolled her eyes and took a sip of her beer, bothered by how bothered she was, both by what had happened and by what Andrea had said.

Liz scoffed. "She doesn't hate you. And who cares if she does? It was an accident. You apologized. What more does she expect?"

"I should probably have offered to have her shirt cleaned."

"Are you kidding? That stain's never coming out."

Kendall turned to her. "Thanks."

"Hey, I just call 'em like I see 'em. You ever try to get red wine out of a white shirt?"

Kendall answered by taking another sip. Liz was right, of course.

Liz was quiet for a moment, and when she spoke, it was softer than usual. "Ken, are you sure you want to keep up with this teaching thing? I mean, this woman makes you kind of miserable. Maybe you should just back away." She shrugged and took a sip of her beer.

Kendall shook her head adamantly. "No. No way. I am not going to just give up because she's kind of a bitch."

"Kind of?"

Kendall lifted a shoulder. "I said I'd do it and I will."

Liz shook her head. "I knew that's what you'd say."

Kendall didn't respond. Instead, she sipped her beer and watched the small group in the kitchen, her eyes on red hair, even though she wanted to be looking elsewhere. After a beat or two, Liz interrupted her staring.

"So, what are we drinking today?"

Kendall held up her glass, a smile splitting her face. "We are drinking the Stone Fence IPA."

Liz made a face. "Blech. Bitter."

"Now, Elizabeth. India Pale Ales are an acquired taste. You have to work up to them."

"Yeah, I prefer not to have my taste buds blown off my tongue."

Kendall laughed. "Yeah. It's an intense beer. I didn't like it when I first started drinking beer. I had to build up to IPAs."

Liz held up her glass. "I'll stick to hard liquor, thank you very much. Captain Morgan is my dream man."

Kendall sighed loudly and shook her head. "I wish you'd give me a chance. I could walk you through it, help you learn about beer."

"I got all the beer education I needed in college. Mainly this: it's awful stuff."

Shaking her head, Kendall argued. "No. See, you can't count any college beer experience. In college, you were most likely having a Budweiser or a Coors Light. That's not beer. That's beer-flavored water and all that college kids can afford."

Liz lifted her hand and opened and closed her fingers and thumb like a mouth. "Blah, blah, blah. You've told me all this before," she said with a grin. "I don't like beer, Ken. Accept it."

"Never!" Kendall replied, a matching grin on her face. "I will convert you. I swear it. You wait."

"Do you think you can convert the redhead?" Liz asked, eyebrows raised.

Kendall followed her gaze to where Andrea stood. She'd moved a bit in the circle, rotated around so now, instead of her back, Kendall could see her profile. It was a nice profile. Straight nose, strong chin, bold eyebrows. *Nice neck*, Kendall thought as her eyes traveled down from the chin. When she glanced back up, green eyes locked with hers and Kendall blushed furiously. The heat in her face was so intense, she was sure everybody could see it, and she quickly looked down at the bottle in her hands in an attempt to hide her face.

"Yeah, I saw that," Liz said quietly. "Nobody else did, though." She bumped Kendall with her shoulder and chuckled.

Kendall shook her head. "God."

CHAPTER FIVE

The house smelled divine. That's the first thing Andrea noticed when she walked in the door of her sister's house. The second thing was that her niece and nephew were bigger than they'd been the last time she saw them. That made her feel an uncomfortable combination of sad and guilty. It didn't last long, however, as both kids screamed her name and threw themselves at her, wrapping their little arms around her thighs, ridiculously happy to see her.

"Wanna play Barbies with me, Aunt Andrea?" Brittany asked. She was seven and looked just like her mother, her hair the exact same chestnut color, her eyes just as green.

"No. She wants to play cars," five-year-old Ben said, his red eyebrows meeting in a V above his nose.

It went downhill from there, the elation over seeing Aunt Andrea plummeting into arguing over who got to play with her. Luckily, Julia showed up before any damage could be done. She stepped into the fray like a seasoned pro, pushing the kids arms' lengths away and saying, "Aunt Andrea is here to have dinner with us. How about we're on our best behavior so she sees what good kids you are?"

They hung their heads for about four seconds, then ran off together to their playroom. Andrea watched them in fascination and shook her head with a smile.

"I know," Julia said, chuckling. "Their moods change with the wind. I'm still not used to it."

Andrea handed over a bottle of Merlot. "I think this will go well with the stew. Thanks for having me."

"Oh, honey. We're not waiting for the stew. Come with me."

Andrea followed her sister through the house, which was warm and welcoming, neat but not spotless, cozily lived in. Andrea fought the desire to flop herself onto the couch with the pillow askew, prop her feet up on the coffee table littered with magazines, and turn on the TV; that's how inviting her sister's house was. At the same time, it freaked her out a bit, because she could never stand to have her own house in such disarray. It would make her want to scream.

Trailing after Julia, she entered the kitchen/dining room combination, where the table was set for five, and the warmth of the room enveloped Andrea like her grandmother's hugs did when she was a child.

"Where's Phil?" Andrea asked, taking the proffered corkscrew from her sister's hand.

"In his workshop in the basement." Julia lifted the lid from the crockpot and the mouthwatering scent of beef, potatoes, and vegetables grew stronger.

"God, that smells good," Andrea said. "Glasses?"

Julia pointed at a cupboard and said, "I made rolls, too."

Andrea's head snapped around. "Grandma's rolls?"

Julia grinned as she nodded. "In the oven as we speak."

"I think I've died and gone to Heaven." Andrea poured wine and handed Julia a glass.

"I wanted you to be happy to be here so you'd come back."

The words warmed Andrea's heart at the same time she felt the familiar ribbon of guilt she'd felt at the front door. "I'll always come back, Jules."

"Okay. Come back more often then." Julia grinned to take any sting out of the words and touched her glass to Andrea's. "I'm glad you're here now."

"So am I."

The afternoon and evening went much too quickly, as it always did when Andrea managed to spend time with the family members she was closest to. Brittany and Ben both tried to outdo each other with tales from school. Turned out, Brittany was something of a numbers whiz. Andrea looked at her sister quizzically.

"I have no idea," Julia responded. "It certainly didn't come from me."

"Me, neither." Andrea sipped her wine.

"Um, hello?" Phil said from his spot at the table as he finished off his second bowl of stew, his spoon dwarfed in his enormous hands, the muscles of his forearms rippling beneath the rolled-up sleeves of his flannel shirt.

"Oh, that's right. I had help making these kids, didn't I?" Julia grinned.

The adults laughed and Andrea caught the look of love Phil shot across the table at his wife, who smiled back at him. Andrea often found herself torn when she spent time at her sister's house. She envied what Julia and Phil shared. Their life, their love, their home and children. They were a team. A partnership. A united front on most issues. And a large part of Andrea wanted to have that, wanted to have the solidity of a spouse in life and love. It was very similar to what she felt when she looked at Gretchen and Kylie.

But there was also a very large independent streak in Andrea's soul. She wasn't quite sure where it had come from, but she relished it, held tightly to it, and guarded it with everything

52

she had. Losing herself in somebody else was not in her plan. She did not want to be one of those women who looked to her significant other before answering a question. One of those people who couldn't make plans without consulting another person. She liked being in charge of herself, of her life, having to answer to nobody. *She* was the only person she wanted to be in control of her world.

She and Julia had had many a conversation about the whole thing, amazed at how differently the two sisters—only three years apart and raised in the same household with the same issues—looked at life. Andrea was reasonably sure her desire to take care of herself stemmed from her parents' divorce and watching her mother completely fall apart, utterly unable to take care of something as simple as paying the electric bill, she'd been that dependent. Andrea wondered if somehow, her eleven-year-old brain had taken it all in and mentally vowed never to allow herself to be put in the same situation. Julia, having been fourteen at the time of the divorce, was already well on her way to becoming who she was today, so her development wasn't as affected.

At least that's the conclusion they'd come to.

Phil's deep baritone voice cut into Andrea's ruminations. "Hey, Andrea, I'm thinking of making a bonfire out of all my Buffalo Bills paraphernalia. I'm sure you've got some to add. What do you say?"

Andrea laughed. "Are you kidding me? I've got a couple thousand dollars' worth of jerseys and sweatshirts alone."

Phil pushed a hank of brown hair out of his eyes and shook his head as he helped himself to a second roll and ripped it open so he could mop his dish clean with it. "I don't want to give up. I really don't. But it's been fifteen years since we made the playoffs." He looked up from his dish and his brown eyes locked with Andrea's. "*The playoffs.* That's not even getting any further than that. Worst drought in NFL history." He shook his head some more. "It's hard to be disappointed year after year. I didn't even want to watch the Super Bowl this year."

"But you did," Julia pointed out.

"I completely agree, Phil," Andrea said with a grin at her sister. "But…I've been a Bills fan since I was a kid. So have you."

"Yeah. I know."

"We can't be fair-weather fans, can we? That's not cool."

"I hate that," he said. "I hate when people only root for their team when they're winning."

"Me, too." Andrea followed Phil's lead and helped herself to another roll, making a mental note to spend an extra fifteen minutes on the treadmill tomorrow. She paused, made a show of thinking hard. Finally, she said to him, "I say we hold off on the bonfire. For now."

Phil sighed, bit off some of his roll, and chewed thoughtfully, as if this were a very serious life decision. After long moments, he nodded. "Yeah, I suppose you're right."

"I know we say this every year, but let's see what next season brings."

"I'd like next season to bring us a quarterback that doesn't suck."

"Amen to that." Andrea held up her wine and touched it to Phil's water glass. At exactly that moment, Ben spilled his juice down the front of him. Julia jumped up to grab a towel and started to blot at the mess, and Andrea had an immediate flash of Kendall Foster clumsily swiping at Andrea with a towel. It was only then that Andrea remembered the look on Kendall's face.

She was mortified. *And I snapped at her. Actually, I accused her of doing it on purpose. Nice work, Andrea.*

Ben's mess was cleaned up in a matter of moments, and Julia shooed him upstairs to change his shirt. "That happens once a week," she said matter-of-factly. "That boy would drop his own head if it wasn't attached to his shoulders."

Brittany found that absolutely hilarious and burst into a fit of giggles, which were apparently contagious, as soon all the adults were laughing with her.

It was nearly nine o'clock by the time Andrea finished reading two bedtime stories to each child, and she was shocked to feel nearly as exhausted as they were.

"And they are down," she said proudly to Julia as she descended the stairs. "I'm beat. I don't know how you do this every day."

Julia chuckled as she pushed herself off the couch and out from under Phil's arm to meet her sister in the foyer. "You get used to it," she said simply.

Andrea reached for her green scarf and wound it around her neck before donning her wool pea coat and matching gloves. "Thanks so much for dinner."

"Anytime. I'm really glad you came." Julia opened her arms and hugged Andrea tightly. "Let's not wait so long between visits, okay?"

"Promise."

"You always promise. I mean it."

"Yes, big sister."

Julia bumped her playfully. "Be careful driving, all right? The news said it might be a little slick."

"I'll be careful."

"And send me a text when you get home."

"Now you sound like Mom."

Julia gasped in mock-horror. "How dare you!"

Andrea laughed and gave her another tight hug. "Bye, Phil." She waved into the living room.

"Be safe, Andrea," he replied.

The cold air tried its best to steal her breath from her lungs as she made her way to her car. Traffic was light, and she wondered at each car that she passed. Was the driver like her? Somebody who'd just visited a warm and cozy family and was now going home alone?

She was shocked to realize that, for the first time since she could remember, the idea of her empty driveway, empty house, empty bed, made her just a little bit sad.

♒

Tuesday morning dawned bright and sunny, and for the first time in nearly two months, Andrea allowed herself to entertain the idea of the end of winter. February was funny like that in upstate New York. You could get a gorgeous, sunny day in the low forties, which would allow you to breathe easier knowing winter was almost over. Then the next day, you could get six more inches of snow and there would be cursing and irritation and frustration, not to mention shoveling.

"God, I hate February," she muttered as she poured her coffee. Then she looked down at her feet and her voice went into immediate baby-talk mode. "But I love you. Yes, I do. Yes, I do." The little gray and white kitten put his paws up on her pant leg and mewed the tiniest, most ridiculously cute sound Andrea had ever heard, and she reached down to scoop him up. She nuzzled him against her face. "Good morning, Mr. Zeke. You did very well last night. Yes, you did." She made kissy faces at him for several seconds before she caught herself, grinned, and set him down.

It had been a good decision. She thought about it now as she scooped a little canned food into one side of Zeke's dish, then added some dry in the other. Kylie had introduced her to Lisa Drakemore at the party Saturday night and they started talking about Andrea maybe getting a cat. They'd discussed it for a long while, and Andrea admired how devoted to the animals in her shelter Lisa was, but how not pushy she seemed with Andrea. She wanted her to be sure a kitten was what she wanted. Not for a second did Andrea feel pressured.

So yesterday, she left work and drove to the shelter. Where she'd spent nearly three hours trying to decide on an animal. There were dozens upon dozens of cats and kittens, and for a little while, she felt almost heartbroken that she couldn't take them all home with her. She'd been mortified to feel her eyes mist over and had to turn away from other people more than once.

Zeke had been one in a litter of seven. They were all variations of gray and white, but he was the only one with white paws and he'd looked up at her from his pen with the sweetest eyes she'd ever seen. The choice had been made for her.

Luckily, the shelter had a store as well, so Andrea had been able to get the essentials for his first night with her. Today, she planned to run out of work a teeny bit early and hit the nearby pet store for more. Glancing down, she sipped her coffee as she watched him gobble up his breakfast, and she suddenly felt an overwhelming surge of happiness. Squatting down, she scratched along his neck and he looked up at her, a glob of brown food clinging to his pink little nose.

"You're adorable," she said affectionately as she wiped the food away with her thumb.

Living in an older city home had its advantages, one of them being the rustic and charming pocket door that separated the foyer and stairs from the rest of the house. Once she was all ready for work, she set out some toys, a blanket, and a scratching post, tossed a couple treats on the floor, and closed Zeke onto the first floor, calling a goodbye to him as she pulled the side door shut behind her. She was going to have to figure out the litter box location at some point, but for now, the kitchen was as good a place as any. It wasn't like she had company very often. Or ever.

Having to don her sunglasses for the ride helped her hold on to her good mood, even though she was a little worried about the day, specifically her eleven o'clock appointment. She hadn't forgotten the party or how rude she'd been to Kendall Foster. She'd actually intended to apologize that night, but Kendall had left before Andrea had worked up the nerve.

What is it about that woman that brings out the worst in me?

It stayed on her mind for the entire morning, and by ten-thirty, she was relatively shocked that Kendall hadn't canceled their appointment. At ten-fifty, the receptionist at the front desk buzzed Andrea to let her know that "Kendall Foster from Old Red Barn Brewcrafters" was here. It was the first time she'd actually paid attention to the name of Kendall's brewery, and it made her smile.

With a tug on the handle, Andrea quickly opened her bottom desk drawer and took out her bag so she could grab her compact. Checking the small mirror quickly, she smoothed a fingertip over each eyebrow, then applied a fresh coat of lip gloss. Tossing it all back where it came from, she stood and looked down. Her gray slacks were neatly pressed, a subtle crease lining each leg. The light blue cowl-neck sweater fell just below her hips, and she fidgeted with the collar until it felt right. With a deep breath, she left her office.

The hall to the lobby was a straight shot, and once she turned the corner and headed down it, she could see Kendall waiting. She was looking out the window and didn't see Andrea's approach. She wore gray slacks similar in color to Andrea's, but her sweater was a black V-neck, the sleeves pulled up to mid-forearm and revealing a silver watch on one slim wrist. Her black boots had a modest heel, her hair was down and tucked behind her ears just like last time, and when she turned to meet Andrea's gaze, the blue of her large eyes was almost startling. Andrea swallowed hard, then smiled.

"I see the sun is still shining," she said too loudly, she thought, as she held out her hand. "I wasn't sure it would last when I saw it this morning."

Kendall stood and shook Andrea's hand. Hers was cool to the touch, but soft, her grip firm. "I thought the same thing," she said as she picked up her bag and coat from the leather couch.

They walked down the hall side by side, Andrea waving and smiling to people here and there. Once in her office, she went directly to the small table and pulled out a chair for Kendall. She wasn't certain, but she was pretty sure she saw Kendall squint in suspicion. But she said nothing and took the chair.

As Kendall pulled out her laptop and got herself situated, Andrea cleared her throat and spoke. "Listen, Kendall, about Saturday night..." The sentence dangled and after a beat, Kendall looked at her and raised her eyebrows in question. Andrea wet her lips. "I apologize. I seriously overreacted. I was..." She took in a deep breath, let it out. "I was nervous about being there and I took that out on you and I shouldn't have. I'm really sorry."

Kendall was quiet for a moment. She punched some keys on her laptop, then turned to Andrea. "What were you nervous about?" Her voice was quiet, gentle even. Placing her forearms on the table, she waited.

"Well, to be honest, it was the first time in a long time I'd been to a party by myself." There. It was out. *That wasn't too bad.*

Kendall chuckled. "Me, too."

"You too what?"

"It was the first party I've been to alone in..." She looked up at the ceiling. "Six months? Eight? Something like that. I mean, I was with my friend Liz, but not *with* her."

"Well. I hope I didn't spoil it completely for you." Andrea was surprised to realize she meant every word.

Kendall really did have a great smile. "Of course not. And I'm still sorry for the wine. I hope I didn't spoil the party for you either."

"You didn't. In fact, I'm incredibly glad I went." Andrea hopped up from her chair and went around to her desk to grab her cell. "I met a woman who works at one of the shelters."

"Oh, Lisa? She's awesome."

Andrea nodded. "I went home with this handsome young man last night." She turned her phone so Kendall could see one of the nine hundred photos she'd taken in the past eighteen hours.

"Get out," Kendall said as she took the phone and held it closer. "Oh, my God, is he the cutest thing on the planet?"

Andrea beamed like a proud mama.

"What's his name?"

"Zeke."

"Zeke. That's perfect. Oh, my God, I want to cuddle his little face." Kendall said the last sentence in baby talk startlingly similar to what Andrea had used that morning, and it made her grin. They scrolled through several more photos, each of them using voices three octaves higher than normal.

"I have to go to the pet store this afternoon and pick up some more stuff for him," Andrea said as she finally put the phone away. "I got him a few things from the shop at the shelter, but I want to get him some more. I'll have to wander a little bit, see what there is. I've never had a cat before. I'm not totally sure what I need."

"I can help," Kendall said, and her smile was open and friendly. "I've had cats and dogs my whole life. I've got a cat now. In fact, I got him from Lisa as well."

"Really? You'd do that for me?"

"Of course. That's what friends are for." Kendall blushed gently as she said it, and Andrea watched her tuck her hair behind an ear as her gaze darted away.

"That would be great." Andrea held up a hand. "As long as I'm not putting you out or anything."

"It's no trouble. I'd be more than happy to help you go kitty shopping. Tell me when and where and I'll meet you."

"The pet store on Monroe? Around three-thirty?"

"I'll be there."

Andrea nodded and smiled. "Okay."

"Good. That's settled." Kendall clapped her hands and rubbed her palms together. "Let's get to it then, shall we?"

"Yes." Andrea shifted in her chair and propped her forearms on the table as she watched Kendall tap keys on the laptop. She had really beautiful hands, small and graceful with neatly filed nails and smooth-looking skin, and Andrea found herself staring at them until Kendall started talking.

"Okay. All beer essentially falls into two categories: ales and lagers."

Andrea nodded.

"Ales are heavier, more intensely flavored. Lagers are clean and crisp." Kendall hit a key and the slide changed. As she started talking about amber ales and pale ales and stouts and wheat beers, Andrea found herself shifting her focus back and forth between the picture on the PowerPoint presentation and Kendall's mouth. And whenever she focused on Kendall's mouth, she heard very little; she only saw. Even white teeth and full, glossy lips. *God, she's got a great mouth.* She would blink quickly several times, refocus on the slide, and try to concentrate on what Kendall was saying. And then her eyes would slide back to Kendall's mouth and it would happen all over again.

At one point, Andrea realized that Kendall had stopped talking. Her eyes snapped up to Kendall's who looked...amused? Did she look amused? Andrea swallowed hard.

"I sent this to your e-mail as well, so you can look back over it later if you...missed anything."

"Okay," was all Andrea could manage.

Kendall checked her watch. "I think that's good. You okay with it all?"

Andrea nodded with great enthusiasm. "Yes. Absolutely."

"You're sure? Because lesson number three is tasting. You ready for that?" There was a mischievous twinkle in Kendall's blue eyes.

Andrea couldn't help but smile back at her. "I'm ready."

"All right then. Should we schedule it for the end of a day? And where would you like to do it? Probably not a good idea to drink beer in your office." She laughed. "You can come to my place. I can come to yours. We can find a neutral spot. What feels best to you?"

"Let me think on that and get back to you, okay?" Andrea heard herself say, as the idea of being anywhere else alone with Kendall felt very strange in this moment...and just a little bit dangerous.

Kendall nodded, apparently not picking up on Andrea's indecisiveness. "Absolutely. You let me know." She slid her laptop into the bag and stood up to put on her coat. "In the meantime, kitten paraphernalia. I'll see you on Monroe Avenue at three-thirty, yes?"

"Yes." Speaking of being alone with Kendall.

Kendall held out her hand. "Thanks, Andrea."

"Thank you." Andrea was acutely aware of every tiny millimeter of Kendall's skin nestled in her hand, and her heart rate picked up speed.

With a smile, Kendall left the office.

Andrea stood in the middle of the room, slowly exhaled the last of Kendall's perfume she'd breathed in, and closed her eyes. "Oh, so very, *very* inconvenient," she whispered to the air.

⁖

Kendall glanced at her watch for the fourth time in the last fifteen minutes. It was two-thirty. She'd need to leave for the pet store in about half an hour. Picking up her bottle of water, she returned to doing the same thing she'd spent most of the day doing: staring off into space and trying to analyze her meeting with Andrea this morning.

Three or four times, Kendall had toyed with canceling. Saturday night's incident was awful, and Andrea had been downright rude. Much as the brewery would benefit from having its products in Hagan's, Kendall had integrity, and being lambasted on a regular basis by the head of beer distribution wasn't something she was willing to accept. It was a conclusion she'd come to early Sunday morning as she lay in her bed, wide awake since three.

"That's it," she'd whispered to her empty bedroom. "I'll cancel."

But Monday had dawned sunny and bright, and Kendall had gone to work and made terrific progress with some distributing prospects and she began to think that Saturday hadn't been so bad. The sunshine again this morning helped alleviate her concerns and she'd decided—not for the first time—that she was going to be the bigger person, that she was not going to let an inexplicable personal conflict affect her business dealings. She could handle Andrea Blake. She always had. So she'd put on her favorite black sweater, the one that made her look slim, smart, and casually professional, and she'd gone to the meeting.

And Andrea had been so...*different.*

The apology hadn't really come as that big a surprise. Any decent person would have issued one, and Kendall was happy to accept it. It was the rest of it that had her a little freaked. The smiling, the chatty small talk, the pictures of the kitten, the staring.

"She was totally staring at my mouth." Kendall said it aloud, causing Buster to lift his head from his dog bed. Kendall glanced at him. "She was. I'm sure of it."

Kendall was thoroughly confused.

"Okay." She rubbed both hands roughly over her face. "Enough."

Buster watched her for a long moment. When she picked up the handset to her phone and dialed a contact's number, he was apparently satisfied that she was going to get some work done and settled back down on his bed.

The beeping of her cell phone pulled Kendall out of the project she'd been working on to remind her she needed to hit the road. A quick stop into the ladies' room allowed her to take a good look at herself in the full-length mirror on the back of the door that she'd made her brother install. "I have to make sure I look good for meetings," she'd told Rick by way of reasoning. He'd simply rolled his eyes, chalked it up to a "girl thing," and had the mirror hung up. Now, she stood in front of it and examined herself much more closely than she normally did.

She still wore the black V-neck. Frankly, she felt good in it. It was one of those articles of clothing that made her feel more confident simply because she knew she looked good. After this morning's meeting, she'd scooted back to her own place and had changed from her gray dress slacks to washed jeans and high black boots. Now she gave her hair a quick brush, touched up her makeup, and added a fresh spritz of perfume, all of which she kept in the medicine cabinet in the ladies' room. As there were only three women on the Old Red Barn Brewcrafters staff, she didn't worry about leaving it all in there.

Reclasping a silver hoop earring she was about to lose, she blew out a nervous breath, surprised at the butterflies in her stomach. "No big deal, Kendall," she whispered. "No big deal. Just a friend helping a friend. Relax."

And with that, she felt a little better.

The parking lot at the pet store was sparsely populated when Kendall pulled into a spot at 3:25. She immediately saw Andrea getting out of her black Toyota, sunglasses perched on her face and sunlight glimmering off her wild hair, and the butterflies were suddenly back in full force. Tightening her fingers around the steering wheel, she closed her eyes and counted slowly to five. "Jesus, get a grip."

"Hi there," Andrea said with a grin as Kendall slid out of the driver's seat. "Right on time, as always."

"I can't stand to be late for anything," Kendall said, trying not to stare. God, Andrea looked good. She still wore the same clothes from this morning, but with a black wool pea coat and white gloves with a matching white scarf. She looked sleek, very put together, and ridiculously sexy. Kendall swallowed hard and dragged her gaze toward the store's front entrance. "Shall we?"

Once inside, Andrea grabbed a cart and life became easier for Kendall. Focusing on pet products was a good way to occupy her mind. "Okay. Let's do food first. Do you have an idea what you want to feed him?"

Andrea squinched up her face as she thought, and it created a little divot at the top of her nose. "Something natural. I don't want to feed him something loaded with fillers and preservatives."

"I am happy to hear that." Kendall hooked her fingers over the front of the cart and pulled it toward the food aisle. Once they had both wet and dry food chosen, Kendall asked the next question. "Litter box?"

"I have one. Just the temporary stuff they gave me."

"Where is it?"

"Kitchen."

Kendall immediately shook her head. "No. You don't want it there."

Andrea made a face. "Yeah, I figured."

"Basement? Bathroom?"

"I was thinking the basement, but I'd have to leave the cellar door open and I'm not sure I want to do that."

"You could put a cat door in," Kendall suggested, and pulled the cart along to the correct aisle.

"I have no idea how I'd do that."

Kendall grinned. "Well, lucky for you, it's not that hard. And I can help if you need it." She tried to pull her gaze away, but Andrea held it, and another one of those sizzles passed between them, just like the first time. Kendall cleared her throat. "Okay. Next?" She turned and pulled the cart in no particular direction, simply to get them moving.

"I'd like to get him one of those stands to put in front of the window so he can see out," Andrea said from behind her. "You know what I mean?"

Kendall nodded and headed down the correct aisle.

"Wow. You know this store," Andrea commented with a chuckle.

"Lots of pets in my family. My whole life."

"Yeah? I always wanted a dog growing up, but my mother thinks animals are dirty." Andrea ran her hand over the carpeted top of one of the cat trees.

"Really?"

Andrea tossed a wan smile over her shoulder. "Afraid so."

"Well, that makes me sad for little, tiny Andrea."

"Me, too."

They were quiet for a beat, then Kendall said, "But you have Zeke now."

"I do. I have Zeke now. And I think Zeke deserves this—." She bent to look at the tag. "Cat tree. Don't you?" She turned to Kendall, a wide grin on her face, and—much to Kendall's horror —she felt her knees go weak.

"I do."

Into the cart went the cat tree.

Forty-five minutes and nearly three hundred dollars later, they were loading Andrea's trunk full of stuff.

"I have never seen such a spoiled cat," Kendall commented as she set the last bag down and chuckled.

"Well, maybe you should. See him." Andrea seemed to busy herself with closing the trunk and finding her keys. Her eyes focused on her hands as she pulled on her gloves, she continued. "I was thinking. About lesson number three. Why don't you come to my place? I'll make dinner and you can meet Zeke and then you can teach me more about beer." She looked up then, and Kendall was surprised to see something very much like vulnerability resting there in her eyes.

Kendall wet her lips. With a nod and a smile, she said, "That sounds great."

"Good." Andrea smiled back and the two of them stood there in slightly awkward silence. Finally, Andrea spoke. "I need to check my schedule, so let me get this stuff home and… Can I text you details?"

"Sure."

"Okay. Great. What's your number?"

Kendall rattled it off as Andrea punched it into her cell. Kendall's phone rang from inside her coat pocket, but then stopped.

"There. Now you'll know it's me." Andrea walked around to the driver's side of the Toyota and Kendall backed toward her own car. Over the roof, Andrea grinned. "Thank you so much for all your help, Kendall. I really appreciate it."

"You're welcome," Kendall said simply. "I had fun."

"Me, too. I wasn't sure if I would."

"Neither was I."

They stood like that again, holding one another's gaze, before Andrea finally said, "Okay. I'll text you." She lifted one white-gloved hand. "Bye."

"Bye."

CHAPTER SIX

Andrea's house was adorable, at least from the outside. Kendall took it in as she pulled into the driveway Friday evening. In a nicely maintained city neighborhood, Kendall guessed it was probably built in the 1930s, as many of the houses here were. The siding was a neutral beige, all the trim cream and burgundy. The driveway led back to a matching one-car garage that sat in the back of the yard. Judging by the bushes and flowerpots peeking out from under the snow, Kendall suspected in the summer, the landscaping was bursting with color.

In the back seat of the car, Kendall had stashed a small cooler, her laptop bag, and a bottle of wine as a thank you for the upcoming dinner. Looping straps over her shoulders and pocketing keys, she headed up the front steps. The door opened before she had a chance to knock.

"Hey there. Come in." Andrea stood back to allow Kendall entrance, and Kendall immediately wondered how it was possible for Andrea to put on washed, worn jeans and a green ribbed turtleneck, and look positively radiant. Her hair was loose and everywhere, and she had a pair of cozy-looking suede slippers on her feet.

Kendall gave her body a shake. "Temperature's dropping out there." She set her stuff down in the foyer and unzipped her coat. Andrea took it from her, hanging it on a nearby hall tree as Kendall took off her shoes.

"I have an extra pair of slippers," Andrea suggested.

"You do?"

From around the doorway, Andrea produced a fleecy pair of navy blue slippers. "Nobody's worn them but me. My sister got me these for Christmas." She looked down at those on her feet.

"I'll take 'em. Thank you." There was something strangely intimate about wearing something of Andrea's, but Kendall pushed the thought to a back corner. Handing Andrea the bottle of wine, she said, "This is for you."

Andrea accepted it, their fingers brushing, Kendall trying not to notice. "I love this wine," she said as she looked at the label. "It's one of my favorites."

"Hey, who do you think you're dealing with? I pay attention to the kind of wine I spill all over somebody."

Andrea laughed, a light, very feminine sound, and gestured for Kendall to follow her.

The living room was decorated in comforting, inviting colors, a chocolate brown couch with green and beige throw pillows beckoning to Kendall to come sit. The hardwood floors shone, an area rug in beiges, greens and burgundies breaking things up just a bit. A gas fireplace sat on the far wall, a fire burning cheerfully. There were very few knick-knacks and only a couple photographs, and everything was very neatly in its place.

"This is gorgeous," Kendall said as her eyes scanned the tan walls and pictures of two kids that hung there. Suddenly, a furry little streak of gray shot into the room from around a corner. Kendall laughed. "Zeke, I presume?"

"Zeke," Andrea confirmed and scooped him up. "Come here, rascal."

"Oh. My. God. He is so cute." Kendall shifted her stuff to one hand and got in close because there was no way she was *not* going to nuzzle that kitten. Too late, she realized how close her face would be to Andrea's, and every ounce of energy she had went into focusing on the cat and not the intoxicating scent of Andrea's perfume. *Not* the light pink gloss of her lips, mere inches from Kendall's. *Look at the cat*, her head shrieked at her. *The cat. Only the cat. Look at the cat!*

"Isn't he?"

"Did he sleep last night?" Kendall must have found just the right spot under Zeke's chin to scratch, as the cat closed his eyes, lifted his head slightly, and started to purr. "Oh, the motor's running."

"He did. I heard him running around a couple times, but no large crashes and I didn't wake up to any of my furniture shredded to ribbons, so he did okay."

Kendall scratched for another moment, and when she shifted her gaze up to Andrea's face, it was caught by jade green framed with dark lashes. She took an involuntary step back, then hoped Andrea hadn't made the connection. If she had, she didn't let on.

"Okay, handsome. Go play." Andrea kissed Zeke's head, then set the kitten on the floor and led Kendall to the kitchen. A breakfast bar separated it from a small formal dining room.

"Well, this isn't typical of a city home," Kendall commented on the layout as she set down her goods and took a seat on one of the stools.

"No, it's not. I had my brother-in-law tear down this wall when I moved in. The house felt so dissected and choppy with each room being all closed off. I wanted to open it up a bit."

"This is great." She watched as Andrea went to the stove and lifted the lid from a large stockpot. The kitchen was suddenly filled with the scent of chicken and warmth. "Oh, my God, what is that amazing smell?" she asked, lifting her nose to catch more of the aroma.

"I made chicken soup," Andrea said, giving a half-shrug. "I hope that's okay. I just figured it's so cold and soup is perfect for this weather. I also made bread to help soak it up."

"You made chicken soup and homemade bread?"

"I did."

"I may never leave," Kendall said with a grin. Andrea smiled back at her and that sizzle happened yet again. Kendall cleared her throat. "Do you cook a lot?"

Andrea had turned back to the stove, so answered with her back to Kendall. "I do. I love to cook."

"And how long have you been at Hagan's?"

Andrea stopped stirring to squint up at the ceiling. "Oh, God...I started when I was fifteen. Stayed part-time while I was in school, then back to full-time...sixteen years?"

"Holy cow."

"I know, right?" Andrea laughed. "My goal is to have my own store. Manage it."

"It takes this long?" Kendall thought sixteen years seemed a long time to wait for a promotion, but she admittedly knew nothing about how large retail operations worked.

"We don't open a ton of new stores. And the current managers tend to stay in their positions until they retire."

"It's that good a job, huh?"

"I wouldn't keep waiting like I have if it wasn't. We've got a couple new stores opening in the next few months. One in Pennsylvania and one in Maryland, I think. North Carolina, maybe. I might get lucky."

"You'd move out of state?"

Andrea shrugged. "If it was the only way for me to get my own store? Yes."

"Well, if that's what you want, then I'll keep my fingers crossed for you." Kendall reached for the cooler she'd brought. "How 'bout we get started? I've got some good stuff for you to try." She pulled out several bottles of beer, each a different brand and style. Andrea crossed the room to the breakfast bar, and the trepidation on her face made Kendall burst out laughing. "Just trust me. Okay?"

Andrea nodded, the hesitation replaced with an uncertain smile. "Yes, ma'am."

"That's what I like to hear." Kendall also pulled out two pilsner glasses. "Lots of beers taste better in different glasses, but for tonight, we're just going to use these."

Andrea came to stand next to Kendall and leaned her forearms on the counter as she looked over the bottles. Their shoulders touched and Kendall was reminded of Gina from the bar after volleyball standing the same way, and how very different the reaction of her body was to each of the women. While she did everything she could to put distance between Gina's arm and her own, Kendall actually shifted a millimeter so her shoulder pressed into Andrea's just a bit.

"Do you want to start now or wait until we eat?" Kendall asked, her stomach flipping in a pleasant way. *God, I feel like I'm sixteen. What is my problem?*

"Well, the soup needs another fifteen or twenty minutes, so why don't we start?"

"Okay." Kendall glanced at her laptop bag, then at Andrea, then back.

Andrea chuckled. "What?"

"Well, I brought a whole PowerPoint presentation for this, too, but…it seems kind of silly now."

Andrea waved a hand at her. "Leave it. I'm a smart girl. I can pay attention." Then she winked at Kendall before she pushed off the counter and went to stir the soup. "Teach me."

Kendall inhaled slowly and let it out as quietly as she could. When she'd agreed to teach Andrea, she hadn't counted on the physical attraction to develop so unexpectedly and intensely, and now she wasn't sure what to do about it. If anything. *No,* her brain screamed at her. *You do nothing at all about it. Not a thing. This is business.* With a subtle nod, she took that thought to heart and did her best to shift into business mode.

"Okay. We're not far from the past holidays, and that's good because some of the seasonal beers are best for beginners like yourself."

Andrea returned to her perch, settling herself once again very close to Kendall. "What do you mean by 'seasonal'?"

"Well, lots of brewers make special batches for different seasons, usually in limited quantities. Summer brings out a lot of beer brewed with fruit, especially citrus, to give their beer a lighter, more refreshing taste. Fall touts lots of pumpkin ales and that leads into the holiday season, where many beers are brewed with all kinds of spices."

Andrea's eyebrows raised. "Really? I had no idea. I don't really pay attention."

"That's why you have me."

"Oh, is that why?"

Kendall glanced up at her playful tone and was snared yet again by those green eyes. Wetting her lips, she pulled out a bottle opener and reached in front of Andrea for the first bottle. *Business. Stick to business.* "The holiday seasonals are pretty much gone now, but we hoarded a bunch at our brewery, so I brought some for you to try."

"They're not all yours." It was a statement, and Andrea sounded surprised as she looked over the bottles, turning each to scan the labels, and must have noticed that only one came from Old Red Barn.

"Of course not," Kendall said, furrowing her brow. "I'm not going to feed you just our beer. That wouldn't be fair. I promised to teach you about *beer*, not just about *my* beer."

"So…this is from a competitor of yours?"

Kendall shook her head. "Oh, no. We don't think of it like that. Well, I'm sure some of us do. But my brothers and I don't think about us all being in competition. We all just want to make good beer and share it." She met Andrea's eye. "And make a profit. Let's not be ridiculous. But we make great beer and so do some other breweries. We taste everything, and there are some that we really like that aren't ours. We try to learn from our fellow brewers, and we like to share methods and ideas. Not a terribly common business view, but there it is." She popped the top off the first bottle, took the glass, and poured, starting down the side of the glass, but ending up in the center in order to create a sufficient head of foam.

Andrea watched carefully, and her head tilted just slightly to the side.

"Okay." She handed the glass to Andrea, but didn't let go. "Hang on. Tasting beer is a lot like tasting wine. You need to get the entire effect. That's why a glass is always better than drinking from a bottle. It breathes; it lets you take in the aroma." She let go of the glass. "Take a sniff."

"Really?"

"Just like you would with wine." Andrea did as asked, then took another sniff, and this time, she was paying attention.

76

Kendall could tell by the gentle hardening in her eyes, the slight downturn of her brows. "What do you smell?"

Andrea pressed her lips together in thought, took a third sniff. "Cinnamon."

"Mm-hmm. What else?"

"A little lemon?"

"Uh-huh. And?"

"Maybe…rice? Which is weird." Andrea looked up at her like a child hoping she got the right answer. She did.

"Weird but correct. How does it look?"

Andrea held the glass up to the light. "It's a little cloudy."

"That's the sign of a wheat beer."

"Kind of a dark gold color. The foam is thick on top."

"Good. Perfect. Now take a sip."

Andrea hesitated just enough to make Kendall grin. Then she put the glass to her mouth and tasted, coming away with a tiny bit of foam on her upper lip. Kendall swallowed hard, and tucked her hand subtly under her thigh to keep from reaching up to wipe it away.

Andrea opened and closed her mouth several times, analyzing the taste, then took another sip. "You know. This isn't horrible."

Kendall laughed. "Coming from somebody who doesn't like beer, I think that's a compliment. Can you see why it's a seasonal beer?"

Nodding, Andrea said, "The flavor…it's very…warm. The cinnamon, maybe a little nutmeg. Very wintery. Very Christmas. It's got a little bit of spice."

"Everything is better with a little bit of spice. Don't you think?"

Andrea held her gaze and nodded. "I do."

Kendall was pleased. "Very good. Okay." She pulled another bottle forward, then reached for the glass, which Andrea held away from her.

"No. I want this."

"You do?" Kendall raised her eyebrows.

"It's good. It's like beer, but…not."

"Well, all right then."

"Are you going to have some?"

"Me?"

"I don't want to be the only one drinking here, Kendall."

Something in Andrea's face, the way she said Kendall's name, something in her expression, just the slightest bit of a pout—or maybe Kendall was completely inventing it in her own mind— but something tugged at her. Low in her body. *Low* in her body. "Okay. I'll join you." She pulled an IPA from the cooler, one she'd brought for herself, and poured it into the other glass.

Andrea set hers down, crossed the couple steps to the stove and stirred the soup, then bent to pull the bread from the oven. Kendall stared at what was a nearly perfect ass for several seconds before realizing what she was doing, and, yanking her gaze away, looked intently at the ceiling instead.

"What are you looking at?"

Kendall glanced back at Andrea, who was now squinting up. "Oh, um, yeah. Your light. It's nice."

Andrea shrugged. "Thanks."

"That smells fabulous. What can I do to help?"

"You can put our beers on the table and grab me the soup bowls." Andrea flicked the oven mitts off her hands and gestured toward the dining room with her chin.

"On it."

Kendall could not say enough good things about the meal. The soup was hearty, warming, and had just enough of everything to make it perfect. "This bread?" She held up her third slice so Andrea knew just which bread she was talking about. "This bread is ridiculous. *Ridiculous.*"

Andrea's laugh settled in the pit of Kendall's stomach, caused a flutter there. "Is that a good thing?"

"It's absolutely a good thing. Ridiculous in a good way." As Kendall buttered the slice, she said, "Do not let me eat another piece. I mean it. I'll have to go buy new pants." She noticed Andrea's glass was empty and she pointed to it with her butter knife. "You liked it."

"I did. Surprise." Andrea grinned.

"Well, we need to try the next one then. Are you ready?" At Andrea's nod, she went to the cooler and pulled the next beer. "This is a Hefeweizen. It's German. I brought a raspberry one because I thought a little bit of fruitiness would increase its chances of you actually liking it." She winked at Andrea as she poured.

Andrea held the glass up to the light. "Definitely cloudy. A tiny bit of color there, from the raspberries, I assume."

Kendall nodded. "Some fruity beers are brewed with much more fruit. Those are lambics. You'll probably really like them, but I didn't have one to bring. Next time."

Andrea quirked up a corner of her mouth at the comment, then brought the glass to her nose. "Oh, I can definitely smell the raspberries." She sipped and really seemed to take her time analyzing the flavor. "I can tell this is a different beer, but not terribly different."

"Hefeweizen is also a wheat beer, like the last one."

"The raspberry is really subtle. There at the beginning, but gone after I swallow."

"It's on the front, not the back."

"Yes. Exactly."

"You like it?"

"I do." The surprise was evident in Andrea's eyes as she took another sip.

Kendall laughed. "Okay. You drink that and we'll taste another." She popped the top on another bottle, used her own glass, and poured the much darker beer.

"Oh, that one's pretty," Andrea breathed.

With a grin, Kendall informed her, "This is a coffee stout. There are also chocolate stouts. When they make a stout, they roast the malt or the barley first, so it has a bit of a burnt taste." She held the glass up, admiring the thick creaminess of the head, the deep, dark brown of the beer. Andrea was right. Stouts were pretty. She handed the glass to Andrea, who went over it like an old pro, holding it up to the light, then sniffing it.

"I can smell the coffee immediately."

"It's pretty prevalent."

Andrea took a sip, and it was only a second or two before she made a face that had Kendall laughing out loud.

"Is that a no?" she asked as Andrea handed her the glass.

"That is most definitely a no. Blech. I feel like I need to wipe off my tongue like Tom Hanks in *Big*. I'll stick to my fruity beer, thank you very much."

"Yeah, I wasn't sure how that one would go over. I'll drink it."

And that's how the evening progressed. Andrea drank the beers she liked, handed those she didn't over to Kendall. Several sips into her fourth full glass, a shandy, Andrea said, "I think I may be a little drunk."

"Yeah, that would be one of the drawbacks—or benefits, depending on how you look at it—of craft beers. They tend to have a higher alcohol content than your average, run-of-the-mill Budweiser. In fact, that last one you had was..." Kendall squinted at the bottle, feeling slightly tipsy herself. "Almost nine percent."

"Is that a lot?"

"Regular beer is about four percent, so..."

"So, yes. The answer is yes."

"The answer is yes."

Zeke took that moment to make his third appearance of the night, zipping through the room chasing his little stuffed mouse toy in what Kendall had dubbed a "drive-by." Both women giggled as the kitten disappeared under the dining room table, only to reappear out the other side, the neon green toy in his mouth.

"He is freaking adorable," Kendall said. When she pulled her eyes from Zeke to glance in Andrea's direction, she found her staring. "You okay?"

Andrea blinked several times. "Yes. Yeah, sorry. I'm good." She cleared her throat. "Listen, Kendall. I have a guest room and a couch. And..." She let her eyes wander over the table, allowing the empty bottles to speak for themselves.

"And I probably should not be driving." Kendall finished the thought.

"Yeah." Andrea nodded.

Kendall had been having such a good time, she hadn't really paid attention to her beer consumption. But Andrea was right. She wasn't drunk, but she was pretty buzzed, and getting into the driver's seat in this state was not smart. "You're sure you don't mind?"

"Not at all. I'd rather you're safe."

"Thank you."

"Of course." Andrea stood, teetered ever-so-slightly, and picked up her glass. "So, if you're staying, let's go sit on the couch where it's more comfortable. Want to watch a movie or something? It's early and it's Friday."

Kendall watched as she walked by, the jeans looking even better on Andrea than they had when she first opened the door. Kendall took another large gulp of her beer and followed her hostess.

Once they were side by side on the alarmingly comfortable couch with their slippered feet up on the coffee table and their remaining beer in their hands, they settled in by mutual agreement to watch the *Friends* marathon on one of the cable channels. Determining who knew the show better proved to be a challenge, as each of them quoted her share of lines correctly. Kendall seemed to have a knack for cracking Andrea up, and she decided in pretty short order that the sound of Andrea's laughter was something she liked very much. When their beers were gone, the empty glasses ended up on the coffee table, and Andrea remarked on the cold weather as she pulled a huge afghan off the back of the couch and covered them both with it.

Kendall couldn't remember the last time she'd been so completely comfortable.

Sleep came as a total surprise, and when Kendall next opened her eyes, there was an infomercial on the television for a super-duper blender of some sort, and Andrea was snuggled up against her. With a squint at her watch, she saw it was 2:43 in the morning. They'd obviously shifted and slid, as Kendall was lying to her right, her head on a throw pillow, her legs still propped on the table. She was stunned to note that her arm was wrapped protectively around Andrea's shoulders, and Andrea was sleeping soundly, her head up under Kendall's chin as if it was the most natural position for them to be in. Auburn curls were everywhere, and Kendall placed a gentle kiss on the top of Andrea's head before she even realized she was about to do it.

An internal battle started then, Kendall's brain warring with her body. Her brain said she should get up, go, leave, run. Now. This was a bad situation. This was supposed to be business. How could she ever expect a fair shot at getting her product into Hagan's if she had an unfair advantage? Her body, however, wouldn't move. It was warm and comfortable and…happy. Yes, happy. Happy to be holding on to a beautiful woman. Happy to be curled up on a comfy couch, under a soft blanket, sharing body heat. And Andrea smelled so good, like coconut and oranges. *Has to be her shampoo*, Kendall thought as she moved her head enough to sink her nose into Andrea's hair and inhale.

Slight movement caught her eye, and it was only then that Kendall noticed Zeke all curled up in the crook of Andrea's knees. "Well, now there's no way I can move," she whispered, and that was all the convincing she needed. The remote was too far away for her to reach without disturbing everybody, so she left the TV on, and moved her hand to bury her fingers in Andrea's hair. Andrea shifted slightly, took a deep breath, and snuggled in closer to Kendall, who swallowed hard, then took her own deep, relaxing breath, and closed her eyes. It wasn't long before she drifted off again.

❧

Something was tapping her face.

Lightly. Softly. But insistently.

Kendall struggled up through the thick underwater feel of being heavily asleep as the tapping continued. Cheek. Chin. Forehead. Cheek again. When she was finally able to open her eyes, she was confronted with a gray, furry face with a white chin and a little pink nose. Blue eyes looked at hers for a beat before a tiny paw tapped her nose.

"Well, good morning, Mr. Zeke. What an effective alarm clock you make."

The kitten cocked his head as he listened. Kendall shifted her hand under the blanket, and that became Zeke's new target as he launched himself at the bump it made.

The smell of coffee and the coolness of realizing she was alone on the couch hit Kendall at the same time. Squeaking floorboards overhead told her where the mistress of the house was, and Kendall was surprised she hadn't felt Andrea get up. Then she wondered what position they'd been in when Andrea had awakened and how freaked out she'd been about it.

And then *she* started to freak out about it.

Sitting up quickly, she frightened the kitten, who bolted off the couch like a shot. Kendall stood and straightened her clothes, which had become annoyingly twisted around her body. Then she folded the blanket and looked around frantically for her shoes before remembering that she was wearing Andrea's slippers in place of her boots.

A glance over her shoulder told her the kitchen was clean—how in the world had she slept through *that*?—and her cooler was set neatly on the dining room table. Avoiding the mirror on the dining room wall, she collected it and hauled it to the front door where she began exchanging slippers for boots.

Andrea came down the stairs just as Kendall was setting the slippers neatly near the door. She stopped, one hand on the banister. "Hi," she said, and everything about her, from her stance to her voice, was tentative, uncertain.

"Hey," Kendall replied, unable to hold eye contact. "Um, I've got an early meeting, so I should get going."

"On a Saturday?" Andrea asked, but didn't question further.

Kendall closed her eyes for a brief moment, mentally cursing her apparent inability to keep track of the days of the week, before sputtering, "Um, yeah. Sometimes it's the only time my brothers and I can make our schedules work." *Oh, nice, Kendall. Smooth lie. Very smooth.*

"Oh. Okay." Andrea nodded and Kendall was convinced she sounded more relieved than skeptical.

"Thank you for dinner," Kendall said. "And for the slippers."

Andrea smiled. "You're welcome. Thanks for the lesson and the tasting." She brought a hand to her head with a wince. "And the slight hangover."

Kendall chuckled. "Yeah, sorry about that. I didn't think you'd drink all the ones you liked."

"Isn't that what you're supposed to do with beer you like? Drink it?"

Kendall grinned and zipped up her coat.

"Do you want some coffee to take with you?" Andrea remained on the stairs.

"No, that's okay. I'll get some on my way home…err…to the meeting. But thank you."

"I'll call you," Andrea said as Kendall opened the front door and had her face slapped by the cold air.

Kendall nodded. "Great. Thanks again, Andrea." She walked as quickly to her car as she could, wishing she'd taken the time to warm it up first. But she had to get out of there. She couldn't explain it. She just had to.

The SUV complained slightly in the cold, but finally turned over, and Kendall let it run for a few minutes as she pulled on her gloves and glanced in the rearview mirror. Her hair was a flattened mess and the mascara she hadn't removed before sleeping left attractive black smudges on her lids.

"Oh, aren't you a lovely sight to wake up to?" She sat back roughly in her seat and blew out a breath she could see. When she glanced back at the house, she was pretty sure she saw the curtain move slightly.

She jammed the car into reverse and fled the scene.

CHAPTER SEVEN

"Oh, shit."

Andrea lowered herself down onto the couch, cradling a cup of coffee in both hands. She blew on it before taking a sip and watched Zeke as he ran around under the dining room table like his tail was on fire. He zipped her way and ran up her pant leg before she even saw him coming. She laughed and set down her coffee, then scooped him up.

"What do I do about this, Zekey-boy? Hmm? I can't have a thing for this woman. It's not cool, given our jobs." Zeke batted her on the nose, sans claws. Then he struggled until she set him down, and he was off and running again. Andrea shook her head with a grin as she picked her coffee back up and took another sip. Glancing at the neatly folded afghan, her mind tossed her a flashback from barely three hours ago.

She was warm. So comfortably warm and relaxed that she actually fought waking up, struggling to keep her eyes closed, to stay in the sweet oblivion of slumber. But her efforts were fruitless and her lungs took in a large, slow breath and her eyes finally blinked their lids against the sunlight beaming directly on them. She was lying with her head turned to the left, and under her ear she could hear the soft, steady beating of a heart, feel the gentle rise and fall of restful breathing. There was a warm, protective hand resting on the small of her back, under her shirt and against her bare skin, and her leg was thrown casually over another. Afraid to actually look, she was reasonably sure her left hand rested very happily on a breast.

Andrea took it all in, afraid to move until she had stock of the entire situation. She barely remembered falling asleep—they'd been watching Friends, *hadn't they? And she certainly didn't remember being this close to Kendall. Touching Kendall. Lying on top of Kendall with Kendall's breast in her hand. Because that's exactly what she was doing right now. Just about lying on top of Kendall. Kendall, who was sleeping soundly and peacefully, her arm wrapped around Andrea as if they slept like this all the time.*

Being very careful, Andrea lifted her head and looked up. Kendall was sound asleep, one arm bent near her head, her full lips parted just a little bit. Her blond hair tousled across the throw pillow, and her head was turned slightly to her right, giving Andrea a full, perfect view of her long neck, the smooth-looking skin, the line of her jaw, the small gold hoop in her earlobe. Andrea's body reacted immediately and she had to fight to keep herself from exploring more of the softness under her hand. She knew if she didn't get up, get away, now, *she would do something they'd both regret later. She did allow herself another few moments to just look—God, Kendall was a beautiful woman—before swallowing hard and then very slowly and very carefully extricating herself from her cocoon.*

She took another sip of coffee now as she recalled just how cold she'd suddenly felt once away from Kendall's body heat. Away from Kendall's body. The woman obviously slept like a log because she hadn't moved. Andrea went on to clean up the kitchen and then headed upstairs to take a shower, and Kendall never shifted once. The memory of it brought a tender smile to Andrea's lips and it took a beat or two before she forced it away.

"This is not something to be smiling about," she said aloud, and Zeke stopped his stalking of a shoe to glance in her direction. "Seriously, Zeke. I mean it. This is not funny." Dropping her head back against the couch, she talked it out with her kitten, who at least had enough manners to creep back over to the couch and jump up onto the back so he could bat and nibble at her hair while she spoke. "She's in competition with other brewers. There can't be any impropriety. You know?" She turned to look at Zeke, whose blue eyes were wide. "Her company deserves a fair shot, and if anybody finds out she's getting...special treatment from me, there could be trouble. Repercussions. For both of us. Right?" He studied her, as if really analyzing her question, before bopping her on the nose with a tiny paw. She couldn't help but laugh. "Well, I guess I just leave it alone now. I told her I'd call her but...I probably shouldn't. We tasted enough and she's taught me enough where I can probably educate myself more on my own. I also realize that I'm talking to a cat, but I'm doing so to sort it all out in my own mind. I am not crazy." She scratched Zeke's little head. He'd apparently had enough deep conversation for the moment because he pushed off the couch and flew into the dining room.

Andrea shook her head. "Well. At least it's over..." Her voice trailed off and her coffee cup stopped halfway to her mouth as her eyes fell on what Zeke was playing with now: the strap to Kendall's laptop bag, which sat leaning against a table leg where Andrea had set it this morning.

"Oh, shit."

⋙

"Shit." Kendall tore through her car, throwing papers and bags out of her way. "No, no, no, no." Snow brush. Extra gloves. Boots. Gym bag. Her laptop was nowhere to be found and she was searching her car for no reason because she knew exactly where it was. "Okay, Universe. You win. You've had your fun. You can stop fucking with me now. Please?"

The entire ride home from Andrea's, she'd vowed that was it. This ridiculous attraction she had for the woman couldn't continue. She was a business acquaintance. That they happened to not only fall asleep on each other, but slept wrapped up together for the entire night, was beside the point. Andrea had obviously woken up and panicked; how else was Kendall to look at it? She'd been up, showered, and dressed before any conversation took place. That was pretty clear. It said, "We're not going to discuss the previous night. We were drunk, tired, and today, we're moving on." It made perfect sense to Kendall.

Except for when she thought back to waking up at two in the morning with Andrea wrapped up in her arms and how she hadn't wanted to move.

"Stupid, stupid, stupid," she muttered as she pulled back out of her car and smacked her head on the doorframe. "Damn it."

The crunch-squeak of cold, cold snow under tires made her turn her head. Liz's Honda was pulling up alongside Kendall's SUV.

"I'm late," Liz said as she got out of her car. "I know. Sue me."

Kendall blinked at her. "Late for what?"

"Aw, come on, Kendall. Tell me you didn't forget." Liz's dark hair was spiked up in front and shiny with product. She wore a dark coat and a red scarf and smelled just a little heavily of cologne. It wasn't her typical Saturday morning outfit, and that's what kicked Kendall's memory in.

"Breakfast! The cute waitress." Kendall nodded, held up a placating hand. "I didn't forget. Just give me a minute. Come up."

"You totally forgot," Liz muttered as she followed Kendall up the outside stairs to her apartment. The building had originally been a large barn, but was converted into a roomy garage nearly fifteen years ago. The second floor was then remodeled into a small but adorably functional apartment and Kendall had moved in almost three years ago.

"I didn't forget," Kendall lied as she slipped her key into the lock. "I'm just…running a little behind this morning." She pushed through the door as a black ball of fur sat front and center and began a mournful yeowling. "Hi, Ollie. I know. I know. I'm sorry." She kicked off her boots and went straight to the kitchen situated against the far wall. As she pulled out the bag of cat food and poured some into the small bowl in the corner, Liz gasped dramatically, one hand over her mouth, the other pointing an accusing finger at Kendall.

"You haven't been home! You were out all night!" She said it as if she'd just solved the most complicated math problem of all time. Kicking off her own shoes, she crossed the room and flopped over the arm of the couch, then propped her head on her fist. "Spill."

Kendall shook her head and sighed in defeat as she watched her cat dive into his food dish like he hadn't eaten in weeks. There would be no pacifying Liz until Kendall gave her every detail; she knew better than to fight it. "Fine," she said, drawing the word out to make her annoyance clear. Then she told Liz the entire story, from the invite to the amazing food to the beer to the glaringly obvious attraction they each had for each other to the falling asleep on the couch.

"Wow," Liz said on a dreamy breath. "It's like a romance novel."

"Yeah, and this morning was the bucket of cold water thrown on the whole thing."

"What do you mean?"

"I mean I woke up alone on the couch."

"Maybe she just didn't want to wake you." Sitting up in excitement, Liz added, "I bet she watched you sleep. They always watch the other one sleep."

Kendall quirked a brow at her. "They?"

"In the rom-coms. One always watches the other one sleep. It's romantic."

"It's creepy."

"Quit stomping all over my fantasy, Kendall." She made a gesture to continue. "You woke up alone. Then what?"

Kendall told her how the kitchen had been cleaned and Andrea had been completely showered and dressed and had barely come all the way downstairs before Kendall left.

"Okay, first of all," Liz ticked off fingers as she spoke, "you sleep like the dead, so it's no wonder you didn't hear anything. Second, she made coffee and offered you some. And third, it sounds a little bit like you sprinted out the door before she even had the *chance* to come all the way down the steps."

Kendall stared at her for a beat before saying simply, "Shut up, Liz. You weren't there."

Liz took that to mean, correctly, that she was on the right track. "Why are you so freaked about this?"

"Because it's business." Kendall crossed the small room and dropped onto the couch next to her friend. "She has the power, not so much to make or break my company, but to at least help it make a significant profit. I can't have it look like I'm trying to influence her decision."

Liz looked at her for a full five seconds before busting out laughing. "What do you think this is, a gangster movie? That it's common practice for people to try to bed the beer distributor in order to get a place on her grocery store shelves? That one of

Matt's guys from Stark Brewers is spying on you and may whack you for getting too close to said beer distributor?"

Kendall allowed herself to be stung by Liz's laughter for a split second before grudgingly agreeing with her. "When you put it like that, it does sound a little bit overdramatic."

"A little bit?"

Kendall bumped her with a shoulder. "Shut up. You're making me feel stupid."

"That's because you are *being* stupid. And I thought you hated this woman."

"I never hated her. I disliked her a great deal. Before. Anyway, I thought she hated me."

"And yet you spent the night on her couch with her sleeping on top of you. Frankly, I'm a little disappointed you didn't take advantage of the situation at two o'clock this morning."

Yeah, so am I, Kendall thought, but kept it to herself.

"I think you should call her," Liz said, her face completely serious now.

"Yeah?"

"Yeah. It's been a while for you. Just...feel her out. See where she stands on the whole thing. Can't hurt."

"As it turns out, I'm going to have to call her, regardless." At Liz's confused expression, she continued. "I left my laptop there."

Another bark of laughter burst from Liz's mouth. "You *are* living a romantic comedy. That shit only happens in the movies, I swear."

Kendall shook her head, but couldn't help laughing along with her. "It's ridiculous, isn't it?"

"Totally. It's also your shot." Liz held her gaze, then gave a gentle smile and a half-shrug. "You *have* to call her."

"I do."

"The decision is pretty much out of your hands."

"It is." They sat quietly, letting the facts sit with them. Finally, Kendall slapped her hands on her thighs and stood. "Let's go scope out your waitress, shall we? Let's focus on your love life for a change."

Kendall did a quick tidy up, teeth brushing, and change of clothes, and thirty minutes later, they sat in a booth at Julian's, one of the most popular downtown restaurants in the area. It was very busy—Kendall was surprised they didn't have to wait to sit —and it smelled deliciously of bacon, maple syrup, and homemade waffles. Julian's wasn't fancy. In fact, it was rather plain in its décor of wooden tables, orange vinyl booths, and deep green carpet. But the food was good hearty fare, a little Greek, a little Italian, a lot of American, and the place was almost always at least three-quarters full. Breakfast was an especially busy time of day, as Julian's homemade Belgian waffles were legendary.

Also legendary was Liz's crush on a certain Julian's waitress by the name of Marcy, who happened to work their table that morning, as luck would have it.

"Can I get you ladies something to drink? Coffee? Tea? O.J.?" Marcy's smile was contagious as she stood at their table, notepad in hand, pen poised to take their order. She had a silver ball on a rod pierced through the end of her right eyebrow and a diamond stud in the left side of her nose. Her short-sleeved shirt revealed too many tattoos on her left arm to count, and her short hair was purple today. Kendall was pretty sure it had been green on their last visit.

"Coffee for me would be great," Kendall said. After a beat of silence, she kicked at Liz under the table. "Liz? Coffee?"

"Oh. Um. Yes. Please. Coffee. Yes." By the time she raised her wide blue eyes in Marcy's direction, the waitress had turned to leave. Dejection was clear on Liz's face.

"What is the matter with you?" Kendall hissed at her. "You didn't even look at her."

Liz dropped her head into her hands with a groan. "I know. I can't! I don't know what happens to me. She gets close and suddenly, my brain won't function."

Kendall grinned at her friend.

Liz looked up at her, saw the expression. "What?"

"You're very cute like this."

"Like what?"

"Lovesick."

"Stop it."

Kendall continued to grin, then saw Marcy on her way back. "Here she comes," she whispered. "Make eye contact, for God's sake."

"Here we go," Marcy said, setting down their coffees and depositing several little containers of cream onto the table. "Ready to order?"

"Liz? You go first," Kendall directed, widening her eyes slightly across the table.

"Okay. Um…I would like a waffle please. With strawberries." Liz cleared her throat and looked up.

"Excellent choice," Marcy said. "Would you like whipped cream on that?" She managed to capture and hold Liz's gaze, and when she mentioned the whipped cream, she arched one eyebrow ever so slightly. Kendall rolled her lips in and bit down on them to keep from laughing out loud.

"Yes, please," Liz said in a small voice, and her throat moved as she swallowed.

"Another excellent choice," Marcy said, then winked. "And you?" She turned to Kendall.

"I'll have the same thing. No whipped cream, though. Liz can have it all."

"Perfect. I'll be back in just a bit." Marcy gathered the menus, shot a last look at Liz, and was gone.

"Oh, my God," Liz whispered. "What just happened?"

"What just happened was we were not-so-subtly told that your crush on Marcy is reciprocated."

"You think so?"

Kendall cocked her head and gave Liz a look. "Were you not just here fifteen seconds ago?"

"What do I do now?"

"You ask her out, weirdo."

"Hey." Liz pointed at Kendall with her spoon before stirring sugar into her coffee. "You had a gorgeous woman sleeping on top of you all night and you did nothing, so let's think twice about who's calling who a weirdo."

"Touché," Kendall said with a grimace. "Okay. I'm out." She held her hands up in defeat. "You do what you want."

Marcy delivered their dishes not long after that, Liz's loaded with what was obviously extra whipped cream. The restaurant was packed and she was off immediately.

Liz and Kendall ate their breakfast and chatted about nothing important. When they each set down their forks in surrender, Kendall saw Marcy heading their way. She gave Liz a look, widened her eyes slightly, but said nothing.

"Can I get you guys anything else?" Marcy asked.

Kendall shook her head. "Nothing for me, thanks. Liz? Is there something you'd like?"

"Yes. Um..." Liz cleared her throat. "This is going to sound...forward. Maybe. But, would you...would you like to...maybe..."

The stuttering was apparently as painful for Marcy to watch as it was for Kendall because she interrupted Liz with, "Grab coffee with you? I'd love to. I'm off here at three. Meet me outside?"

The combination of relief and joy that spread across Liz's face in half a second flat was almost comical. "Great. That's great. That's perfect." Liz nodded as she spoke, kept nodding even when she was done.

Marcy set the check face down on the table. "See you at three, Liz." And she was off again.

Liz stared after her for a moment. When she turned back to Kendall, her eyes were wide and sparkling. "I did it," she whispered.

"You did," Kendall said happily.

"I did it."

"I am very proud of you, my friend."

"What time is it?" Kendall held her watch so Liz could see it. "Oh, my God. I don't have much time."

Kendall squinted at her. "Liz. You've got more than four hours."

"That is *not* much time." She wiped her face and threw her napkin down, grabbed her stuff and the check. Glancing back at Kendall, who hadn't moved, she snapped her fingers. "Let's go. Let's *go!*"

Kendall laughed. "I'm coming, Romeo. I'm coming."

At least one of them had made a move.

∽

Kendall did whatever she could to keep herself occupied for the rest of the day. She was avoiding the ultimate issue here—that she needed to get in touch with Andrea—and she knew it. But that didn't keep her from reading the news on Huffington Post on her phone, playing Candy Crush, and surfing Netflix to see if there was something new to watch. And all the while she was keeping herself busy doing meaningless things, in the back of her mind was the image of Andrea sleeping comfortably alongside her, all tousled hair, parted lips and warm skin.

"How the hell did I end up here?" she asked aloud more than once, because the truth was, she could still feel Andrea in her arms. She could still smell her hair and hear her soft, even breathing. And she wanted to be back there. She wanted to turn back time, go back twelve or fourteen hours and do what she wanted so badly to do right now. Because Andrea couldn't give her that look or ridicule her or yell at her if Kendall was kissing her senseless, now could she?

Dropping her face into her hands, Kendall groaned loudly, earning her a look of irritation from Ollie napping on a windowsill. She propped her chin on a palm and just watched him for a moment, trying not to think any longer about anything, but it was futile.

"I have to get my computer back, Ollie. There's no getting around that. I need it for work." With a sigh, she picked up her cell phone, just as it began ringing in her hand, startling her so much that she dropped it. Grabbing it from the floor, she glanced at the screen, shocked to see Andrea's name there. "Holy shit, how weird is that?" Taking a deep breath, she mentally tried to pull herself together, though why she was freaking out, she was uncertain. She cracked her neck by stretching her head to one side, then the other, finally muttering, "Screw it," and hitting the Talk button. "Hello?"

"Kendall?"

"Yes."

"Um, hi. It's Andrea. Andrea Blake."

"Oh, hi, Andrea." *That's it. Play it cool. You barely remember her.* "How are you?"

"Good. I'm good." There was a pause and Kendall was pretty sure she heard a swallow. "Listen, you left your laptop here."

"I did?" *Good. Feigned surprise. You hadn't even noticed because you have not been thinking about her at all. Certainly not all day long.*

"Yeah. I leaned it against the dining room table while you were sleeping and you must not have seen it."

While I was sleeping... Kendall thought back on Liz's words, how she was sure Andrea had watched her sleeping, and something about that idea sent that familiar flutter through Kendall's stomach. And then it ventured lower.

"Oh. Huh. I hadn't even realized I was missing it." Kendall had no idea why she was lying, but she kept up the story. "I have a desktop here at home, but yeah, I'm going to need the laptop for work."

"I figured. Well, I can bring it by if you need it tonight. Or you can certainly come by here. You do know where I live." Andrea's voice held a hint of a smile and something else... flirtatiousness?

"That's true." Kendall wet her lips, suddenly feeling weirdly nervous. "Um, okay. How about I swing by tomorrow. Is there a time that's better than not?"

"I'm going to be here all day tomorrow. I've got some paperwork to get done. Any time is fine."

"Okay. I'll text you when I'm on my way. Is that okay?"

"Perfect. I'll see you tomorrow, Kendall."

The way Andrea said her name, softly, almost tenderly, was enough to turn Kendall into a puddle of goo. She stared at the phone in her hand long after she'd ended the call, painfully aware that she was completely turned on.

This was bad.

This was very, very bad.

Wasn't it?

CHAPTER EIGHT

Kendall was stalling and she knew it. Reaching across the table to stab another pancake she didn't really want, she asked her mother what was new in her life.

"What's new in my life?" Cathy Foster squinted at her, at the odd question, but responded anyway. "Oh, my life is very exciting, I have to admit." She grinned as she smoothly flipped the four pancakes in the pan on the stove. As if realizing she did, in fact, have something to talk about, she added, "My book club meets tonight."

Kendall tried not to show her relief at having something to talk about, something to take her mind off her impending trip to Andrea's house. "What are you reading?"

"The latest Stephen King," her mother said. "Honestly, I think the man's disturbed."

"Disturbed and richer than God," Jim Foster commented from behind his Sunday paper.

Kendall grinned at her father, then asked, "Did you read the whole book?"

"Of course she did," her father answered for his wife. "She complains how scary it is, but she won't put the damned thing down. She sits up in bed with the covers all pulled up under her chin. Like a blanket's going to protect her from a deranged killer or an angry ghost." He lifted a shoulder in defense and chuckled as Cathy swiped at him with her dish towel.

"He's a very good writer," she explained. "It's just...you have to wonder about somebody's mind when they can come up with such...warped ideas."

Jim folded the section of paper he'd been reading, set it down, and picked up the next. As he did, he glanced at his daughter from across the table. "What's on your agenda today, Kendall?"

Kendall chewed her bite of pancake. She swallowed and said, "I need to go visit a friend."

"What friend?" Adam asked as he came in from the mudroom.

"God, you move like a cat," Cathy muttered. "I never hear you come in."

Adam crossed the room and kissed her on the cheek. "How do you think I was able to sneak out and back in all those nights as a teenager, Mom?"

Cathy laughed and gave him a swat with her dish towel as well, her weapon of choice since her children were little.

Kendall hoped the subject had moved on, but Adam persisted. "What friend?" he asked again as he grabbed a dish and piled it with four pancakes, then scooped the remaining bacon from off the plate in the middle of the table.

"Andrea." Kendall said it quietly, hoping to gloss over it.

"Andrea Blake?" Adam's sandy eyebrows went up to meet his hairline. "She's your friend now? I thought you hated her."

"No. I don't hate her."

"Or...no, wait. She hated you. Right?" Kendall stayed silent. Adam did not. "Wait...didn't you just tell us the other night about how mean she was at volleyball? And that she'd basically blackmailed you into giving her a beer education?"

Kendall shrugged. "Turns out, she's not so bad." She kept her eyes downcast. Adam had always been able to read her like a book and she was hoping to avoid his scrutiny.

"So, you just visit her now?"

"She…has my laptop."

"What? Why does she have your laptop?" Adam chewed as he pawed through the paper, earning a whack from his father as he grabbed for a section not yet read.

Kendall stood, took her plate to the sink. "I left it there by accident." She turned on the water, hoping to drown out any reply, wanting Adam to leave it alone. He, of course, was her big brother. Leaving things alone was not something he was capable of.

"Left it where?"

"At her house."

"You were at her house? When?"

"Friday." Kendall rinsed her dish and put it in the dishwasher, keeping her back to the table. She could feel her mother's gaze next to her.

"I thought you were meeting with her at her office."

"I did. Tuesday."

"And yet she ended up with your laptop Friday. At her house…" Adam scrunched up his face, pretending to think really hard as he let his voice trail off like a detective in a murder mystery, slowly putting the pieces together for the viewers.

Kendall shot him a look. "I wanted her to taste some different beer and didn't think we should do that at her office. Okay, Mr. Nosy?"

"Friday during the day? Or Friday at night?" He was completely messing with her now, and she knew it, felt her face heating up. He'd been able to push her buttons since they were kids, and he relished it.

"People work during the day, jerkface."

"Ah-ha. So Friday *night* then."

And right on cue, her father joined in.

"You know," Jim said as he tipped one corner of his paper down so he could make eye contact with his son. "Now that I think about it, I got up early yesterday morning and Kendall's car wasn't in her driveway. I thought that was odd."

"Dad!" Kendall sounded just as young as she felt in that moment.

Jim grinned, winked, and went back to his paper even as Adam turned to Kendall, mouth agape in feigned shock.

"You were out *all night?*"

Kendall looked for help. "Mom...?"

"Oh, you two leave her alone," Cathy said, but it was halfhearted and she was hiding a grin.

Suddenly, Kendall was twelve again, the youngest in the family and the only girl, sure the entire world was against her. She groaned and stomped out of the kitchen, grabbed her coat off the hook on her way out the door, and continued stomping until she reached her apartment.

Inside, she scooped up Ollie, much to his dismay, and cuddled him close to her face as she focused on her breathing, worked on relaxing and letting go of her anger. She loved her brother. She loved her entire family deeply. But Adam could always make her feel like a child, even at thirty years old, and he rarely knew when to let up. At the same time, she wasn't sure why his teasing her about Andrea bothered her so much. He could certainly accuse her of far more horrible things than spending the night with a beautiful, sexy woman. In fact, it was almost flattering, her family thinking she was sleeping with Andrea. Who *wouldn't* be flattered?

That was just it, though, wasn't it? She couldn't sleep with Andrea. Even if she wanted to. Which, she was enough of a grown-up to admit, she absolutely did. But it would cause problems. For Kendall. For Andrea. For Kendall's business. Possibly for Andrea's job. No, they were adults. They had to look at the big picture. Sex might be nice. *Nice?* Kendall thought. *Um, no. Sex with Andrea would be awesome.* Somehow, she knew that. But it was not a good idea. It was complicated. Very, very complicated. Best to keep it all platonic.

A glance at the clock told her it was almost ten. Time to get herself showered and ready to make a quick trip into the city.

An hour and a half later, there were no less than six shirts strewn across Kendall's bed. She was on her third pair of jeans. She pulled the soft purple shirt with the waffle weave and hood over her head, then surveyed herself in the full-length mirror. It wasn't bad. The fit was snug, but not tight, and reached her hips. A gentle V-neck showed a teasing peek of skin, a glimpse of collarbone. The sleeves were long enough to reach Kendall's palms, something that drove her mother crazy, but Kendall loved. She nodded once at her reflection, then went into the bathroom to apply a little bit of makeup and straighten her hair. When she finished with those things, she spritzed on some perfume and stepped into black ankle boots.

"Not bad," she said quietly as she checked the mirror once more. Immediately, she rolled her eyes as she held her arms out to the sides, then dropped them with a slap against her hips. "What am I doing?" Seeing Ollie stretched out on the bed in the mirror, she spun around and asked the question directly to him. "What am I doing, Ollie?"

The cat gave her a lazy blink, then yawned widely.

"Yeah, thanks for nothing," she muttered. Deciding not to spend any more time analyzing her own behavior, she snapped up her phone and typed out the text before she could change her mind.

Hi. I'm free. Is now okay to pick up my computer?

She had barely set it down when it beeped that there was a reply.

Now is perfect. I'm here all day. ☺

Kendall stared at the smiley. Andrea did not seem like the smiley type. At all.

It wasn't until Kendall looked up at the mirror again that she noticed she was also smiling.

❧

Kendall had made the mistake of stopping in at her office in the barn and ended up taking care of a couple of small issues while she was there. Nearly an hour had gone by before she got back in her car and made the short drive to Andrea's. Light flurries swirled around in the air, leaving a dusting of snow on the roads. Not enough to plow, but enough to make drivers a bit more cautious in their travels. She pulled into Andrea's driveway a little bit after one o'clock and shifted her car into Park.

A flick of her wrist turned off the engine. Kendall looked in the rearview mirror and took a deep breath. She tucked her hair behind her ears, swallowed down the lump of nervous energy in her throat, and opened the door.

"Just picking up a computer," she muttered, the words floating away on her frosty breath. "We're all business here. All business."

The street was a quiet one, which was a nice feature in a city block. The houses were all similar to Andrea's, two- and three-stories, many with front porches, most with vinyl siding. They sat fairly close together, but that was also the nature of the beast when living anywhere but the suburbs. Kendall climbed the two front steps and rang the doorbell, puffing out her cheeks as she released a breath and worked to morph into—and stay in—her work demeanor.

She cleared her throat as the door opened and a somewhat frustrated-looking Andrea stood there dressed in black yoga pants and a green long-sleeved T-shirt with a Nike swish emblazoned in white across the front. In her hand, she was holding what appeared to be a Sawzall. "Hey, Kendall. Come on in." Andrea stood back and held the door open before Kendall had a chance to think.

"Hi," she said, and stepped into the warmth of the house. With a glance down at Andrea's hand, she raised an eyebrow and asked, "What're you doing with that?"

Andrea groaned. "Nothing. Not a damned thing. Certainly not what I'd intended to do with it."

"Which was?"

"Install the cat door to the basement."

"Ah, I see."

"It seemed like it'd be so easy, but…" Her grimace showed a hint of embarrassment as she shook the saw. "I don't love power tools. They kind of scare me."

"Understandable." Before she could stop to think, Kendall said, "I could do it. If you want."

The relief on Andrea's face was immediate. "You could?"

With a nod, Kendall said, "I grew up on a farm with two older brothers. I'm pretty good with power tools."

"Oh my God, I would so owe you," Andrea said, and though it was a perfectly innocent remark, Kendall felt that pang of arousal in her stomach.

"It's no problem." She kicked off her snowy boots, and when she looked up, Andrea was handing her the same slippers she wore Friday. There was something—again—almost intimate in the gesture, in Andrea's gentle smile as Kendall took them and stepped into them. Shucking her coat, she said, "Take me to this door."

Zeke was in the dining room wrestling with his stuffed mouse. Kendall saw him and dropped to her knees.

"Hi, little cutie pie," she said in the tiny voice she reserved for speaking to babies and animals. Zeke came right up to her and she scooped him into her arms. "Did you get bigger?" she asked him, kissing his furry gray head. "I think you did. Yes, I do. Yes, I do." When she glanced up, Andrea was smiling down at her with an unreadable expression on her face. "So. Cat door." Kendall stood back up as Andrea pointed.

She'd done okay so far, Kendall noted, as she got back down on her knees and did a cursory inspection. Andrea had outlined with pencil exactly where she wanted the opening to be. It was an old wooden door, but not too terribly thick.

"I just…" Andrea held up the saw when Kendall glanced her way. "How do you get this through the wood?"

With a nod, Kendall stood. "A valid question. One I happen to have the answer to." She dusted off her hands. "You have a Sawzall. Do you have a drill as well?"

Andrea's green eyes lit up. "I do."

"Then we've got this covered."

Less than forty-five minutes later, the cat door was in and functional, and Zeke was tentatively trying it out. He pushed at the flap with his paw, then jumped back when it moved. Andrea and Kendall spent the next half hour with treats and toys, doing what they could to coax him through until he finally got the hang of it. They both burst into applause when the kitten pushed his way through and scooted down the basement stairs to his litter box.

"Nice work, partner," Kendall said with a grin as she held up a hand for a high-five.

Andrea dutifully slapped it. "Hey, you did most of it. I just assisted."

"Assisting is ultra-important."

"Well. I couldn't have done it without you." Andrea's face grew serious. "Thank you."

"You're welcome."

"Hey, are you hungry?"

"I could eat."

"How do you feel about soup again? And maybe grilled cheese?"

"I could live on your soup." Kendall grinned as she leaned her forearms on the counter. "And what kind of crazy person doesn't love grilled cheese?"

"Good. I'm on it. Consider it a thank you from me to you."

"You don't have to do that," Kendall said.

Hand on the refrigerator handle, Andrea looked at her. "Unless…you have plans. Someplace to be today. I didn't even think to ask—"

"I don't." Kendall said quickly. She shook her head, and her voice went soft. "I don't have anyplace else to be."

Their gazes held and there was that sizzle again. "Okay," Andrea said, just as quietly. "Good. Soup and sandwiches then."

They managed to talk about safe things while Andrea put the soup on to heat up and they cleaned up the mess from the cat door. Movies, music, and books were all easy topics—and they seemed to be in agreement on all three as far as likes and dislikes. They each preferred independent films to Hollywood's blockbusters. Both were excited that pop seemed to be making a resurgence. And mysteries were their novels of choice, though Kendall was also a sucker for a good romance.

Once the soup and sandwiches were ready, Andrea reached into the refrigerator and pulled out a Stone Fence IPA. She held the bottle up, tipped it back and forth so Kendall could see it.

"What are you doing with that?" Kendall asked on a laugh.

Andrea shrugged. "I thought it would be a good thing to have in the fridge, just in case we had another class." She made air quotes around the word "class," and Kendall felt the strong pull of affection. Andrea grabbed glasses out of the cupboard, handed one to Kendall, and then used a bottle opener to pop the top. "Why is it called Stone Fence?"

Kendall poured the beer as Andrea retrieved plates and napkins, and they took seats side by side on the barstools. Andrea opened a raspberry shandy for herself. "Are you having a beer? Just to drink a beer?" Kendall's eyebrows went up in surprise.

Andrea's cheeks pinkened just a bit, something Kendall found adorable. "I like it," she said with a shrug. Gesturing to Kendall's beer with her eyes, she made an expectant face.

"Oh. The name." Kendall picked up half her sandwich. "All our beers are named for something to do with the farm."

"Old Red Barn," Andrea said.

"Well, we couldn't exactly call it 'Foster's.'" At Andrea's puzzled expression, Kendall smiled. "There's already a Foster's beer. It's Australian."

"Oh."

"So, the big red barn is the main building on my parents' property. It used to be a working farm when my dad was a kid, but that gradually fell by the wayside. We have a Treehouse Lager because there's a treehouse where my brothers used to hang out when they were kids."

"Not you?"

"I did when they weren't around. They wouldn't let me in if they were there. In case you hadn't noticed, I'm a girl." Kendall laughed.

"Oh, I noticed," Andrea said, then bit into her sandwich, avoiding eye contact.

Kendall swallowed the bite she'd been chewing and picked up her spoon. "There's a stone fence along one side of the property that my grandfather put up. He hauled each and every one of the flat stones that make it up."

"Wow."

"Yeah, it's pretty impressive. We also have Rusty Truck Ale. My dad has this old—."

"Let me guess," Andrea interrupted. "Rusty truck?"

Kendall grinned. "How'd you know? Yeah, it's the one eyesore that drives my mother crazy. My dad's a very neat guy, but this red truck has been up on blocks next to the middle barn ever since I can remember."

"The middle barn?"

"Yeah, that's the next building down in size. It used to house the dairy cows. Then it was converted into a garage. And then we built an apartment on the second story that's totally cute. It's where I live."

"Really? You still live at home?"

Kendall bristled slightly. "Well, not at home. It's my own apartment."

Andrea held up a hand. "I'm sorry. I don't mean to sound judgmental. I just know I couldn't live anywhere near my mother. But that's me." She chuckled in an obvious attempt to keep things light.

"I mean, my parents are nearby, but it's my own place," Kendall said, trying not to sound defensive. And also trying to forget how her mother walked in any time she wanted to and collected Kendall's dirty laundry or delivered clean. She made a mental note to tell her to stop.

Andrea smiled. "Well, it sounds adorable."

"It is. You should come see it some time."

"I'd like that."

Kendall took a bite of her sandwich, cheese dripping onto her hand, her heart hammering in her chest. As she licked the cheese from her finger, she glanced at Andrea, whose eyes had gone dark as they focused on Kendall's hand. A quick flick up and they were staring at each other.

"Andrea—."

"I know," Andrea said and blew out a breath as she tore her eyes away. "I know. It's not a good idea."

Kendall shook her head slowly. "It's not. It wouldn't look right. For either of us."

"Impropriety. Special treatment."

"Exactly."

"But…" Andrea stood and crossed the kitchen to the fridge, pulled herself another beer and held one up for Kendall, who nodded. She popped both caps, handed Kendall hers, and sat on the barstool. She poured her beer and took a large swallow of it.

Kendall looked at her expectantly. "But?"

Andrea wet her lips and Kendall had to look away. "But… you feel it. Right? It's there? It's not just me?" She waved a finger between the two of them, in the two feet of space they'd carefully kept between them all day.

Kendall shook her head, inhaled deeply, and let it out very slowly. "No. It's not just you."

Andrea absorbed that for a moment. "Well. At least there's that."

"It's so weird," Kendall said with a chuckle. "I thought you hated me."

"I thought *you* hated *me*," Andrea said, joining in with the laughter.

"Well, after that volleyball game? I did, just a little bit."

Andrea wrinkled her nose. "Yeah, that's me. My mother says I'm mouthy. I can't seem to help it."

"You never could."

"True. But then the meeting happened."

Kendall covered her face with her hand. "Oh, God, I know. I'm so sorry about that. I just couldn't believe my bad luck, having you walk in as the head of beer distribution the day after that volleyball game. I mean, what are the odds?"

"Slim."

"Very slim. And I felt terrible about what happened."

"And then the party. And that wine."

Kendall dropped her head to the counter with a thump. "I'm *really* sorry about that."

"I know." Andrea was laughing now. "And I was an asshole. *I'm* sorry about *that*."

"Man, is it any wonder we each thought the other hated us?"

"It's really not." Their laughter gradually quieted. Andrea studied the beer in her glass. After a beat, she looked up at Kendall. "You understand, right?"

"Understand what? Why we can't...do anything about... this?" Kendall made the same encompassing gesture as Andrea had.

"Yes. It's just...I've worked so hard to get where I am at Hagan's. I want my own store. That's always been the goal: to manage my own store. Beer is the last department I need to head up before I'm eligible. Any hint of..."

"Impropriety," Kendall supplied.

Andrea made a face. "I'm starting to hate that word."

"Me, too."

"But yes, any hint of it and my chances of promotion could go out the window. They have very strict rules about such things. Hagan's is a progressive store, but with some values that are a little old-fashioned." She was quiet for a long moment and her eyes seemed to focus on something Kendall couldn't see, something in her head. "When I woke up Saturday morning..." Her eyes went wide and she brought her fingers to her lips as she turned to look at Kendall. She shook her head and whispered, "I had to do what was right."

"I get it. I do." Kendall tried hard not to feel the weight of disappointment that was crushing her chest, and was hit with the sudden need to lighten the mood. She held up her glass with a grin that she suspected did not reach her eyes. "Hey. To doing the right thing."

Andrea looked at her for a moment before touching their glasses together.

❦

114

"I should've gotten out of there right then," Kendall said into the phone later that evening.

"Yeah, you should've." Liz was eating something. Kendall could hear her chewing. "But?"

Kendall sighed deeply and flopped on the couch on her back, her legs hanging over the arm. Ollie climbed up and made himself a bed on her chest. "I couldn't. I just wanted to be around her as long as I could. I ate a second bowl of soup I didn't need just so I could hang out longer."

"Jesus, you've got it bad."

"I know! I have never, ever felt such a physical attraction to anybody in my life. It's all I can do not to reach out and touch her every single time I see her."

"I don't get why it's such a bad idea. Just take the woman to bed already."

Kendall tried to hide her annoyance with her friend. "I told you before. It's not that simple. You don't work in the trade business, so it doesn't make sense to you. She could get in trouble, possibly lose her job. I don't want to be responsible for that."

"Um, retail is trade." Liz was insulted. Kendall could hear it in her tone, so she tried to backpedal.

"I know, I know. I meant…okay, it would be like you sleeping with one of your customers and then giving her a better deal on her phone bill than the people you're not sleeping with."

Liz managed a Verizon store, and was hit on by customers—men and women alike—a shocking number of times. "You say that like it's never happened." When Kendall laughed, Liz said, "I still say you're making way more of this than you need to."

Kendall's laugh turned to a groan. "Liz, what am I going to do?"

"I told you. Take the woman to bed."

"And I told you. I can't."

"Then you only have one other option. Don't see her. Avoid her like she has a contagious disease." Kendall was quiet, which prompted Liz to ask suspiciously, "What did you do? Tell me."

"I invited her to see the brewery," Kendall said in a small voice.

"Kendall. Why?"

Kendall shrugged, even though Liz couldn't see it. "I don't know. It's part of the beer education. I want her to see the process."

"That's bullshit and you know it. She doesn't need to see the process."

Kendall covered her eyes with a hand. Liz was right.

"Are you trying to torture yourself? Because that's what this is going to end up being for you. Torture. Seriously, Kendall. You're like an alcoholic wandering around a liquor store just for the fun of it. What's the matter with you? Call her up and cancel. Just…stay away from her."

Kendall nodded. "I know. You're right." At the same time, the voice in her head was saying, *I don't know if I can.*

❧

"*…and I don't have a choice. I have to go. So…I'm really sorry for the short notice, but I have to cancel your visit to the brewery today. I'll get back to you to reschedule later in the week. My apologies…you take care of yourself, Andrea.*"

Andrea played the message back for a third time. Apparently, there was some brewers' trade show type thing that Kendall's brother was supposed to attend, but for some unknown reason, he backed out and Kendall was going in his place. It was a little too last-minute—and a little too convenient—for Andrea to accept it for anything other than what it most likely was: a made-up reason not to see her. The last part of the message, said in a very soft and tender voice, made it pretty clear.

She couldn't really blame Kendall. After their discussion on Sunday, being around each other had been easier and harder in equal measure. How was that even possible?

Before she could dwell any longer, Brady Kerner knocked on her doorjamb. "Did you see the e-mail?" he asked without preamble.

"Which?" She'd checked her e-mail a bit earlier, but shifted her gaze to her monitor.

"Just came through. Three new stores opening in the next six months."

Andrea looked up and blinked at the empty space where Brady had stood. He had a habit of doing that. Appearing, saying his piece, leaving. He irritated the crap out of a lot of people that way. Her included. She shook her head as she scrolled through her inbox to the e-mail he was talking about. Attached to it was an official press release. Construction on three new Hagan's stores would begin within the next month. One in northern Maryland, one in the Philadelphia area, one in Raleigh, North Carolina.

This could be her chance.

If she knocked it out of the park during her stint as head of beer distribution and made it abundantly clear that she was not only interested in, but qualified for, the management position of one of the new stores, she might have a shot.

The news went only a little way in making her feel better about Kendall canceling on her, which surprised her and she said as much later as she sat across from Kylie having lunch.

"This is big news. I might finally get my own store. Why aren't I more excited? I should be more excited."

"Well," Kylie said, stabbing a green pepper with her fork. "If I had to guess, I'd say this girl has thrown you for a loop."

Andrea sighed, but didn't say anything.

"Okay, so wait," Kylie said, holding up a hand, a forkful of salad in the other. "You had a meeting scheduled for when?"

"Late this afternoon," Andrea replied, ripping a piece of bread into chunks. She dunked one in her soup. "I was going to leave the office and meet her at her family's brewery so she could give me a tour, show me around. She's been teaching me about beer."

Kylie chewed her salad and scrutinized Andrea, who shifted under her gaze. "This is the same woman who spilled an entire glass of red wine on you at my party, like, what? A week ago?"

"Yes."

"I thought she hated you. Or you hated her. Somebody hated somebody. That's the impression I got."

Andrea shrugged. "I know. Things change."

Kylie squinted at her for a moment. Then she set her fork down, propped her elbows on the table and her chin on her clasped fists. "Okay. From the beginning. Because I think you've left out some details. Otherwise, you've been purposefully vague." Kylie's blue eyes held Andrea's green ones and it was only a couple seconds before Andrea looked away.

"Damn it."

Kylie grinned. "You cannot out-eye contact me, Andrea. You know this."

"I do."

"So? Tell me what's going on. All of it."

Andrea's shoulders dropped in defeat and she slowly told Kylie all about Kendall. How they initially knew each other, the volleyball game, the brewers meeting, the party, the teaching, the trip to the pet store, and the impromptu slumber party.

"Okay, so wait." Kylie held up her hand in an exact duplicate of her earlier position. "You fell asleep together on the couch?"

Andrea nodded.

"And you woke up on top of her?"

"Pretty much." Andrea could feel the blush heat up her cheeks. "And my hand was…in a really good spot."

"And then you…" Kylie made a rolling motion with her hand, gesturing not only for Andrea to continue the story, but to tell her what she wanted to hear. Which was not what Andrea told her.

"And then I slipped off her and out from under the blanket and cleaned the kitchen."

Kylie steepled her fingers, tapped them together lightly, then rested them against her lips. "I see."

"You think I'm an idiot."

"No!" Kylie's eyes went wide. "Not at all. This is a work thing. There are rules. I get it, believe me."

"You do?"

Kylie furrowed her brows. "That's how Gretchen and I met. Didn't I ever tell you that?"

It was Andrea's turn to go wide-eyed. "No, you didn't. I mean, I know you worked together. Right?"

"Better. She was my boss."

"What?" A sense of relief washed through Andrea like a wave. "So, you do get it." Having somebody who understood her decision and the reason for it was something Andrea didn't realize she missed until it was presented to her.

"Oh God, yes. We had a hell of a time." Kylie sucked on the straw in her Diet Pepsi.

"It's so hard," Andrea said. "I mean, we don't really know each other very well. We haven't had a lot of time together. But..." She let her voice trail off and swallowed hard.

"In the meantime, the physical attraction is killing you."

"*Yes.*" Andrea reached across the table and closed her fingers around Kylie's forearm. "Thank you so much for getting that. I mean, it's possible we'd get to know each other better and discover that we're really not all that compatible. But as it stands, I just want to..." She lowered her voice. "Rip her clothes off with my teeth."

Kylie barked a laugh. "I can so relate to that. Gretchen would show up to work in these sexy business suits, all high heels and regal authority. God."

The two of them gazed off into space for a moment, before making eye contact and dissolving into laughter.

"Look at us," Andrea said. "All dreamy sighs and fantasies."

"Good times," Kylie said.

"So, what ended up happening?" Andrea picked up her soda and toyed with the straw. "You're together, so obviously something happened."

"Gretchen left her job." Kylie shrugged matter-of-factly.

"Ah."

"Yeah."

"Well, I don't want to leave mine. And Kendall's family owns hers, so I don't think she'll be leaving any time soon."

"Right." Kylie sipped her soda. "This is mostly about your job, though, right? I'm betting her family doesn't care who she sleeps with."

Andrea lifted a shoulder. "Yeah. The ball's really in my court. Which she's been great about. She totally gets it."

"So, you've talked about it." Kylie leaned forward.

"Yes. At my house on Sunday."

Kylie waited, eyebrows raised.

"She forgot her laptop on Saturday when she left, so she came to get it."

"And you just happened to start talking about how much you wanted her?" Kylie asked with a wink.

"No, I was trying to put in the stupid cat door and couldn't figure out what I was doing. So Kendall did it for me."

"Ah, I see now. A pretty girl running a power tool."

Andrea's cheeks flushed. "What *is* that?" she asked as they both laughed. "Anyway, there was a moment when it was really clear that we were on the same wavelength, so I brought it up and she totally got it. She absolutely understood why it wasn't a good idea for us to pursue anything."

Kylie nodded slowly as Andrea spoke. "Well, she gets points for that."

"I thought so, too. She's got integrity. Which, of course, makes me like her more." Andrea grimaced.

"But she canceled today."

"Yeah. On purpose, I think. She told me to take care of myself, which is pretty much code for goodbye, yeah?"

Kylie tipped her head from one side to the other. "Could be."

"That's how it sounded. And I get it, Kylie. I do. I completely understand. But God, it makes me sad. And a little angry. It's been a long time since I met somebody who holds my interest the way Kendall does, and doesn't it figure she's somebody who's off-limits? It's so unfair."

"Seems to me you only have the two options. Leave it alone or go for it."

"It does sound that simple, doesn't it?" Andrea asked, not happy with either choice.

"Yep."

They went back to eating their lunch, what was left of it, and moved on to other topics. All the while, though, Andrea's mind kept replaying their conversation, breaking it down into the simplest of terms as Kylie had. Leave it alone or go for it.

She wasn't sure she was strong enough for either.

CHAPTER NINE

As February slid into March, Mother Nature seemed to tire of the cold weather as much as everybody else and eased up. The morning had dawned sunny and in the high forties headed to near sixty. The majority of the snow was gone, melting the world into the soggy brown mess that defined March, but that also meant warmer weather was on its way. The positive effect of impending spring was obvious in almost everybody Andrea passed on her way into work. It was a nice change from the dark moods and examples of Road Rage she'd been dealing with since the end of January. She was scheduled to visit a handful of stores today in the area, and the sunshine had her looking forward to spending time in the car and out of the office.

Andrea had settled seamlessly into her role as head of beer distribution despite the early bumpiness of the road. Her constant research—along with all the details Kendall had taught her—increased not only her confidence level in her knowledge of beer, but her enjoyment of it. She'd continued to buy different types and taste them. Some she enjoyed. Others she poured down the sink. But she could now hold her own in a conversation about today's microbreweries and craft beers.

Having met with all sixteen of the craft brewers in the area, Andrea had finally met with her staff, and together, they'd chosen the three that would have their day on the shelves of all Hagan's stores. Of course, they would only get to stay if they sold well enough, but it was always a cool feeling to let a vendor know he or she now had shelf space.

It came as no surprise to Andrea that Old Red Barn Brewcrafters was one of the three, and it had nothing to do with her feelings about Kendall. The beer was good and it sold well. Part of Andrea's job was to research a product's sales history, so she made several phone calls to various bars and restaurants around the city to see which beers sold best. Turns out, Old Red Barn was a beer-lovers' favorite, especially the Stone Fence IPA (which Andrea just could not get down no matter how many times she tried). Though it had been incredibly tempting to call Kendall on the phone and deliver the good news (almost) in person, she'd taken the coward's way out and sent an e-mail, keeping it professional and neutral. In return, she'd gotten a thank you e-mail from Kendall, one that was just as professional and neutral. Andrea didn't know why she was disappointed that Kendall had been just as cool as she had.

Kendall...

As so often happened, Andrea's gaze drifted to the window, to the sunny day outside, to the blue sky and the birds that had seemed extinct three weeks ago but now were back in droves, poking their beaks into the softening ground and chattering like they hadn't seen each other in ages and were catching up with their little bird friends. She and Kendall had had no contact other than those two e-mails since Kendall had canceled the tour of the brewery. This only confirmed Andrea's suspicions that Kendall had been cutting off contact, and while she understood everything about why, she still felt stung. It was completely illogical. Irrational. But there it was.

"Andrea?"

The voice startled her from her thoughts, and her body jerked. She turned a sheepish grin to Jean Sherman, the admin for the six department heads that were housed in this section of the building.

"Sorry," Jean said, holding up a hand. "I didn't mean to scare you." Jean was a widow in her early sixties, neat as a pin both in appearance and work space, and was alarmingly efficient.

Andrea waved a hand, gesturing her closer. "My fault for zoning out."

Jean crossed the room and handed Andrea her mail. As she turned to go, she stopped and squinted at her. "Are you all right?"

"Yeah. Why?"

"No reason. You just seem…a little distracted lately. That's the third time this week I've startled you." She grinned. "How about if I stomp my feet when I enter from now on?"

"Perfect." Andrea smiled at her as she left the office.

A little distracted lately.

It wasn't like she could deny it. It was true. She'd gone on with work and life just fine. She'd made a valiant effort to spend more time with her sister's kids, going so far as taking them to a movie last week. She'd done a boatload of beer research every night at home and really felt like she knew her stuff now. She'd played with Zeke constantly. She'd done everything in her life she always had. And yet…

And yet.

In the back of her mind there was always the shadow of a beautiful blonde with full lips and a gentle smile, hair tucked behind her ears, standing with her back against the wall in the corner, head canted slightly to the side, arms folded across her chest, feet crossed at the ankle, blue eyes sparkling with some mischievous secret knowledge. Always there, no matter what

Andrea was doing or thinking. Kendall was always there in the background.

With a sigh and light jostle of her head, Andrea forced herself to return to work, to focus on other things. It was a tall order, but she managed to do it for over an hour. When it was almost time to head out and make her store visits, she gave her e-mail a quick check. There was one from the office of Roger Hagan.

Roger Hagan was a hometown success story and one of the most recognized names in upstate New York. Hagan's grocery stores had been started by his father, Henry Hagan, who focused hard on customer service. He was one of the first local businessmen to make it clear how important it was to take care of your customers, that if they didn't feel valued, they would not return. When Henry passed away in the seventies, the stores went to Roger, who had grown up under his father's wing and knew exactly how to keep the core values intact while using his more modern way of thinking to help grow the business. Under his watchful eye, the number of Hagan's locations had quadrupled in less than twenty years. The respect he received from the entire community was legendary. He was big on charity; he donated tons of money to various causes and sponsored large events that helped raise funds for things like cancer research, AIDS prevention, and new community buildings. The man was a local god.

So an e-mail from him in her inbox was an unusual occurrence for Andrea. What made it more unusual was when she opened it and saw that it was addressed only to her. There were no other names in the address list. There was nothing to indicate there were maybe a bunch of others copied. It seemed to be meant only for her.

She read it quickly. Then she swallowed hard, cleared her throat, and read it again. Slowly. And then again.

She picked up her cell, dialed Julia's number, and read it again, this time aloud.

"So...does that mean what I think it means?" Julia asked, obviously trying not to sound overly excited until she was certain.

"It means they've been keeping track of my time here and they think I'm ready to manage my own store."

"That's what I thought it meant!" Julia's voice was a squeal so high-pitched Andrea pulled the phone away from her ear with a laugh. "That's fantastic! I'm so proud of you, Andrea. This is amazing. What happens now?"

Andrea rubbed her fingertips against her forehead. "Well, I have to let them know whether or not I'm interested."

"Which you are."

"Which I am. Then I guess they will decide where I might want to go or where they may need me."

"So...you'll get one of the new stores? I don't know how this works."

"Not necessarily." Andrea sat back in her chair and watched the birds again as she spoke. "The current managers usually have the option to move to a new store. They have seniority."

"And if somebody does move, that would leave an opening for a manager that would need to be filled."

"Exactly. So really, I could end up anywhere."

"Even out of state?" Julia asked. It was apparent she was trying to be nonchalant about asking the question, but didn't quite get there.

"Possibly."

"Would you go?"

"I might." Andrea didn't want to say an unequivocal yes because she didn't want to freak out her sister. But she knew in her heart that she most likely *would* go. Just about anywhere.

◆

Things at Old Red Barn Brewcrafters had picked up in a very big way, and for that, Kendall was grateful. It was shocking how quickly it had happened, and it kept her busy. She was on the phone a huge percentage of the day, and when she wasn't, she was either meeting with Rick and Adam about marketing strategies or she was visiting customers and bringing new samplings for them to try.

The placement in Hagan's had been cause for a mammoth celebration. Getting on their shelves had been a major goal from pretty much the opening day of business, and Kendall's brothers made no secret of how proud of her they were for getting it done, going so far as to have a cake made for her in the shape of a beer bottle, which they shared with the staff the day after the news arrived.

That news had come by e-mail. Kendall wasn't sure why she'd expected anything different. She'd been the one to cut things off with Andrea, and she'd done so in just as impersonal a manner, leaving a voicemail message on Andrea's work phone, despite having her cell number, because of course, she was hoping to get a recording and not have to actually talk to Andrea herself. Like a grown-up. The brewery had been keeping her ridiculously busy, but every now and then, Kendall would find herself staring off into space, daydreaming about a tall, gorgeous woman with waves of auburn hair and green eyes that looked at her so intensely she was sure Andrea could see right into her head, read her thoughts as if they were written on her skin.

It took her over a week to admit to herself that she missed Andrea. And even that was weird because how could you miss somebody you'd barely spent any time with? It seemed silly. Childish. Irrational. They'd been in each other's company a total of a handful of hours, really. And their reasons for not delving into things to see where they'd take them made perfect sense. Perfect, logical, understandable sense. There was no reason they couldn't be friends. They were mature adults. They liked each other. A friendship was fine.

Except there wasn't one.

Kendall had said in her message that she'd reschedule the canceled tour of the brewery, and she'd meant it at the time, even though her excuse for canceling had been bogus. She figured she'd just give herself some time, things would settle down, and she'd reschedule. But time went on and her thoughts around Andrea weren't any different. Or any cleaner, frankly. The physical pull was almost too much to bear, and Kendall knew herself well enough to understand she needed to stay away for a while or she might do something that would ruin any chances of a friendship in the future.

But it had been nearly three weeks.

And Andrea had given Old Red Barn one of the spots in Hagan's. Kendall was happy about that. She liked to think she knew Andrea at least well enough to understand that she wouldn't use her personal feelings to influence her business decisions, so Kendall was ecstatic that their beer had earned a place on the shelves. Rick was looking into buying a couple more tanks so they could increase their product output, as reception had already been stellar.

It was a Wednesday evening, and Kendall had worked late. Not that working late was an unusual occurrence when you worked in a small family business. But she was tired and starving by the time she got back to her apartment with a Tupperware container full of chicken and potatoes her mother had saved her from dinner. She planned to eat, soak herself in a hot bath with a glass of wine, and fall into bed. She was halfway through step one when her cell rang. Seeing Liz's name on the screen, she answered.

"Where in God's name have you been?"

"It's nice to hear your voice, too, Elizabeth." Kendall could almost see the cringe on Liz's face at being called by her full name.

"I was beginning to think maybe you fell into one of those giant vats of beer and drowned, never to be heard from again."

"Well, would that be such an awful way to go?"

"I suppose not. But your friends would miss you." Liz's voice went serious. "Like me. I mean, it's not like I bug you about it that often, but you've been completely MIA for more than two weeks. Even on the weekends."

Kendall sighed. "I know. I'm sorry, Liz. It's just been so busy here. In a good way. The phones have been ringing off the hook."

"I know. I know. I get it. I just worry about you. Are you eating? Are you getting enough sleep? I miss your face is all."

Kendall grinned. Liz could give her a hard time on just about anything, but she really did understand how time-consuming her job could be. The fact that she complained at all, even teasingly, told Kendall she really had neglected her friend. "I am sleeping. And I am currently shoveling my mother's roasted chicken into my face as we speak, so yes, I am eating as well." She softened her voice. "And I miss you, too."

"Good. Then you can make it up to me."

"Uh-oh," Kendall said with a laugh. "What did I just let myself get roped into?"

"St. Patrick's Day. Tomorrow night at McGillicutty's."

Normally, the idea of going out to a crowded bar on a weeknight would make Kendall wince in discomfort, but much to her surprise, Liz's invitation sounded great. The fact that Kendall had completely forgotten about the Irish holiday told her a night out was just what she needed after working her ass off for so many days in a row. "You're on. Though you know my rule."

"You are not drinking green beer." They said it in unison and then laughed.

"So," Kendall said as she stabbed a piece of potato with her fork. "How are things going with your little waitress?"

"I was waiting for you to ask," Liz said, and Kendall knew simply by the change of tone in her voice that things were good. "She's amazing. Seriously. This is…" She heard Liz take a deep breath, then let it out slowly. "This is a little scary."

"Yeah?"

"Yes! I just…I like her so much, Kendall. So much. She's funny and sexy and sweet…"

"Why, Elizabeth Sheridan, are you," Kendall feigned a loud gasp. "Falling in love?"

Liz laughed, but Kendall could hear the nervousness behind it. "I might be," she said quietly.

"Oh, Liz." Kendall's voice was just as quiet. "That's terrific."

"It's terrifying. That's what it is."

"Yeah." It was all Kendall could offer. "You okay?"

"I'm great. Marcy's coming tomorrow. That's okay with you, right?"

"Oh, God, of course. I look forward to getting to know her a little better."

"Well, good," Liz said with a chuckle. "Because she wants to get to know you better, too. I think she questions some of the stories I've told her about you."

"Hey!"

The laughter helped ease some of the seriousness the conversation had taken on, and they spent the next twenty minutes talking about superficial things. Liz carefully steered clear of the subject of Andrea, and Kendall loved her for it. By the time they finished talking, promising to meet at McGillicutty's by five ("Seriously, Kendall, it's going to be packed as it is. Be on time."), Kendall's dinner was gone and she was more than ready for that hot bath she'd promised herself.

These were the times it was hard not to let her mind drift. The thought crossed her mind as she lay in the tub, water just this side of too hot covering her body, fluffy bubbles up to her shoulders making the bathroom smell like strawberries. The idea of a bath was to relax her muscles, to let her mind float to wherever it wanted to, to just...be. And her muscles very much appreciated it. Her mind, however...her mind tended to float off to the same place it usually did...

Visions of auburn hair and green eyes and creamy skin... long legs and full lips...that sultry voice and a sexy smile that spoke of a secret of some sort hiding just behind it.

Kendall had barely become cognizant of what she was doing before her body tightened with the orgasm, her hand gripping the side of the tub, the other moving between her legs as her eyes squeezed shut. She rode it out for several seconds before gradually relaxing, letting her breath out slowly, and swearing softly.

Ollie peeked his head over the side of the tub to peer at her with his big green cat eyes.

"It's none of your business what I'm doing," she said to him. He looked at her for another beat before turning to exit the bathroom. Kendall rested her head back against the fiberglass and rubbed a hand over her face. "Oh, goddamn it." She reached for the wine glass she'd set on the stool next to the tub and took a healthy sip, not wanting to take any part at all in analyzing why her brain constantly went to Andrea as fantasy material. It certainly wasn't helping her accept her decision to cut things off. And Andrea hadn't tried to get ahold of her after that, so she obviously agreed with it. So why did her mind and body insist on betraying her on a regular basis with thoughts of what it might be like to be intimate with somebody she couldn't have, somebody that pretty obviously seemed to want her as well, but was off-limits? True, Kendall had been the one to cut off contact with her cowardly e-mail, but—and she only grudgingly admitted this to herself now—she was more than a little disappointed that Andrea hadn't tried to get in touch with her anyway. Which was silly. And she knew it.

Things would change.

She kept telling herself that. Things would change. Given enough time, they would. They had to. She wasn't sure how much longer she could go on throwing herself into her work so she didn't have to deal with what was constantly in her head. As she lay in the tub, her breathing finally reaching a normal rate, she thought, *This is exhausting.*

※

The crowd at McGillicutty's was dense and noisy. Kendall really hadn't expected anything less, but trying to get from the front door to the corner of the bar where she could just make out

Liz's form made her feel like a salmon swimming upstream. The conversation was more a collective dull roar. Kendall could hardly make out any individual discussions. She shimmied sideways, held her hand up to keep a large man from backing right over her, and got her purse stuck between two older gentlemen who'd both moved at the same time. After what felt like a Herculean effort, she was spat out of the crowd and next to Liz, who spoke much too loudly to be sober.

"Kendall! You made it! And..." She glanced at her cell phone on the bar to check the time. "Only four minutes late. A new record for you."

"Oh, no. I was on time," Kendall said as Liz folded her into a hug. "Early even. It took me ten minutes to get from the door to here." She looked around at the mass of people filling the space, just standing around holding their drinks. "How the hell did you manage to get a spot at the bar?"

"I got here early."

"How early?"

Liz took a moment to squint again at her cell. "Um...around noon? I think?"

Kendall's eyebrows shot up. "Noon? Jesus, Liz, no wonder you're already drunk." With a laugh, she dropped her arm around Liz's shoulders and ordered the new beer from Stark Brewing that McGillicutty's had on tap.

"It's the holiday of my people, Kendall. I must celebrate. It's my duty."

"I completely understand. Where's your little waitress?"

"Bathroom."

Looking around, Kendall realized she probably wouldn't be able to see Marcy even if she was close, as she was petite and McGillicutty's crowd seemed to be eighty percent large, white men. There were a couple small pockets of people with women in them, but overwhelmingly, the customer population was male. "I hope she's driving."

"She is."

Kendall's beer arrived and she touched her plastic cup to Liz's. "I see they spared no expense on the glassware today."

"Drunk people break stuff," Marcy said as she sidled up to them. "Oh, my God, there are a million people here. Hey, Kendall."

Kendall smiled. "Hi, Marcy. How's life?" Marcy wore faded skinny jeans with holes in the knees, brown Ugg boots, and an orange sweater that was surprisingly complementary to her purple hair.

"Life is great." Her grin was wide as she tucked her hand under Liz's arm. The affection in her eyes was apparent, and Kendall felt a startling pang of envy when she saw it. "How about with you?" Marcy asked. "Liz tells me you had a big deal go through at work and you've been crazy busy."

"Liz speaks the truth."

"You own a brewery."

"My brothers and I do, yes."

"That is so freaking cool."

Kendall felt herself puff up a little with pride, as usually happened when somebody expressed amazement at her chosen career. "Thanks. It's fun. Hard work, but fun."

It was difficult to be heard above the din of the crowd, but Kendall leaned close to Marcy's ear and they talked about the brewery, how it got started, what Kendall's job was. Liz popped in every so often, but mostly just watched the two of them converse, which Kendall could tell made her friend very happy.

Though it didn't seem possible, the crowd continued to grow. Kendall watched in amazement as the four bartenders on duty ran their asses off, keeping hands filled with bottles and cups filled with alcohol. A waitress stopped by to pick up a tray loaded with cups of green beer, and Kendall smiled and shook her head. The beer dyed green generally tended to be the cheap stuff, and she felt a small amount of pity for the people drinking it, as they were sure to have massive hangovers tomorrow. As her eyes followed the waitress's path, watching her lift the tray high above her shoulders and impressively maneuver her way through the crowd, Kendall's gaze was snagged by a burst of color in the far corner of the bar. A burst of…not really red…more like…auburn.

No. It couldn't be.

What were the chances? There were countless numbers of Irish pubs in the city. What were the odds that Kendall and Andrea would end up at the same one? Kendall craned her neck and stood on tiptoe, but the color was gone, lost in the undulating sea of people.

She turned back to Liz to find her furrowing her brow. "What?" Liz asked her.

Kendall shook her head. "Nothing. I thought I saw Andrea, but…it's nothing."

Liz and Marcy exchanged a look that made it clear to Kendall details of her non-existent love life had been shared. "Where?" Liz asked, and stood up on the rungs of her barstool so she could see over the crowd.

"Nowhere. It doesn't matter. Never mind." Kendall waved a dismissive hand and made a valiant move to change the subject. "So, Marcy, tell me about you. How long have you been at Julian's?"

It worked, and Marcy's voice seemed to pull Liz's focus back to their little threesome as Marcy talked about how she worked at Julian's to pay for cosmetology school. Liz watched her with such joy in her eyes that Kendall felt her heart warm for her friend. And despite her envy, she was thrilled Liz had found somebody. Marcy seemed intelligent and funny with a good head on her shoulders. Talking with her was enjoyable.

Kendall's ears had adjusted to the constant hum of the bar, and after half an hour, she was able to concentrate on the voices of Liz and Marcy without having to strain while trying to read lips. That's why it was so surprising when the third voice spoke in her ear and not only did Kendall hear every word, she *felt* every word. As if they entered her ear and travelled through her brain, down her spine, and settled in her unexpectedly tightened stomach.

"Looks like you need a refill."

Liz's eyes went wide in front of Kendall, and she suddenly looked completely sober. Kendall took a moment to swallow down the lump of nervousness that had appeared out of nowhere in her throat. Then she made her best effort to look completely casual as she turned to her right and met those stunning green eyes.

Andrea was leaning one elbow on the bar, her head calmly tilted to one side as she grinned at Kendall. She was obviously wearing work clothes; the black pantsuit and ivory shell made her look sleek and dominant, like she could have anything she wanted from anybody she asked. Kendall took her time raking her eyes over Andrea's figure. She couldn't see the shoes, but knew they were heels, as she had to look up a little bit higher than usual to meet Andrea's gaze.

Holding up her near-empty plastic cup, she said, "Well, what do you know? Looks like I *do* need a refill."

"Allow me." Andrea took the cup, their fingers brushing lightly, and signaled the bartender. When he returned with a full cup, Andrea handed it back to Kendall, then held up her own glass. "Happy St. Paddy's Day." They touched cocktails.

"What are you drinking?" Kendall asked, eyeing the brown liquid. "And how come you get a real glass? How do you rate?"

"I rate because I'm not drinking beer. When you drink real Irish whiskey on St. Patrick's Day, you get a real glass. That's how things work in the world." Andrea winked and Kendall felt the tightening in her stomach increase. It was not unpleasant.

At the loud sound of throat clearing behind her, Kendall closed her eyes briefly, then turned to her friends. "Um…Andrea, these are my friends, Liz and Marcy. You guys, this is Andrea."

Liz stood up so fast her barstool almost fell over as she stuck out her hand. "Nice to meet you. I've heard a lot about you." Then she leaned in a little closer and stressed, "A lot." Kendall smacked her shoulder and gave her a look. "Okay, not a lot," Liz amended. "Maybe a little." She held her thumb and forefinger an inch apart. "Just a little bit." Marcy nodded a greeting, then helped Liz sit back down and strategically placed herself between Kendall and Liz to give her more privacy. Kendall made a mental note to thank her later.

Andrea seemed to take it all in stride and continued to smile at Kendall. She said something, but a group of guys next to them burst into raucous laughter and Kendall only saw Andrea's lips move. She inched closer until she could smell Andrea's perfume. Andrea grasped Kendall's upper arm and pulled her nearer still, and suddenly her mouth was moving against Kendall's ear.

"I asked how you are." Andrea pulled back to meet Kendall's eyes.

With a nod, Kendall pulled her back in, suddenly grateful for the noise and the necessity to get so close to Andrea. "I'm good. How about you?"

"Oh, you know. Busy with work."

"And how is Mr. Zeke?"

Andrea's smile grew as she spoke about her kitten. "Oh, my God, he's growing so fast. His newest thing is to make himself a bed under the pillows on the couch. He curls all up and I can only see his tail. Look." She fumbled in her pocket and pulled out her cell phone, then navigated through until she found pictures. Leaning close to Kendall, she scrolled through about five of them.

"Wow, he *has* gotten big," Kendall commented.

"You should come visit him." Andrea spoke with her eyes still on the phone's screen and continued to scroll as Kendall looked at her.

"I'd like that," Kendall was shocked to hear herself respond. "And I still owe you a tour of Old Red Barn, you know."

Andrea looked up then, and their eyes locked.

Held.

Sizzled.

"Yes, you do," she said so softly that Kendall only understood from reading her full lips.

Before the conversation could go any further, two people seemed to stumble into them, having pushed their way through the crowd.

"We thought you might have gotten lost," a tall, clean-cut guy said as he laid a hand on Andrea's shoulder. His tie was askew and he had a sport coat draped over his arm.

"Or just sucked into the vortex of drunk people in an Irish pub on St. Patrick's Day," said the woman next to him with a laugh. She looked to be around forty, her dark hair pulled into a complicated twist at the back of her head.

"No, I just ran into a friend," Andrea said, her eyes lingering on Kendall's as if she realized the moment was broken and she was trying to commit Kendall's face to memory. "Kendall Foster, these are two of my coworkers. Steve Baker and Annabeth Sawyer."

They shook hands all around.

"This place is a mob scene," Steve said with a laugh as he lifted his cup of green beer to his lips.

Kendall nodded. "Yeah, not my ideal way to spend my free time, but I've been really busy and friends asked me to come, so..." She let her voice trail off.

"Andrea, a couple more people arrived while you were gone." Annabeth jerked a thumb over her shoulder. "You coming back to our table?"

"Yes," Andrea said. She looked at Kendall and her expression seemed to say she'd rather stay and talk with her. Kendall felt warmth low in her body. "I should go."

"Sure. I'm glad you came to say hi." Kendall touched Andrea's upper arm, let her hand linger.

"I wasn't kidding about coming to visit Zeke."

"And I wasn't kidding about the tour."

For one brief moment, it was as if the entire room had emptied, quieted, stilled. Nobody existed except the two of them, and their gazes held fast. Until Steve bumped Andrea's arm and pointed to a new glass with fresh whiskey on the bar in front of her.

"Come on, red. The others are waiting." He gave her a tug as Annabeth led the way into the crowd like a diver plunging into the water.

Andrea set down her glass, took the new one, winked at Kendall, and turned to follow Steve, all in one fluid movement. Then she disappeared into the swarm of bodies.

Kendall stood and stared at the spot where she was.

"Wow." Marcy's voice was close. Kendall turned to face her friends and noticed Liz was missing. At the questioning arch of her eyebrow, Marcy said, "Bathroom."

"Puking?" Kendall asked.

"That would be my guess." Marcy moved to sit on Liz's stool. "Well, that woman was beautiful."

Kendall gave a nod as she signaled the bartender for one more beer.

"And you're not dating her…why?"

"It's complicated."

Marcy propped her chin in her hand. "Yeah, I know. Liz told me. But she is very obviously into you."

Kendall's eyes widened.

"Oh, please. Don't act like you don't see it."

With a chuckle, Kendall said, "Oh, no. I see it. I just didn't realize other people did."

"Honey, if she could have kissed your face off right here in the middle of this crowded Irish pub and not caused a scene, she totally would have."

"Well." Kendall shrugged, then took a large, cooling slug of her fresh beer to calm her racing heart. Once she'd pulled herself together, she mirrored Marcy's stance and they looked at each other.

"Uh-oh," Marcy said. "Is this where you give me the if-you-hurt-her-I-will-hunt-you-down-and-kill-you speech?"

"Oh, no. I'm much more subtle than that," Kendall said with a wink. "No, I just want to make sure you know how awesome Liz is. She's my best friend and she puts on this tough, badass air, but she's really one of the sweetest, gentlest, most sensitive people I know."

"Me, too." Marcy's smile was tender.

"And if she loves you, she loves you with everything she has. There's no halfway for her. She's all or nothing."

Marcy sipped her Coke. "Yeah, I'm getting that about her."

"And if you hurt her, I will hunt you down and kill you."

"There it is," Marcy said with a laugh.

Liz returned, looking much better than earlier. They both looked at her expectantly.

"Everything okay?" Kendall asked, eyebrows raised in question.

"I am ready for round two," Liz said, pumping her arm.

Marcy and Kendall both shook their heads.

"Hey," Liz said as she bellied up to the bar. "Where'd your hot redhead go?"

"First of all, she's not mine," Kendall said.

"First of all, she could be if you snap your fingers."

"That's what *I* told her," Marcy said with a laugh.

"Great minds," Liz said and gave Marcy a quick kiss on the cheek. Turning back to Kendall, she said, "Secondly, she *is* hot and she *is* a redhead. Two out of three ain't bad, baby. So, where'd she go?"

"She's here with work friends," Kendall told her, craning her neck to see if she could snag a glimpse of Andrea and her crew. She couldn't. Too many people. "She might even be gone by now." Working hard to keep the disappointment out of her voice, she wasn't sure if she'd been successful. When she stopped searching and turned back to her friends, Liz was giving her a knowing look. Kendall narrowed her eyes in warning.

"So, I think I've had enough of green beer for a while," Liz said, clapping her hands once and rubbing them together. "How about some whiskey?" She signaled the bartender.

"Thank God you're not like this all the time," Kendall said with a laugh, glad to have the subject changed. When the bartender pulled two glasses out, Kendall shook her head. "None for me, thanks."

Kendall switched to soda not long after that, and the rest of the evening went on enjoyably. Liz was right; it had been too long since she'd spent time with her friend, and Marcy turned out to be a lot of fun to be with. Overall, Kendall had a better time than she'd expected to, even if she spent more of it than she cared to admit surreptitiously looking around the bar for a glimpse of wavy auburn hair.

She was disappointed.

After helping to pour Liz into Marcy's car and waving them out of the parking lot, Kendall took her time driving home. Her buzz was long gone (she wouldn't have driven otherwise), and she spent her time behind the wheel recalling the conversation with Andrea. The proximity of their bodies, the smell of Andrea's hair, her skin, her perfume. The intensity in her eyes. Not to mention what had to be an amazing figure hidden beneath that sexy business suit.

"Nothing has changed, Kendall."

She said it out loud just to be sure she understood. It didn't matter how sexy Andrea had looked. She could have approached Kendall in a lacy black bra and matching panties (a visual that made Kendall light-headed for a moment) and still nothing would have changed. They were still in the same boat as before.

Although…

Were they? With Old Red Barn already in Hagan's, *were* things still the same? Would there still be the same worry about impropriety? The choice was already made. Old Red Barn had secured a place in Hagan's. So…didn't that mean things actually *had* changed?

After all, Andrea had been the one to broach the subject of them getting together. Kendall flashed back again to the bar, to Andrea inviting her to come visit Zeke. Was she just being polite or did she mean it? And when Kendall had played along, telling her she still owed her a tour, Andrea had been receptive to that as well.

Kendall's brain hurt by the time she pulled into the driveway to her parents'. The lights were on upstairs, she noticed as she drove past their yellow house and pulled on along to her own apartment.

Ollie raced to see her, and she couldn't help but smile. It was nice to have somebody happy about her arrival. On the small island counter in the kitchen was a bag of groceries and a note from her mother. Kendall picked it up, read that there was now milk, eggs, and cheese in her fridge in addition to the bread, bananas, and potato chips in the bag on the counter. Gratitude and irritation swirled inside her in equal measure as she recalled Andrea's initial surprise—and slight disapproval, Kendall was sure she'd felt it—at the idea that she still lived at home. And despite the fact that she did have her own apartment, her own space, it was almost like living at home. It was her parents' property. She paid them rent…not nearly as much as she probably should. And her parents had a key, as evidenced by the occasional magically appearing groceries or clean laundry.

Maybe it was time to make a move.

It wasn't the first time she'd had this thought. She loved her parents. They were awesome people who accepted her and adored her. And though bringing somebody home to her apartment wasn't something she could do often because the *entire* family would know (and tease her about it), that was not the reason she thought about moving.

"I'm thirty years old," she whispered to the empty bathroom as she stripped out of her clothes and turned on the shower. Being in a crowded bar for hours made her feel grimy. She pinned her hair up and stepped under the hot spray. "I'm thirty years old," she said again. "And essentially, I live with my parents." She blew out a loud, frustrated breath before letting the water pelt her face.

Maybe it was time to at least *think* about making a move.

CHAPTER TEN

The week flew by like leaves in an autumn windstorm, and before Andrea could even take a breath, it was Friday. Jean had been in and out of her office no less than ten times, and even Brady couldn't seem to stay away. The weather was making its much-anticipated—and much beloved—move from winter into spring. The sun was shining. Geese flew overhead as they returned to upstate New York. Attitudes everywhere had greatly improved. It was as though the general population was fully tensed during winter, shoulders lifted and pressed tightly against ears to conserve warmth, and now that winter was leaving and warmer weather was on its way, muscles relaxed, shoulders lowered, people were happier.

Andrea was now fully immersed in her job, and her confidence level was up where it should be. She was certain that was due in no small part to the correspondence she'd been having with Roger Hagan's office. She'd expressed her very deep interest in managing her own store and even though it was now a "sit tight and wait" sort of thing, she felt invigorated. Elated. Happy.

She took a seat at her desk for what felt like the first time all afternoon. Calls on her cell, trips to stores, and a meeting with her staff had sucked up most of her day, and it was only as she dropped into her chair that she became aware of how much her feet ached. Kicking off her pumps under her desk, she grabbed her mouse and woke up her computer.

Twenty-seven new e-mails.

With a groan, she began to scroll, deleting the junk, filing things she could deal with later, clicking on...she stopped as the name Old Red Barn Brewcrafters snagged her eyes.

Andrea had done an impressive job of putting last week's St. Patrick's Day surprise meeting with Kendall in a box and on a shelf in her brain labeled Can't Handle Right Now. Being so busy had been a huge help, and she'd gone so far as to take work home with her every night this week in order to keep her mind from wandering into forbidden territory.

She wet her lips and clicked on the e-mail to open it, not sure why she suddenly had butterflies in her stomach. It was time-stamped about two hours ago.

Andrea –

It was very nice to run into you again last week. If you recall, we touched on you taking a tour of Old Red Barn Brewcrafters. I am happy to arrange that for you anytime, if you wish, but I wanted you to know that we've been running over the weekends as well as during the week, albeit with a skeleton crew. I say this because it's much less busy then, and you would really be able to get a sense of our process.

Let me know if you'd like to come by on Saturday or Sunday and we'll set up a time.

Thank you once again for choosing us as one of the Hagan's beer vendors. We are grateful and promise never to disappoint you.

I hope you're well.

Sincerely,
Kendall Foster
Sales/Marketing

Andrea stared at the name for long moments, fighting the weird urge to run her fingertips over it. Suddenly, it was as if the box she'd shelved slid off, hit the ground, and spilled its contents all over the floor of her mind. Kendall's eyes like a summer sky, her flawless, creamy complexion, the sexy line of her neck, the little quirk of a smile she'd get. All of it assaulted Andrea, and she knew she should stay away or she'd be completely swept up. At the same time, she didn't want to. She had no real excuse. The danger of being unethical was pretty much gone.

So, why the hesitation?

Without allowing herself to overanalyze things any further, Andrea hit the reply button and quickly typed a note that she'd love to take a tour tomorrow. What time was good? She clicked Send before she could second-guess her decision. Then she sat, staring at the screen, tapping her fingers on the desk, and nibbling at a thumbnail.

Kendall had to have been sitting at her desk looking directly at her e-mail because a response came inside of three minutes suggesting a time of noon and the address.

Andrea could not keep the smile off her face.

✖

Kendall was grinning like an idiot and she knew it as she walked from her office out into the hall and through the doors into the brewery, Buster on her heels. Sun streaked cheerfully through the high windows, leaving squares of light across various spots on the concrete floor. She found Rick near one of the fermentation tanks and caught his attention.

"Here are the orders for next month," she told him, showing him the printout in her hand. "You know, since we're doing so well lately..." She let the sentence dangle hopefully.

"You want a tablet. I know. You're right. Go get one."

Kendall blinked at him. "Really?"

"Yes, really. Do it soon before I change my mind." His voice was stern, but his eyes held a playful glint.

"Awesome. Thanks, Rick." She turned to go, then stopped. "Oh," she said, facing him again. "Who's on tomorrow?"

Rick lifted one shoulder. "Skeleton crew. Mike probably. Me."

"Not Adam?"

"No. He's got tickets to a hockey game." Rick studied her. "Why?"

"Andrea Blake from Hagan's is coming by for a tour." Kendall's attempt to stay nonchalant obviously failed as her brother squinted at her.

"You're being careful, right Ken-Doll?" His Big Brother Voice was evident.

Kendall made a face, shooting for casually unconcerned. "Careful about what?" Rick studied her, and after a beat, she was fighting the urge to squirm. He'd been able to do that since they were kids.

"Adam says you like this girl."

"Well, maybe you and Adam should mind your own business." She knew as soon as the words were out that she'd given herself away. And that she'd stung him.

Rick simply nodded, kept his eyes on her face for another excruciating moment, then turned back to the tank. "He's just doing the big brother thing. Looking out for you. So am I."

Kendall watched him climb the ladder and immediately felt guilty for being annoyed by the two of them. "I know. And I appreciate it. I'm a big girl, Rick. I can handle myself."

"I don't doubt that," he replied, not looking at her. He said nothing more as he checked the latch, tugged on a hose.

"I just wish you guys could see that." She waited, but he stayed quiet, and she knew she'd hurt his feelings. "So…she'll be here around noon. Will you be able to help me show her around?" Kendall bit her bottom lip and waited for what felt like a really long time.

"I'll be here," Rick finally said, still not looking at her.

"Okay." She wanted to say more, but Rick wasn't an emotional guy and prolonging the discomfort of the situation would only embarrass him. "Okay," she said again as she took a couple steps backward, then turned to go back to her office. She hadn't been looking forward to the afternoon because she had a couple stops to make, customers to visit before she clocked out officially. Both were bars and both would be very busy on a Friday afternoon, but now, instead of dreading the trips, she welcomed them, was grateful for them, as they would (ideally) keep her mind off tomorrow.

A quick stop back at her apartment allowed her to change into a clean pair of skinny jeans, a navy blue sweater with a significant plunge in the neckline, and high brown boots. A touch of makeup, some silver hoop earrings, and a spritz of perfume, and she was good to go. She could imagine feminists everywhere shaking their fists in outrage as she used her femininity to sell her product, but the bottom line to Kendall was that it worked. She never went overboard. She had scruples, for God's sake. But time and experience had taught her that a male bar owner was more likely to buy beer from her than from Adam, especially if she "prettied herself up a bit," as Adam had called it, just to annoy her. It was a simple fact, though, that it worked, so she wasn't going to apologize for it.

It drove Liz crazy.

In the car now, Kendall chuckled as she slipped on her sunglasses, remembering how appalled Liz had been when Kendall told her one of her customers had asked her on a date.

"He was kind of sweet about it," she told Liz.

"It was a business meeting, Kendall. It's disgusting." Liz shook her head, her eyes dark with anger.

It was hard to explain the mentality of bar owners, brewers, and the like to somebody who wasn't privy to the inner workings of the community. It was different. There were different rules, different codes of honor. People in the "real" business world just didn't get it.

Kendall was all right with that. She liked this world.

Captain Jack's was, as Kendall had expected, fairly busy, but she managed to locate a decent parking spot. Inside was dark, of course, and she stood at the doorway while her eyes adjusted, fully aware that the eyes of every one of the dozen men sitting at the bar had turned her way to see who'd just come in.

"Kendall!" Jack Pickett was the owner, a bulky man with a head of luxurious-looking white hair and a matching moustache. Learning he was the owner of a bar would surprise nobody, as his protruding belly and reddened nose made his love of all things alcoholic pretty clear. But he was neat and fair and kind and Kendall liked him very much.

"Good to see you, Jack," she said as she stood on the brass foot rail of the bar between two regulars so she could reach over to hug him. "How are the grandkids?"

Jack immediately pulled out his cell phone. His enormous hands and sausage-sized fingers made navigating difficult, but he finally managed to pull up a new photo for her. Three towheaded children smiled at her.

"Aw, they're getting so big," she said, and Jack puffed up with pride. Then he filled a glass with ice and pushed the button to dispense Diet Coke for Kendall.

"This pretty little lady your mistress, Jack?" asked the gentleman to Kendall's left. He sat on the same stool every afternoon at this time, and he asked the exact same question every time Kendall came in.

"She's much too good for me, Sully," came Jack's exact same answer.

Kendall bumped Sully with her shoulder, playfully but carefully, as the man was so thin a stiff wind might blow him off the stool.

"How's business, Jack? What do you need?" Kendall asked, pulling up a screen on her cell phone, which reminded her that she was going to go get a tablet this weekend, which in turn, widened her smile.

"Gimme one of the Stone Fence. That stuff sells like crazy. And I think the Rusty Truck is getting low. What's new? Anything to impress me?"

"Rick just brewed up a batch for spring. He's calling it Yellow House Peach Wheat. It's a smooth easy-drinking wheat beer, like Blue Moon, but he's added a tiny bit of peach and just a hint of pomegranate. It's really good."

"Sounds froo-froo," Sully muttered as he hid a grin.

Kendall feigned an insulted gasp, pressed a hand to her chest. "Sully. How could you say such a thing? You hurt me."

Sully chuckled.

"It's good. I promise. I tried it last week and wanted more, but Rick wouldn't let me have it." Turning back to Jack, she said, "Tell you what. I'll send over two cases of bottles. You know my brother doesn't mess around. He knows what he's doing. If your customers don't like it and you can't sell all of it, I'll buy what's left back from you. Fair enough?"

Jack gave a nod. He was no dummy. And Kendall knew it would sell. It was *good*.

Kendall took down the whole order, then made time to sit with the regulars, drink her Diet Coke, and chat them up. At this hour, most of them were older men. Some retired. Some widowed. Some who just didn't want to go home after work. Kendall talked to each and every one of them. It was important to her. It was how she got to know her clientele, what they liked to drink, what they didn't. She stayed for a good half an hour, then bid her goodbyes to Jack, Sully, and the gang, and made her way to her next appointment.

Pumpkinhead's had a ridiculous name and a silly logo—a pumpkin with a smile and a beer stein—but it was a very cute little joint that catered to a neighborhood crowd with a very eclectic mix of people. Twenty-somethings, middle-agers, retirees, bowling leagues, softball teams, girls' nights out. You name it, they gathered there at some point during the week.

Rodney Kemp was the owner, and one look at his enormous round body and shock of red hair and it was clear where the name of the bar had come from. Like Jack Pickett, Rodney was jolly, kind, and always lit up when Kendall came through the door. Rather than an across-the-bar hug, she and Rodney high-fived each other. Before her butt hit the stool, he asked, "What's the newest? What's your brother brewing up for spring? Don't lie to me. I know he's working on something." She told him all about the Yellow House Peach Wheat. The second she finished the description, he slapped his palm flat on the bar. "Yes. Order me some."

Kendall loved this part of her job. She might dread the idea of the driving and the socializing when she was at the office, but only because there was usually a ton of other things to be done. Once she was in one of her customers' establishments, she felt alive. This was where she did the real work. This was where she worked her ass off to fit in, to show these bar owners—overwhelmingly men—that just because she was a pretty girl didn't mean she didn't know all about beer. She loved to talk brewing with them. There was nothing quite like discussing beer making with a bar owner, somebody as well-versed in the subject as she was, somebody who shared her passion. She figured it must be akin to a chef talking to a food critic or a filmmaker speaking to the owner of a movie house. They loved the same things and sharing that enjoyment was like rooting for the same football team or pulling for the same actor to win an Oscar. It was invigorating.

Kendall stayed at Pumpkinhead's for close to an hour, chatting up Rodney, talking about what beer sold best and what he'd like to see in the future. She always took his ideas back to Rick; Rodney was one of those guys who really knew beer, but also knew business, and kept up on all the latest hits and misses in bar ownership. He took his job very seriously and more often than not, Kendall left their meetings with a lot to think about.

By the time Kendall returned to Old Red Barn, everybody had gone home for the night. It was Friday, after all. People had dates to go on and movies to see and were going out to dinner. Nobody stuck around on Friday night. "Nobody but me," she muttered as she pushed the door to her office open and clicked on a light. With a glance at the empty dog bed, she pursed her lips. Even Buster had better things to do than hang out with her.

Flopping back into her chair, she woke up her computer and scanned through the pages she'd saved on tablet research. She was heavily into comparing two brands when a soft knock came from the doorway.

Kendall looked up, then smiled. "Hi, Mom."

"You're working again?" Cathy said by way of greeting, but her smile was warm and in her hands was a foil-wrapped bowl.

Kendall's eyes lit up. "Ooo, what are you bringing me?" She sniffed the air.

Cathy unwrapped the bowl, took a fork from the pocket of her hastily thrown-on jacket, and handed both to her daughter. "Macaroni and cheese."

"Oh, Mom," Kendall said, taking the fork and digging in before the bowl could touch her desk. "You know this goes straight to my hips. I might as well just glue it there." She closed her eyes and made soft humming sounds as she chewed.

"Yes, I see how that deters you from eating it."

"You can't expect me to fight off such things as cream and cheddar cheese. I am only one woman."

Cathy took the chair at the front of Kendall's desk and lowered herself into it. Kendall watched her as she looked around the office, then down at the dog bed, then at her hands. Swallowing the macaroni in her mouth, Kendall finally said, "What is it, Mom?" Cathy looked at her with feigned innocence, and Kendall simply tipped her head to the side and raised her eyebrows.

With a small sigh, Cathy held up her hands in surrender and said simply. "It's Friday night, honey."

"Yeah?"

"And you're here. In your office. Working."

Kendall nodded. "I do that. A lot. I work here."

"I know. That's what worries me."

Kendall waved a hand. "I'm fine, Mom. Don't worry." She shoveled a forkful of macaroni into her mouth and turned her attention back to her computer monitor.

"Kendall." The tone of her mother's voice left no room for argument. It wasn't harsh, but it was firm. It said, *now you listen to me.*

Kendall turned back to Cathy and waited.

"Ever since you broke up with Janet, you've thrown yourself into your work."

"Mom—" Kendall began, but was cut off by her mother's upheld hand. She closed her mouth.

"Before you go explaining to me how busy you are and how much time and effort and work it takes to keep a microbrewery running..." At Kendall's surprised expression, Cathy chuckled. "Yes, I do hear you when you talk. I'm not deaf, you know. So before you get into those excuses, I know all of that. I've heard it before and I do understand it. Your job is time-consuming. But your father and I are a little worried that you're focusing too much on the brewery and not enough on...you. That's all."

It was very sweet. Touching, even. And not altogether untrue. It was also a bit embarrassing and more than a little unnerving knowing her parents were paying that much attention to her social calendar. Maybe it really was time to find her own place— one that was *not* on her parents' property.

"I'm okay, Mom. I promise. You're right. I am not doing enough outside of work. But you know how the winter is. Nobody wants to do anything or go anywhere. Now that it's warming up, I'll start doing more stuff." At her mother's skeptical look, she reassured her. "I will. I mean it."

Cathy studied her for a long moment, her blue eyes just like Kendall's, holding her gaze as if searching for a reason not to believe her. Apparently, she didn't find one, as she slapped her hands against her thighs and pushed herself to standing.

"All right then. I told your father I'd talk to you."

"You talked to me." Kendall smiled.

"I did." Cathy came around the desk and placed a gentle kiss to the top of Kendall's head. "Don't work too late out here." When her eyes caught sight of the screen, she said, "Ooo, tablets. Are you getting one finally?"

"Yes. Rick gave me the okay today. I need to make a decision and buy one before he changes his mind."

"He won't change his mind, honey. He thinks you're doing a fabulous job." She pointed at the bowl as she turned to leave. "Soak that when you're done or it will never come clean."

"Imagine what it's doing to my intestines," she said with a grin as her mom waved a hand at her. "Thanks, Mom."

Once alone again, Kendall tried to return her focus to her research, but her mind kept drifting back to her mother's words. She was right about one thing: when Janet had left, work was the only thing that kept Kendall from feeling completely lost, from floating off into the ether, untethered and weightless with nothing to hold her. There had been upwards of a dozen nights when she'd actually fallen asleep at her desk, awakened the next morning by the sound of Rick opening and closing the big front door of the barn, and then trying to pretend she'd just gotten in a bit before him. She was pretty sure he never bought it, but he said nothing. Thankfully. She wouldn't have been able to handle the shame.

Her appetite suddenly dwindled, she pushed the half-eaten meal away and sat back, folded her hands over her belly, and wondered when the last time she'd gone out, done something social was. There was the volleyball league, but that was only social if she stayed to have a drink with Liz and her team. Which she didn't always do. Her brain tossed her a quick flash of the last time she had, of Andrea's green eyes watching her from the end of the bar.

Her heart rate picked up.

The next social outing she could recall was the party Liz had dragged her to. This time, her mental replay was of crashing into Andrea, spilling wine all over her, trying to wipe it off. It was amusing now, despite how unamusing it had been then.

St. Patrick's Day. Yeah. That was an awesome outing. She sighed dreamily as she remembered Andrea's lips moving against her ear.

That was it, though. Everything else had involved work.

Unless she counted her two visits to Andrea's house.

Had those been social outings or work? Kendall leaned her head back and studied the ceiling as she used her feet to pivot her chair slightly right, then slightly left, then slightly right. They'd begun as work. The tasting. The retrieval of her laptop. But they'd morphed—easily and unnoticed—into social visits. She recalled putting in the cat door, eating Andrea's homemade soup, falling asleep on Andrea's couch all wrapped around her...

She sat back up quickly and began talking out loud, which felt much weirder without Buster here to at least act as another living thing with whom she might be conversing, rather than talking to herself like a lunatic. "I'm not going there. I cannot go there. I can't revisit that night. I'll just drive myself crazy." She grabbed at her mouse. "Tablets. Electronics. That's what we're focusing on tonight. Work. Come on, Kendall. Just pick a tablet already."

Almost as if she had no control, her fingers flew over the keyboard, typed in an internet address, found a website, scanned for employees, and pulled up the Hagan's employee entry for one Andrea Blake. Her smiling face filled the screen, auburn hair just untamed enough to entertain fantasies, green eyes staring intently at Kendall, one eyebrow slightly arched and a ghost of a smile playing across her lips, as if she knew something Kendall didn't.

Propping her chin in her hand and her elbow on the desk, Kendall just sat there. Looking. Staring. Daydreaming. Fantasizing...

Then she dropped her head to the desk, covered it with her arms, and groaned.

CHAPTER ELEVEN

The Fosters' property was sprawling, especially for this part of the county, and it occurred to Andrea as she passed a cute yellow farmhouse and followed the signs that led her car to Old Red Barn Brewcrafters that the Fosters were sitting on a gold mine of land. The suburbs were encroaching and she was reasonably sure Kendall's parents would get more than a pretty penny for their property...which would then be turned into a housing development faster than they could blink an eye.

The signage was good, and Andrea parked her car in an open spot in a small lot. The name of the beer certainly fit, as she found herself staring up at what could only be described as an old red barn. A *huge* old red barn.

She cut the engine and glanced in the rearview mirror. When that didn't provide enough of a view, she flipped the visor down and used the attached makeup mirror. She'd dressed a bit more casually than she would for work, but didn't want to go too casual, lest she give the wrong impression: that this was not a work-related trip. It totally was.

Wasn't it?

Fixing a small black blur of mascara using her fingertip, she took out her lip-gloss and applied a fresh coat, then tamed a few wild curls that had decided to be unruly today. She closed the mirror and flipped up the visor.

Kendall stood in front of her car, hands on her hips, amused smile on her face.

Busted. Andrea closed her eyes for a second, took in a deep breath and let it out slowly. Then she reached for the door handle.

"Hi there," Kendall said, her voice bright, her face cheery. She looked amazing in faded, low-waisted jeans, a gray Henley, and a denim jacket. Her blond hair was pulled back off her face in a messy ponytail, several strands having already escaped and brushing her face around her ears. She held out a hand in what Andrea could only view as her own show of *This Is Business.* Andrea shook it. It was very warm. And soft. Very, very warm and soft. "I'm so glad you're here."

"Me, too," Andrea said, and meant it.

Kendall gave her a quick once-over. Andrea was sure it was meant to be subtle, maybe undetectable, but Andrea caught it and it made her go a little mushy inside. "So, in case you hadn't guessed, this is the old red barn." She waved her arm like one of the models on *The Price is Right* showing off today's valuable prize.

"I sort of got that," Andrea said with a grin.

"Good. Follow me."

Andrea did not mind following behind Kendall, as the view was pretty spectacular. As soon as she recognized her train of thought, she bit her lip and did her best to banish it. What was wrong with her today? She shook her head and continued walking.

The barn was big, open and airy even in the entryway, and when the front door closed behind them, Andrea could hear a local radio station blaring something by the Barenaked Ladies.

Kendall turned to face her. "So, this is the office area. My office," she gestured to her left. "My brothers' offices." To her right. "Then down here is where accounting is. Over here, where this big space is, will be the tasting room, which I'll show you later. We're not ready yet, but we're working on it. We're hoping to be able to do public tours soon, but we can't serve anything right now. Well, you can taste some today because I'm going to. And you've got an in with the owner." With a wink, she turned and continued on. Andrea stutter-stepped, then followed. *Jesus, get a grip, Andrea.*

A set of double doors led to an enormous open space filled with giant metal vats, skids of boxes and big bags, pipes and hoses running this way and that. It smelled largely, not surprisingly, of beer, and it was chilly. She noticed a handful of other people milling around here and there, tending to one thing or another.

"So…this is where the magic happens." Kendall began to sort of stroll, stopping at different areas to explain what was happening. "We're really pretty small right now. We can only bottle three batches at a time. But we have plans to start expanding this summer, adding onto the back of the barn so we can fit more tanks for fermenting." Andrea followed her for what felt like a very long way to the back corner of the space where huge metal vats, each large enough to hold her car, were lined up. A scruffy-looking man smiled at her and gave a little wave as he walked past. "Okay. This is typically referred to as the brewhouse. This is where the initial stages of beer making take place. Remember our first lesson? Mashing, lautering, boiling, and whirlpooling? All that happens here."

Kendall moved along and Andrea followed. The pride in Kendall's voice, all over her face, was really something fun to see, and Andrea found herself grinning without intending to. Kendall knew this process inside and out and her love of it was evident.

They passed through more doors to what Andrea was pretty sure was the very back of the barn, though the place was deceptively huge. More metal tanks stood lined up, a noodle-like mess of pipes running from one to another, across the high ceilings, everywhere.

"It's crazy, isn't it?" Kendall asked when Andrea met her eyes. "It seems so confusing, but it's really not. Just takes a while to learn it all. So." She gestured to the tanks. "This is the tank room —good name for it, huh? This is where fermentation, aging, and filtration happen." She kept on talking, but her voice seemed to fade away so that all Andrea became aware of was her mouth. Full, glossy, soft-looking lips. Straight white teeth visible with every smile. When the tip of her tongue peeked out to wet her lips, Andrea's breath hitched, which sent her own saliva down the wrong pipe, which sent her into an embarrassing coughing fit. She held up a hand at Kendall's suddenly concerned face, and tried to clear her throat.

"You okay?" Kendall asked, placing a warm hand on Andrea's arm.

Andrea nodded, working to collect herself, her eyes watering. "Yeah. Yeah, I'm fine."

"Let's get you some water." She gripped Andrea's wrist and led her back the way they'd come. "We can get back to the tour in a minute." They walked for several minutes, Andrea feeling better with every step. By the time they reached Kendall's office, she was thoroughly embarrassed, but otherwise feeling perfectly normal. Well, except for the red-hot wave of arousal that coursed through her bloodstream like liquid fire, from her wrist that was warm in Kendall's grip straight up her arm to her shoulder, past her chest and...*down*. Andrea followed as Kendall went in and squatted in front of a mini fridge. Turning back to Andrea, she twisted the cap off a bottle of water and handed it to her. "Here. Drink some of this before I hit you with beer tastings." She grinned and Andrea's stomach tightened as Kendall walked past her to shut the office door.

Things for Andrea went a little hazy after that.

She didn't exactly remember moving or setting down the bottle, but when Kendall turned back from the closed door, Andrea was walking toward her, determination in her steps. Then they were moving together—forward for Andrea, backward for Kendall—until Kendall's back stopped against the office door, a small whoosh of air escaping her when she hit. Andrea hovered there, her eyes unable to focus on anything but Kendall's mouth, her shiny, full lips slightly parted in surprise. Almost in slow motion, Andrea lifted her hand, trailed her fingertips along Kendall's soft cheek. The sound of her own rapid breathing mixed with Kendall's as she ran her thumb gently across Kendall's bottom lip before sliding her hand farther back to grip Kendall's head as she pressed their lips together. She pulled back slightly, looked into beautiful blue eyes. They were dark, heavy with arousal, so Andrea kissed her again.

It started softly, slowly at first, tentatively, as if they were each gauging the reaction of the other. Andrea felt Kendall's hands settle on her waist, thumbs hooking her belt loops to pull her in closer, and she took that as a positive sign. She deepened the kiss some more, pressed herself more firmly into Kendall so there was no space left between their bodies. When Kendall's mouth opened under hers, Andrea took the invitation, pushed her tongue inside and was rewarded with a quiet groan. That was all the encouragement she needed. Grasping Kendall's face with both hands, she kissed her deeply, trying hard to take her time, but wanting nothing more than...*more*. This wasn't just a great kiss. It was an amazing kiss. It was a million times better than she'd imagined...and she'd imagined earth-shattering. This was...it was indescribable. Kissing Kendall was the most wonderfully arousing thing she'd ever experienced in her life, and she never wanted to stop.

She felt Kendall's hands slide up her back, her fingers digging in, and it spurred her on. She grabbed Kendall's ponytail, gently tugged her head back, and launched an oral assault on her neck, Kendall's skin warm and so, so soft under her mouth. She smelled amazing, a combination of her earthy perfume and something that smelled like strawberries, plus a little bit of spiciness that was unique to Kendall and that Andrea couldn't get enough of. Using the tip of her tongue, she licked a hot, wet trail up the side of Kendall's neck to her ear, nibbling the lobe gently with her teeth before returning to that glorious mouth once again. Andrea's other hand had drifted innocently down to Kendall's hip, but now she inched it up until it brushed the side of a surprisingly full breast. Her tongue deep in Kendall's mouth, she moved her hand enough to run her thumb across Kendall's nipple, and even through the fabric of her shirt *and* bra, she could feel it tighten and grow under her touch, feel Kendall's entire body shudder in reaction. So she did it again.

And suddenly, she was stumbling a step backward, Kendall's hand planted firmly against her chest, holding her at arm's length.

"Stop," Kendall said quietly, breathless. "Just...wait. Please."

They stood there, barely a foot apart, lungs heaving, lips swollen, faces flushed with color.

"What's wrong?" Andrea asked, keeping her voice as quiet as Kendall's. "Did I hurt you?"

Kendall shook her head, removed her hand, and Andrea was certain she saw a ghost of a smile. "No. No, you didn't hurt me. It's just…we shouldn't. Not here. Not…we shouldn't."

"I know." Andrea laid a hand across her forehead, amazed by how cold she suddenly was without Kendall's body next to hers. "I'm sorry."

"Don't be."

"I just…I couldn't *not* know what that felt like any longer. It was driving me crazy. I…" Andrea stopped talking, just shook her head slowly as she reached up and touched Kendall's lips with her fingers. "Jesus."

Kendall let her eyes drift closed for a split second before closing her hand over Andrea's and moving it away. "I know. Let's just finish the tour. Okay? Can we do that? My brother knows you're here and he's going to come looking for us before long."

Andrea nodded, cleared her throat, searched hard for business mode, but didn't have a lot of luck. "Yes. Okay. Lead the way." She stepped back to allow room for Kendall to open the door behind her, but their gazes held for a long beat, and that sizzle was there again, but amplified by about a zillion.

Kendall blew out a breath, her hand on the doorknob. She looked down at her feet, seemed to be mentally getting her bearings. She looked up again at Andrea, wet her lips. Andrea gave her a look and a soft groan and Kendall smiled with what Andrea was almost sure was a little bit of satisfaction.

"Sorry," Kendall whispered.

"Liar," Andrea whispered back.

❧

What the hell had just happened? And when could it happen again?

Those were the only two thoughts Kendall could focus on clearly in her mind as she went through the motions of the rest of the tour. She was painfully aware of Andrea, of every move she made, of exactly where she was standing and how close, where she was looking, how she smelled. *Thank God I know this stuff inside and out*, she thought, because concentrating on beer was the last thing on her mind.

Oh, my God, that kiss. Completely unexpected, despite being craved for weeks now, and so dizzyingly sexy. Hot and wet and soft and then not soft. It was quite possible Andrea was the best kisser on the planet. Yeah, it was very, very possible.

She was showing Andrea the bottling area, explaining the process, that part of her brain on autopilot because the rest of her was completely absorbed in arousal. When she glanced at Andrea to see if she was following, she found her staring directly at Kendall's mouth, her eyes hooded. She looked up, their gazes locked, and Kendall felt her entire face heat up as she whispered, "Stop it."

"Stop what?" Andrea asked with quiet innocence. Feigned innocence.

"Stop looking at me like that."

"Can't."

Kendall shook her head, but couldn't keep the grin off her face as they moved along, finishing the remainder of the tour just as Rick approached them.

"Hey," he said, his voice seeming inordinately loud after all the whispering they'd been doing. He held out his hand. "You must be Ms. Blake."

"Andrea. Please." Andrea shook his hand and Kendall thought she did an admirable job stepping back into work mode.

"Rick Foster. It's nice to meet you. Kendall has told me a lot about you."

"Well, don't believe her. I'm actually not so bad." Andrea turned and grinned at Kendall, and Kendall was sure her knees were about to melt.

"What do you think?" Rick looked around the brewery, his pride obvious on his face.

"It's impressive."

"We think so. Thank you so much for getting us into your store. It really means a lot to us."

"It wasn't just me," Andrea explained, in full business manner now. "I've got a staff. They make recommendations. I take those under advisement. Your beers are very popular, high quality, and they sell. That's what we want in Hagan's."

Rick's chest puffed up slightly and Kendall smothered a smile. "Thank you," he said. With a look at his sister, he said, "You guys going to taste the Yellow House?"

Kendall gave a nod. "I was thinking we might."

"Great. I've got to check on the tanks. It was nice to meet you Andrea." He shook her hand again, waved, and was on his way.

Andrea turned to look at Kendall, and just that simple movement sent Kendall's arousal into overdrive again. "I don't know about you," Kendall said with a shake of her head. "But I could use a drink."

"Oh, definitely."

"Follow me."

Kendall led the way to the unfinished tasting room, which held a large bar-like counter, several taps, a smattering of glasses, and two refrigerators. Kendall headed behind the counter and when Andrea moved to follow, she stopped her.

"No." With a finger, she gestured to the other side of the counter. "You go over there. Just…stay over there. On the other side of this very large piece of wood. That will be between us."

The half-grin she gave Andrea must have been just sexy enough because Andrea smiled and said softly, "Yes, ma'am."

Kendall grabbed a couple of glasses, pulled the tap, and filled them. "Okay. This is our new Yellow House Peach Wheat. It's perfect for the impending summer season. It's brewed with—"

"Kendall."

Kendall stuttered to a stop, her gaze on the beer. After a moment, she looked up. "What?"

Andrea quirked up one corner of her mouth as she reached across and took one of the glasses. "Nothing. I just wanted to say your name."

What the hell was happening here? Kendall should just ask the question out loud. Ask Andrea directly. But she couldn't. For some reason, the words just wouldn't come out of her mouth. Instead, she held up her glass and quirked one eyebrow expectantly. Andrea touched their glasses together and sipped, watching her over the rim. Kendall didn't look away. The tension was delicious.

"This is good," Andrea commented, not looking away.

"The beer?"

"That, too."

Kendall set down her glass and kept her eyes on the counter for a beat. Then she looked up and said softly, "Andrea, you're making my head spin here. What's going on?"

For the first time since the kiss, Andrea faltered slightly in her seemingly unshakable confidence. She chuckled lightly, her gaze on the middle distance. "I don't know, to be honest."

Unhappy with that non-explanation, Kendall felt herself getting a little frustrated, a little angry. She kept her voice low, but firm. "You said we couldn't explore this. And you were right. Ethics. Conflict of interest. Impropriety. Remember that lovely word? All that good stuff. And then you push me against the door in my office and kiss my face off? Mixed signals much?" She looked around to make sure nobody was within earshot, pushed her hair out of her face with a nervously shaking hand. "I don't understand."

"I know." Andrea held her hands up, palms forward. "I know. I don't know what came over me. I just…" Her voice drifted off and Kendall could see her throat move with a swallow.

Kendall opened her mouth to speak, but the door swung in and two Old Red Barn employees came in.

"Hey, Kendall," one of them said with a cheerful wave as he approached.

"Hi, Denny. How's it going?"

"Good." He pointed to the refrigerator on the other side of Kendall. "Just grabbing my lunch."

"Oh, sure." She scooted out of the way.

"You trying the Yellow House?" the other guy, Charlie, asked, looking from Kendall to Andrea.

"We are," Andrea said with a smile and held up her glass. "It's fabulous."

"Glad you like it." Charlie beamed, and Kendall knew he'd helped Rick come up with the flavor combination. "I think it's going to sell well this summer." With a wave, he and Denny left the way they'd come. The room was quiet.

"I'd like to talk about this," Kendall said after a moment. "But not here."

Andrea gave a nod. "I would, too." She took a large gulp of beer and used a fingertip to wipe away the excess on her upper lip. Kendall gripped the countertop. "Can you come over for dinner?" Andrea asked, her eyes clear.

"Tonight?" When Andrea nodded, Kendall agreed. "Okay."

"Six?"

"Fine. What can I bring?"

Andrea grinned as she pushed herself back from the counter. "You bring the beer."

CHAPTER TWELVE

Kendall stood on the front stoop of Andrea's house with her heart in her throat. Why was she so nervous? She'd been here before. She was comfortable with Andrea. *Maybe a little too comfortable after this afternoon...* She shook the thought away and tried to steady her racing heartbeat.

She'd changed outfits three times with some help from Liz and Marcy, via Skype. She'd called Liz on the phone in a blind panic after Andrea had left, spilling the entire story about the kiss and this upcoming dinner.

"Okay. There may very well be sex tonight," Liz had said, way too matter-of-factly for Kendall to keep it together.

"Oh, my God, do you think so?" Kendall's voice had been about three octaves higher than normal, a sure sign of her impending implosion.

"Yes, and so do you. Now get a grip, will you? And Skype me so we can see what you're wearing. There's a fine line here you need to walk. Not too prudish, not too slutty."

She'd paraded in front of the webcam for what felt like hours before deciding upon a rather simple outfit. Faded jeans, a V-neck hoodie in black and gray stripes (according to Liz, it was casual and easygoing, but also snug enough to showcase Kendall's "great boobs"), and black boots.

"You're sure?" Kendall had asked for the fifteenth time. "It's not too much? Or too little?"

Marcy's face had popped into the frame on her computer as she pushed her way in front of Liz. "She's right, Kendall. Casual but sexy. And that shirt is amazing on you. Go with it."

After signing off with her friends, she'd taken her time applying makeup, dabbing perfume in strategic spots, and choosing simple yet classy jewelry. Silver hoops in her ears, a chunky silver watch, a hammered silver pendant her mother had given her for Christmas that hung perfectly against the expanse of skin on her chest that the shirt left visible. Hair down, she tucked one side behind her ear and stared at herself in the mirror. Way longer than she should have, which only served to ratchet up her apprehension.

So now she stood on the front stoop, six-pack of beer in one hand, bottle of wine under her arm, fist raised to knock. And she stood there.

And stood there.

And stood there.

There may very well be sex tonight.

"Oh, my God, this is insane," she said finally and rapped on the door.

It was pulled open almost immediately, and Kendall jumped, nearly dropping the wine.

"Sorry," Andrea said, her expression sheepish, and Kendall wondered if she'd been right on the other side waiting to answer the door. The idea made her insides warm. "Hi." The sheepishness gone, Andrea smiled widely, stealing Kendall's breath.

She looked incredible—and had obviously gone for the same "casual but sexy" look Kendall had. Worn jeans that seemed to love her curves, an emerald green ribbed tank under a white button-down shirt with subtle green stripes. A little makeup,

173

some nice jewelry, and a sweet, intoxicating perfume that made Kendall feel woozy on her feet it was so wonderful. Her auburn hair was loose and her cheeks were rosy.

"You look amazing," Kendall said before she could stop herself. She was rewarded by the color in Andrea's cheeks deepening.

"Thank you," Andrea said, stepping back. "Come in."

"Oh, my God, it smells fantastic in here," Kendall said as she set down the beer and wine and took her coat off.

"Thanks," Andrea said with a smile as she took Kendall's coat and hung it up. "Chicken French." Wordlessly, she handed Kendall the same pair of slippers she wore last time. Kendall smiled her thanks. "And I told you beer," she said, eyeing the wine bottle.

"I know. But sometimes, wine is better with dinner. I thought I'd play it safe and bring both."

Andrea gave her a mock-scolding look, but said no more, and Kendall followed her into the kitchen, passing Zeke along the way. He was rolling under the dining room table, the stuffed mouse clutched in his little paws. Kendall set her bottles down on the island and knelt down to play with him. After a few minutes, she got back up and noticed the dining room table was set very nicely, complete with lit candles and cloth napkins. At the sound of a cork popping, she turned to Andrea, who was watching her.

"I'm just going to let this breathe," she said unnecessarily.

"Okay."

The air between them was different. Charged. They both felt it; Kendall could tell by the way they avoided eye contact, said little. It was uncomfortable yet exhilarating at the same time. Kendall couldn't decide if she liked it or not.

"Zeke's getting big," she commented, looking down at the playful cat.

"He is. It's funny how fast animals grow." Andrea's back was to her as she worked on dinner. The conversation stalled.

"Can I help?" Kendall asked.

"You can pour the wine."

"On it."

The Cabernet was noticeably pretty in the candlelight, crimson sparkles reflecting off the glasses. Kendall picked them up and took them into the kitchen where she handed one to Andrea. They touched glasses as Kendall whispered, "Cheers." They sipped, holding eye contact. Andrea's gaze dropped to Kendall's mouth only a second before she leaned in and pressed her lips to Kendall's.

It was a gentle, tentative kiss, almost chaste, and Andrea pulled back after only a few seconds. Then she smiled and turned back to the stove.

Kendall took another sip of wine.

Ten minutes later, they both took their seats at the table.

"If this tastes half as good as it looks and smells, I will be a happy girl," Kendall said as she split open her baked sweet potato and stuffed a pat of butter inside.

"Well, then, I hope it does."

They ate in silence for a while, apparently no longer able to even pretend to converse about mundane things. Kendall was halfway through her chicken breast when she looked up to find Andrea looking at her with such raw sexuality she almost dropped her fork.

"Okay," she said, setting her fork down and wiping her mouth with her napkin. She picked up her wine glass, took a fortifying sip, then propped her elbows on the table. "Talk to me."

"Talk to you about what?" Andrea said, spooning potato into her mouth.

Kendall simply tilted her head to the side and waited.

Andrea rolled her lips in, bit down on them for a minute. Then she, too, set down her fork and picked up her wine. "Okay. You want to talk about today?"

"I'd like to talk about that kiss, yes. I mean..." Kendall rubbed a hand over her face as she tried not to get caught up in a flashback of those moments in her office when she was deliciously trapped between the door and Andrea's warm body. "Where the hell did that come from?"

Andrea looked down at her plate. "I'm sorry. I shouldn't have done that. I—" She stopped talking when Kendall reached across the table and covered her hand with her own.

"Andrea. Are you kidding me? Don't apologize. Please. That's not why I'm here. I don't regret that kiss at all. *At all*."

"You don't?"

"God, no. In fact, I've been replaying it in my head all day."

One side of Andrea's mouth quirked up. "Me, too."

"I guess..." Kendall sat back, searching for words. "I'm just wondering why it happened. We had discussions. We talked about all of it and why it wasn't a good idea. And we agreed. Right?"

"We did."

"And then?" Kendall made a rolling gesture with her hand, encouraging Andrea to pick up the story.

"And then...I don't know. I don't know what happened. I just...had to." Andrea's voice was barely a whisper. "I don't know how else to explain it. One minute, I was fine, in work mode, taking a tour, and the next, I couldn't stop thinking about…what it would be like…with you." She shrugged and shook her head, then furrowed her brows as a look of almost-anger came over her face. "This isn't me, you know," she said, her eyes snapping as she looked at Kendall. "I don't…I don't…do that. I don't just randomly kiss women out of the blue. This is…" She trailed off, looked away as if embarrassed, and swallowed hard. "This is new for me and I don't quite understand it."

Kendall watched the emotions play out on Andrea's face, watched them with rapt attention. She'd always thought of Andrea as—not necessarily cold, but cool. In control. Sexy, yes, but in control. Always. A little bit hard, even. Seeing her so uncertain, so confused about her own behavior, didn't sit well with Kendall. She wanted to fix it, to make it better, but somehow knew that any kind of coddling or sympathy wouldn't be welcomed by Andrea. It would probably embarrass her further. So instead, Kendall decided to take a different tack.

"Well," she said, keeping her voice nonchalant as she sat back in her chair, pushed herself back from the table. She crossed her legs, sipped her wine, and shrugged. "It was kind of bound to happen. Don't you think?"

"What do you mean? What was bound to happen?"

"This. Us. From that first lesson in your office, we started down this path." That statement was more truthful than Kendall even realized until she heard it come out of her own mouth. She waited nervously for Andrea's response.

Andrea held her gaze, but didn't argue. She sipped her wine, never taking her eyes from Kendall's. The air between them crackled.

"And you know what?" Kendall went on, lowering her voice just a touch, feeling emboldened by the lack of opposition from

Andrea's side of the table. "Those reasons we had? For keeping at arms' length from one another? Gone now. My beer is in your store. It's done. There really isn't an obstacle left." She arched one eyebrow as she sipped.

Time seemed to grind to a halt as Kendall waited Andrea out. They sat in silence for what felt like hours, but was surely only seconds, before Andrea set down her wine glass and pushed her chair back slightly from the table. She held Kendall's gaze across the remains of their dinner, the candlelight causing her eyes to sparkle like emeralds. Lifting a hand, she crooked her finger at Kendall and quietly ordered, "Come here."

A zap of erotic electricity shot through Kendall's entire body at the command, and she swallowed hard. After one last sip of wine, she stood and slowly rounded the table. Andrea shifted herself in her seat and patted her own thigh. Without saying a word, Kendall swung one leg over Andrea's, then lowered herself slowly onto her lap.

Kendall's breath hitched as her face came closer to Andrea's, and Andrea's hands settled naturally on Kendall's hips. Given their slight height difference, this position made them almost the same size, Kendall's mouth sitting just a tiny bit higher than Andrea's. This close up, Andrea's face was achingly beautiful, all smooth skin and full lips, her eyes darkened with arousal that Kendall was sure was mirrored on her own face. She wanted to say something. Anything. But the words were stuck in her throat and all she could do was look. And feel. Andrea moved slowly, bringing a hand up to Kendall's face and used one finger to brush a strand of hair from her forehead, tuck it behind her ear. That finger continued to follow behind Kendall's ear, along her jawline to her chin, where it hooked under and pulled until Kendall's eyes drifted closed as Andrea's mouth covered hers.

A LITTLE BIT OF SPICE

The gentle, tentative start to this kiss was much shorter than the last one, and it deepened quickly as tongues and hands came into play almost immediately. Andrea grasped Kendall's head as they kissed, while Kendall dug her fingers into Andrea's waist and tried to pull herself closer, even when she was as close as she could get. Her feet dangled just a bit, her toes skimming the floor. The only sound in the room was that of ragged breathing and the soft meeting of their lips.

I could seriously kiss her forever.

The thought zipped through Kendall's head like a bolt of electricity and once again, she wondered if Andrea might be the best kisser in the human race. The way her mouth made Kendall feel...like what lay beyond the kissing would be enough to completely unravel her—in a good way—but the kissing itself was so intoxicating that she didn't want to rush to that beyond, she wanted to just keep kissing. She'd never had such a reaction to making out with anybody before, and she did her best to just...feel it. Savor it.

Andrea held her face with one hand and trailed a wet, hot path down the side of her neck as the other hand slipped under the hem of Kendall's shirt. When Andrea's fingers touched Kendall's bare skin, they groaned in unison and Andrea closed her mouth over that spot where Kendall's neck and shoulder met, just inside her collar. The tip of her tongue tracked along Kendall's throat to her chin, then back up to plunge back into Kendall's mouth, none too gently this time.

There was something delicious about this position, being in Andrea's lap, with no solid purchase for her feet, no way to shift her body other than to sort of wriggle against Andrea's thighs... something Kendall figured out Andrea liked rather quickly, as each time Kendall moved, Andrea's fingers tightened on the back of her neck and against her ribcage. After the third time, Andrea let out what was almost a growl and wrenched her mouth away. Without preamble, she slid her hands up Kendall's sides, taking Kendall's shirt as she went. Kendall lifted her arms and soon was left sitting in Andrea's lap wearing jeans and a black bra.

Andrea let out her breath slowly as her eyes raked over Kendall's bare torso for the first time. It was shockingly sensual, having this stunningly gorgeous woman looking at her skin, at her bra-clad breasts, and Kendall felt sexy and vulnerable at the same time.

"You're so beautiful," Andrea whispered as she ran a fingertip, feather-light, from Kendall's shoulder across her collarbone, down her cleavage and along her stomach to the button on her jeans, then back up again. Kendall's chest heaved with the increased pace of her breathing and holding onto the hope that she wouldn't simply implode right there in Andrea's lap.

Andrea moved both palms around to the small of Kendall's back and pulled her closer so the apex of Kendall's thighs was pressed against Andrea's stomach. She slid her hands up, splaying them over Kendall's shoulder blades. Looking into Kendall's eyes, she lightly raked her nails down the sensitive skin of Kendall's back, causing a shudder to run through her entire body as her head fell back at the sensation.

"God, Andrea..." Kendall said on a moan.

Andrea repeated the process and Kendall hissed air in through her teeth, her fingers tightening on Andrea's shoulders. Making short work of the bra clasp, she pulled the garment off Kendall and wasted no time palming one full breast as she took the other into her mouth and sucked hard. Digging her fingers into Andrea's hair, Kendall let out a guttural moan as her arousal was kicked ever higher by Andrea's skilled fingers and even more skilled mouth. So all-consuming were the sensations that Kendall didn't notice Andrea unfastening the front of her jeans until her fingers skimmed the wet heat at the edges of Kendall's center, and the moan turned to a whimpered cry of surprised pleasure.

"Oh, my God," Andrea said. "I have to touch you. I have to." She looked to Kendall, who then understood Andrea's access was limited in their current position.

Blinking several times to clear the haze of arousal that hung around them like a fog, Kendall asked simply, "Bedroom?" Extricating herself from Andrea's lap, she stood slowly on shaky legs, eyebrows raised.

"Fabulous idea." Andrea stood and held out a hand. Kendall placed hers in Andrea's and their gazes held for a second until Andrea's slid lower. Kendall was sure she could feel it, as if Andrea were actually touching her, over her shoulders, down across her breasts and stomach, back up. "God," Andrea said, and tried to tug Kendall to her.

Kendall resisted, to her eternal credit, and said again in a hoarse voice. "Bedroom. Or we're going to do this right here on the floor."

Andrea looked down at the area rug under their feet as if actually considering it, before Kendall pulled at her with a grin. Another once-over had Andrea shaking her head. "You apparently don't understand what this view is doing to me."

"Then take me upstairs and show me."

Andrea arched one eyebrow, gave Kendall the sexiest of grins, and nodded once, then turned and pulled Kendall toward the stairs.

Andrea's bedroom was a surprise to Kendall as she stepped through the doorway ahead of her, the room much softer and girlier than she expected for reasons she couldn't explain. Various shades of blue dusted the walls, the curtains, the oval rug under the bed on the hardwood. The queen-sized bed was strewn with an array of pillows in many shapes and sizes, all complementary, all frilly. Most noticeably, the room smelled like Andrea, like her shampoo, her lotion, her perfume. Kendall inhaled the subtle fragrances of coconut, lemon, cinnamon. And then all coherent thought was cut off as warm hands slid around her stomach from behind, and up to cup both bare breasts gently yet possessively. Andrea's body firm against her back, Kendall leaned her head back so it rested on Andrea's shoulder, let her eyes drift closed, and sighed in utter pleasure.

They stayed that way for long moments in the dark bedroom, their bodies warm and close, Andrea's hands knowing and magical on Kendall's breasts. Soon, she trailed one hand up Kendall's sternum to cup her chin and turn her face so Andrea could kiss her. Kendall shifted in Andrea's arms so they were face-to-face, nearly eye-to-eye. She brought a hand up, touched her fingers to Andrea's mouth, as she stared at the full, kiss-swollen lips, never so awed by the beauty of one woman as she was in that moment. There was much she wanted to say, but the words stayed inside, and when she lifted her gaze to meet Andrea's, the green eyes looking back at her were so heavy with desire Kendall had to swallow down the surge of arousal that threatened to combust her.

"You're overdressed," she whispered, and immediately set to work unbuttoning the blouse and pushing it off Andrea's shoulders—which were freckled and gorgeous and Kendall couldn't help herself; she immediately touched her lips to one, kissing the soft skin, pulling Andrea closer, using her tongue to move along the muscle to the curve of Andrea's neck. A small sound escaped Andrea's lips. Not quite a cry, but more than a whimper, and Kendall smiled against her flesh, feeling a surge of power as she reached down to unfasten Andrea's jeans. Squatting in front of her, she pulled them down Andrea's legs, then ran her hands back up as Andrea stepped out of them, balancing herself with a hand on Kendall's shoulder.

Kendall stood and surveyed the glorious body before her. Clad only in the green ribbed tank and pink-and-white striped panties, Andrea was stunning. Her hair was a red cloud around her head, her skin was smooth and creamy, her legs were ridiculous. Kendall simply stood there, staring and slowly shaking her head. Before she could comment, Andrea stepped to her, grabbed her face in both hands, and kissed her senseless.

They moved together after that, like longtime partners in an exotic dance. Clothing came off easily, ragged breaths gave way to moans and small cries. On her back in the bed, Kendall let out a long groan and closed a pillow in her fist as Andrea pushed her thighs apart and settled her naked hips between them, the sensation almost too much to handle. Braced on her forearms, Andrea looked down at her, the moment weighted and solid, and when she moved her hips just a little, Kendall gasped and tightened her legs around Andrea's, pulling her closer still.

Their pace was slow, gentle at first, pleasure spiraling out from Kendall's center, down her legs and through her body like warm water. Her fingers buried in Andrea's hair, she pulled her face down and kissed her deeply, filling her other hand with one of Andrea's small, firm breasts. When Andrea moved a hand between them, slid her fingers down through Kendall's wet heat, and pushed directly into her body, Kendall lifted her hips and wrenched her mouth away with a soft cry of, "Yes…"

"Yeah?" Andrea whispered in her ear as her thumb hit a particularly perfect spot. "Like that?"

"Oh, God, just like that."

"Yeah?"

"Yeah."

"Right there?"

"Yes…"

The rhythm picked up slightly until Kendall was sure her entire body would simply melt into the sheets in one, hot, satisfied puddle. But Andrea didn't let her off the hook that easily. Just as Kendall approached the edge, Andrea slowed her pace. When Kendall's breathing eased, Andrea picked things up again. She managed this three times before Kendall begged, "Andrea…please…"

Andrea smiled down at her, quietly said, "Okay. Come on. Come for me," and tipped her off the precipice into an oblivion of colors exploding behind her tightly closed eyes. Her fingers dug into Andrea's back and she fisted a handful of hair as her entire body tensed and she let out one cry, then held her breath until the waves subsided and she slowly relaxed.

"Oh, my God," she said softly as she worked hard to breathe normally again. Laying a hand across her forehead, she opened her eyes and looked into Andrea's smiling green ones. "That… that was…"

"Pretty amazing."

"Understatement."

Andrea kissed her softly, tenderly. "Yeah?"

"God, yes. And the talking?" Kendall blew out a breath.

"Oh, you liked that, did you?" Andrea asked with a chuckle.

"I had no idea I did. But yes. Very much."

"So noted." Andrea kissed her again.

"Control freak," Kendall added.

Andrea laughed. "It's a problem. I'm not proud." And she kissed her once more.

Kendall pulled back long enough to say, "We're not done," and then deepened the kiss, sliding her tongue into Andrea's mouth as she quickly turned them so they flipped positions. At Andrea's look of surprise at finding herself on the bottom, Kendall grinned. "What? This isn't a one-woman show, you know. I've got plans for you." And with that, she lowered her head, took a nipple into her mouth, and rolled her tongue around it. The groan Andrea gave her in response made her smile wide against the warm skin.

Kendall took her time exploring Andrea's body. With reverence, she touched, kissed, and licked skin, creases, curves. It wasn't long before it was Andrea's turn to plead.

"Kendall. God. You're killing me."

Kendall looked up from the inner thigh she was bathing with her tongue, stopped kneading the breast in her hand. Andrea was looking down her own body at Kendall and their gazes held. The connection crackled between them. "What do you want, Andrea?" she asked quietly. "Tell me what you want."

Andrea dropped her head back to the pillow and covered her eyes with one hand. "Touch me," she said, her voice barely audible. "Please touch me."

"Well, since you asked so nicely..."

Her hands on Andrea's thighs, she gently pushed them farther apart and made herself comfortable. Watching Andrea, she ran her thumb around the swollen flesh, amazed by how wet she was. Andrea sucked in a breath, her chest rising, her fingers grasping at the sheets. Kendall found something incredibly sexy and enticing about Andrea's stomach, the way it rippled as she moved, and Kendall pushed herself up long enough to place a tender kiss on Andrea's belly button before running her tongue back down and through the folds that waited for her.

Andrea's hips rose off the bed as she groaned Kendall's name.

And that was the end of Kendall taking her time.

She sank her mouth into Andrea's center, taking in as much of her as she could, reveling in the feel of her, the sounds, the taste—salty and sweet at once. She sucked Andrea into her mouth as she pushed her fingers inside, and that was all it took. Andrea's thighs fell open, her fingers tightening in Kendall's hair as the orgasm tore through her. Kendall held an arm across her hips, used them to help her stay in place as Andrea moved, her eyes glued to Andrea's face.

She was absolutely, breathtakingly radiant, glorious to watch, and Kendall felt something in her heart shift.

Andrea's muscles relaxed gradually, her hips slowly coming back down to the bed, a spasm making her legs twitch as Kendall removed her mouth and slowly slid her fingers free. Resting her cheek against Andrea's inner thigh, she watched and waited as Andrea recovered, little by little, and her breathing finally returned to normal. Without looking, she held a hand down to Kendall and said, "Come up here."

Happy to oblige, Kendall scooted up Andrea's body until they were face-to-face and pressed a tender kiss to Andrea's lips. Wordlessly, Andrea deepened it slightly, holding Kendall's head to hers, slowly stroking inside Kendall's mouth with her tongue. When they parted, they were both a little breathless, and Kendall collapsed onto Andrea's shoulder.

"God," she said, unable to come up with more words.

"Yeah." Apparently, Andrea was at an equal loss, but she tightened her arms around Kendall and reached down for the covers. Pulling them over their bodies, she placed a gentle kiss on Kendall's forehead. Kendall closed her eyes and tried not to sigh with the contentment that filled her.

They lay quietly for a long while, wrapped up in each other, breathing gently, Andrea's fingers toying with Kendall's hair, Kendall drawing lazy circles on the soft skin of Andrea's chest. By the time Kendall felt herself start to doze, Andrea was already breathing the deep, even breaths of a sleeping person, and any conversation that may have wanted to push out of her stayed tucked away.

CHAPTER THIRTEEN

Spring was almost here.

The thought crossed Andrea's mind as she stood at the kitchen sink, sipped her coffee, and gazed out the window. The sun was shining brightly and birds fluttered and poked at one another in attempts to get to a perch on her full birdfeeder that hung from a maple tree in the backyard. Soon, the collection of birds would go from mostly browns and blacks to splashes of bright color, reds and oranges and yellows showing up with the onset of the change in season.

Moving back to the stove, she picked up a fork and flipped the slices of bacon sizzling in the pan. At the insistence of a little paw batting at her ankle, she squatted down to pick up Zeke, noting the not-unpleasant soreness of her leg muscles, which brought a smile to her face as she buried her nose in Zeke's soft fur.

She and Kendall had found each other again in the night. She'd pulled Kendall from a sound sleep by burying her head between Kendall's thighs, having woken up and watched her sleep for nearly twenty minutes before being besieged by an irresistible need to taste her. Kendall had come hard and fast, and Andrea had underestimated the recovery time needed, as she'd found herself flipped onto her back before she even realized it, Kendall plunging her fingers into Andrea's body with such confident ferocity that an erotic cry of surprised joy had been torn from her throat. Neither of them had spoken a word. They'd simply pushed each other over the edge, collapsed on one another, and went back to sleep.

Andrea had always been a morning person, so the fact that her eyes had popped open by seven, despite the physical workout that had exhausted her body the night before and the precious little sleep she'd gotten, was not a surprise. Propping herself on an elbow and her head in her hand, she'd studied Kendall's sleeping form. She was on her stomach, one arm under the pillow, the other bent so a loose fist was tucked under her chin. She was only covered to her waist, and an entire expanse of bare back and shoulders was exposed for Andrea's pleasure. Unable to stop herself, Andrea reached out and lightly stroked her fingertips across that smooth plane of skin, noting every freckle, every mole, every patch of soft, downy hair. Kendall didn't move, didn't flinch, even when Andrea carefully slipped the covers farther down so she could see the gentle rise of muscle where Kendall's backside began.

The fire had started low in Andrea's body, but it warred with hunger, and finally deciding to let Kendall sleep, she'd quietly slipped from bed, put on her blue pajama bottoms and matching long-sleeved shirt, pinned her hair back and brushed her teeth, and then headed downstairs for much needed coffee and food.

The smell of slightly charred bacon yanked her from her reverie, and Andrea swore as she set Zeke back down on the floor. Placing the overdone slices onto a paper towel, she laid six more in the frying pan, figuring she could crumble the first batch and use them in a recipe later. When she turned to pick her coffee mug back up from the counter was when she noticed Kendall leaning against the doorjamb, looking impossibly fresh in last night's clothes, arms crossed over her chest, and grinning widely, looking for all intents and purposes like the sexiest woman Andrea had ever laid eyes on.

"You roll out of bed looking like *that*?" Kendall asked in disbelief, as if her train of thought had been similar to Andrea's. "So unfair." Her eyes roved down Andrea's body, then back up, stopping not-so-briefly at her chest, before returning to her eyes. "You should wear pajamas all the time."

"I'll keep that in mind," Andrea said, feeling her face flush slightly, and experiencing mixed emotions about the power Kendall seemed to have over her. She turned back to the bacon sizzling in the pan. "Hungry?"

"Starving." And suddenly she was directly behind Andrea, her hands on Andrea's hips, her mouth next to Andrea's ear as she whispered, "Somebody made me work up an appetite last night. And then again at three a.m."

An erotic shudder ran through Andrea's body as her eyes closed briefly. "Me, too."

Kendall wrapped her arms around Andrea's middle and hugged her tightly before letting go. "God, that smells good. Is there coffee?"

Andrea pointed at the pot with the fork. "Mugs are just above. Eggs?"

"Love some. Can I help?"

"Nope. Just sit down and talk to me."

"I can do that." Kendall fixed her cup of coffee, pulled out a stool and sat at the breakfast bar. After several moments of silence, she said, "The sun is shining."

"Mm-hmm." Andrea transferred the bacon to the paper towel to drain, pulled eggs from the fridge. "Scrambled or fried?"

"Scrambled is fine."

"Cheese?"

"Always."

With a nod, Andrea pulled a bowl from a cupboard, set it on the counter near Kendall and cracked eggs into it. A little milk and a few seasonings were next.

"What are you putting in there?" Kendall asked.

"A little oregano. Some garlic salt. A pinch of crushed red pepper."

"Everything's better with a little bit of spice."

"It is." Andrea grinned at the same line Kendall had used during their first tasting together. She used a fork and whisked everything together, feeling Kendall's eyes on her the whole time. And liking it.

"I love your hands," Kendall said, her voice low and husky.

Andrea caught her bottom lip between her teeth at the rush of warmth that ran through her entire body. She looked up and Kendall snagged her eyes, held them. Now she was not only warm, she was incredibly turned on. "Thank you," she whispered, then turned to the stove to make breakfast.

They ate in companionable silence, though Andrea could feel her arousal bubbling just below the surface, and she wondered if this was now a permanent thing.

"These are delicious," Kendall said, shoveling a forkful of eggs onto a piece of toast, topping it with a chunk of bacon, and taking a bite.

"I'm glad," Andrea said with a grin as she watched.

"What?"

"That's a nifty little tower you've made there."

Kendall blushed adorably. "I've done this since I was a kid. Don't make fun."

"I'm not making fun. It's cute."

They grinned at each other and kept eating.

"So," Kendall said after cleaning her plate. "It's Sunday. What's your plan for the day?"

Andrea studied her face, wondering if this was a trick question, but found nothing but sincerity on Kendall's smooth face. Her brain threw her a flash of that same face, head thrown back, mouth open in a soundless cry, and Andrea had to clear her throat in an attempt to collect herself. "Unfortunately, I have some work I need to catch up on or I'm going to be in trouble tomorrow."

Kendall nodded and sipped her coffee. "Same here. We've got a weekend crew working and I promised my brother I'd check in, be present for a while."

"Can you do dinner tonight?" The question was out of Andrea's mouth before she even realized her mind had formulated it, but the smile that spread across Kendall's face was so worth it.

"I can. Why don't you come to my place this time? Though I warn you, we'll be having pizza."

"I happen to really like pizza."

"Well, you're in luck then."

They left it that they'd text each other later to check on work progress. Kendall insisted on cleaning up the kitchen, so Andrea relinquished control—something she rarely did—and sat drinking coffee while Kendall puttered. The view was very, very nice, and Andrea admired the way Kendall filled out her jeans.

When everything was clean and Kendall had her stuff together, Andrea walked her to the front door. Kendall turned to her, one hand on the doorknob.

"I had..." Her eyes looked toward the ceiling as if searching for words. When she returned her gaze to Andrea, her voice went soft. "I had an amazing time last night, Andrea."

Andrea smiled. "Me, too." She reached out, grasped the collar of Kendall's jacket in both hands, and pulled her close, then gently pressed their lips together. She backed off just a touch, then tugged Kendall in tighter and kissed her again. She felt Kendall's arm go around her waist, her hand coming up to cradle Andrea's face as she sucked Andrea's bottom lip into her mouth. Andrea gave a small groan, and Kendall deepened the kiss in response. Arousal flooded Andrea's system in a matter of seconds, and it took every ounce of willpower she had to wrench herself away. She took a step back, holding her hand out toward Kendall in the universal gesture for "stop." Both women were breathing raggedly.

"God, how do you do that?" Andrea asked, trying to catch her breath.

"Do what?" Kendall was just as winded.

"Take me from zero to sixty in about three seconds."

"Hey, I'm not the only one involved here." Kendall's eyes sparkled with mischief as she grinned.

"Yeah, well." Andrea swiped at the corner of her mouth with a fingertip. "You need to go or we'll be having sex right here in the foyer. And it's not warm enough for that."

"Yet," Kendall said as she righted her jacket. "I'll add it to the list."

"What list?"

"The list of places I want to have my way with you."

"There's a list?" Andrea's eyes were wide, even as her heart rate kicked up a notch.

"Oh, yes. There's a list." Kendall winked, leaned in and gave Andrea a quick kiss on the mouth, and pulled the door open. "See you tonight." Then she let her eyes rove down Andrea's body and back up again, quirked an eyebrow suggestively, and was gone.

Andrea stood in the living room and watched out the window as Kendall pulled away, her fingers against her lips that she swore were still hot from Kendall's kissing. "How did this happen?" she asked the empty room and shook her head slowly back and forth. She had piles of work to do, but wondered how she was possibly going to get it done.

Right now, all she could think about was how many hours she had to kill before she could be with Kendall again.

✧

Kendall was getting very little work done at her desk, as every time she looked up, she pictured herself pinned against the door, Andrea's tongue in her mouth. Such a visual made it *very* difficult to concentrate. On anything.

It was going on four o'clock, and thank God for that. She'd come home, showered and changed, and was in the brewery just before eleven, and she'd spent the entire time trying to analyze exactly what had happened the previous day and night.

Not that she was complaining. She was not. At all. In fact, that might have been the best sex she'd ever had. Ever. In her life. And she wasn't sure what to do with that because the biggest question hadn't been answered. Or even asked.

What happens now?

Kendall wasn't one of those stereotypical lesbians who jumped into a relationship as soon as the first kiss was over. She didn't expect Andrea was either. That being said, she did like to know *something* about where things may or may not be headed. The possibility of it being a simple one-night stand was slim, though still there. But the invite for dinner tonight sort of canceled that out. Andrea wouldn't want to see her again—and certainly not so soon—if it had just been a one-time thing. Was it just sex? Were they fuck-buddies now? Kendall supposed that was possible, as there had been zero talk about dating or anything beyond. She wasn't sure how she felt about that… though if it was the only way she could get her hands on Andrea's body again, she might just accept it for a while.

Andrea's body…

Seriously, was there anything more perfect in this world? Her skin, her hair, her hands, her legs, *that mouth…* Kendall closed her eyes and shook her head. This was bad. She could hardly focus. She pressed the heels of her hands into her eyes. Hard.

"Hey, you okay?" Kendall jumped at the sound of Adam's voice. He was in her doorway, a look of concern on his face. "Headache?"

"A little one," she lied. There was no way she could talk to him about any of this. He'd be all over it, all over her, and she'd never hear the end of it.

"Need some Motrin? I think I've got some in my desk."

Kendall smiled at his worry and immediately felt guilty for thinking bad things about him. "No, I've got some. I'm good. Thanks, though."

Adam jerked a thumb over his shoulder. "I'm gonna head out then. Everybody's gone, so lock up when you leave, okay?"

"Will do." He continued to stand there looking at her. "What?" she asked.

"You sure you're okay? You look…weird."

She made a face. "Gee, thanks."

"No, I mean weird, like…sick. Are you sick?"

"I'm just tired. Promise."

He waited another beat before giving in. "Okay. Well, go home. It's Sunday night. Kick your feet up. Watch a movie or something. Relax. You've worked hard this week."

He was gone before he could see the shocked look on her face. Adam was not a sentimental guy. And while it was always nice to have him step out of his normal smartass box, it was also suspicious. She stared after him, squinting. As she did, her cell beeped with a text.

Wrapping up soon. 6?

Kendall felt the smile on her face grow and wanted to roll her eyes at herself, but she couldn't. She was too giddy. She typed back.

Perfect. What do you like on your pizza?

Anchovies.

Kendall squinted at the screen. "No way," she whispered.

Seriously? she typed.

You can just get them on half. ☺

Kendall laughed out loud and shook her head. Andrea continued to surprise her.

You got it. See you soon. She hesitated, then typed, *Looking forward to seeing your face.*

A beat went by. Then another. Just when Kendall figured the conversation was over, the phone beeped.

Looking forward to seeing the rest of you…

᠅

Kendall had buzzed around her apartment like a hummingbird, cleaning, straightening, fixing. Andrea was due any minute and she wanted the place to be impressive. Or at least cute. Charming? Cozy? She'd take anything positive. What she didn't want Andrea to think was that it was messy, crowded, or cramped.

She was standing in front of the full-length mirror on her bedroom door applying lip-gloss when the doorbell rang. Giving her jeans, burgundy long-sleeved shirt, and loose hair a final glance, she headed to the door. One hand on the knob, she took a deep breath, let it out slowly, and opened the door.

How was it that somebody dressed casually could be so damned sexy? It wasn't the first time Kendall had the thought and she almost asked it aloud, but was afraid she might come across as too familiar. Too pushy. Which was silly, she realized a second later, as she'd had her hands and mouth pretty much everywhere on Andrea's body—and vice versa—so what was a little compliment like that going to hurt? But instead, she just looked. Andrea wore jeans with knee-high black boots (frankly, that was enough to kick the sexy meter up about ten notches), a white, cowl-neck sweater, and her coat. Part of her hair was pinned back behind her head, the rest in a loose, auburn cloud around her shoulders, and she smelled amazing. Her eyes were smiling as she said simply, "Hi."

"Hi."

They stood staring at each other and grinning like schoolgirls before Kendall finally collected herself enough to step aside. "Come in."

Andrea stepped through the door, looking around as she did. She handed Kendall a bottle of wine as she stomped her boots off and bent down to unzip them, but Kendall stopped her.

"No." When Andrea looked up at her, Kendall arched one eyebrow and said quietly. "Leave them on. Please."

Andrea wet her lips and Kendall saw her throat move with a swallow. "Well, okay then." She stood and shucked her jacket, gesturing with her eyes to the bottle Kendall held. "I didn't know if you preferred beer with pizza, but I didn't want to come empty-handed. So put that somewhere if we don't open it tonight." Kendall took the bottle to the kitchen as Andrea continued to look around. "Kendall, this is adorable."

"Thanks." Kendall smiled. "People always expect it to be smaller. I mean, it's not huge, but it's bigger than you'd think."

Andrea nodded her head as she wandered slowly toward the couch. The living space was one large room with a kitchen along the wall on the right and an island breakfast bar separating it from the open-concept living room. To the far left was a doorway that led to the bedroom and bath. Windows were on all sides, and two skylights had been installed in the roof, flooding the space with natural light. Kendall tried to see it all through new eyes, Andrea's eyes. Her leather couch was the most expensive item in the apartment, its taupe corner marred slightly by Ollie's claw marks when he was a very small kitten. Thank God he'd discovered his scratching post soon after. Eggplant-colored throw pillows gave a splash of color, as did the eggplant and lavender afghan thrown over the back. The oval area rug was freshly vacuumed, the coffee table and end table just dusted. A cinnamon scented candle warmed up the atmosphere.

Andrea wandered slowly as Kendall watched from the kitchen. At the bedroom door, she peeked in, then turned back to Kendall and waggled her eyebrows. Kendall laughed as Andrea returned to the breakfast bar and took a seat on one of the stools.

"Oh, your stools have backs on them," she observed, looking behind her, and Kendall couldn't stand it anymore. She rounded the counter and when Andrea turned back around, Kendall was right there with a kiss. It was intended to be quick, just a hello peck really, but it was only seconds before Kendall found herself sucked in. Andrea had to lift her head to reach Kendall from her sitting position, and Kendall found her hands wandering to that column of neck, caressing it as the kiss deepened. She felt Andrea's hands on her waist, thumbs sliding under her shirt to rub lazy circles on her bare skin when the doorbell rang, jerking them back to reality like an electric shock.

"Pizza," Kendall whispered, pecked Andrea's lips once more, then went to the door, which opened before she reached it, pulling a small squeak of surprise from her. "Mom. Hi."

"Hi, sweetheart." Cathy Foster pushed in carrying a laundry basket of clothes. "I was just coming to see if you wanted to—" She stopped short when she saw Andrea, whose face was flushed. "Well, hello there."

Kendall closed her eyes briefly, then opened them and swiped her fingertips over her mouth to make sure she didn't have Andrea's lip-gloss all over her face. "Um, Mom, this is Andrea Blake. Andrea, Cathy Foster. My mother."

Andrea stood up and held out her hand, looking for all intents and purposes much more together and relaxed than Kendall felt. Cathy set down the laundry and shook Andrea's hand. "It's nice to meet you, Mrs. Foster."

"Oh, please. Cathy. Mrs. Foster makes me sound so old." She held Andrea's hand as she studied her face before Kendall saw it all click into place. "Oh, *Andrea*. From volleyball." She looked back at Kendall. "And Hagan's."

"Yes to both," Andrea said with a smile, then sat back down.

The three of them languished in somewhat awkward silence for several seconds when the doorbell rang again.

"Busy place," Andrea commented and tossed a wink at Kendall.

Kendall rolled her eyes. "*That* should be the pizza."

It was. She paid the delivery guy as her mother and Andrea chatted behind her. When she closed the door and carried the pizza to the counter, Cathy was expressing her shock at Andrea having been at Hagan's since she was sixteen.

"That doesn't happen often these days," she was saying as Kendall reached up into the cupboard for plates. "People don't tend to stay in the same place for their entire career."

"Very true," Andrea replied. "But it's a great company, they take good care of their employees, and I really like working for them."

"If it ain't broke, don't fix it," Cathy said with a laugh. "That's what Kendall's father is always saying."

Oh, God, Kendall thought. *Time to go.* "Um, so Mom… thanks for bringing the laundry by…" She braced her hands on the counter and leaned forward, letting the sentence dangle, hoping Cathy got the hint. She did, judging by the squinty, unimpressed look she shot her daughter before turning back to Andrea.

"That's my daughter's not-so-subtle cue for me to hightail it out of here. It was nice to meet you again, Andrea."

Andrea chuckled, probably at the mortified expression on Kendall's face. "Same here."

As the door closed behind her mother, Kendall blew out a breath and let her head fall down in relief. When she looked up, Andrea was grinning. "Tell me the truth. Was I just cock-blocked by my mother?"

With a slow nod and a wide grin, Andrea replied, "I do believe you were."

Kendall broke into laughter. "Unbelievable." Flipping open the pizza box, she said, "Let's eat," and then turned to the fridge. "And we are having beer with pizza. It's only right." She grabbed an IPA for herself and a Yellow House Peach Ale for Andrea.

When she turned back, Andrea was making a face, looking down at the pizza. "What's wrong?"

"I think they put anchovies on the whole thing."

"Well, I hope so. That's what I ordered."

Andrea's head snapped up. "No."

"Yes."

"You don't like anchovies on your pizza."

"You're right. I don't. I love them." Kendall pulled down two glasses, grabbed a bottle opener, and popped the caps off both beers.

Andrea fell back onto her stool in obvious disbelief. "Do you know I have *never* met anybody else who likes anchovies? Not a soul."

Kendall grinned and handed her a glass of beer. "Well, now you have." She poured her own beer, then held up her glass. "To anchovies, the salty, joyous, underrated pizza topping we love."

"I will definitely drink to that."

Kendall handed a plate and a napkin to Andrea, then took a slice of pizza for herself. Claiming the stool next to her guest, she sat down. They each took a bite and made twin humming sounds of delight, then burst into laughter.

Andrea took a sip of her beer. "You brought this here just for me?"

"I did," Kendall replied. "I don't really enjoy the fruity stuff so much."

"Because your tastes have matured?"

"I think you're mocking me." Kendall squinted.

Andrea gasped. "I would never!" She took another bite of her pizza. "Is the yellow house your parents'? The one I drove past on my way here?"

"Yeah." She scrunched up her face as she said, "And yes, my mother does my laundry. Not because I ask her to, but because she comes here and gets it while I'm not home. You saw how she just walks in."

"Thank God she rang the doorbell first," Andrea said, raising an eyebrow.

Kendall covered her eyes with a hand. "I don't even want to think about it." She ate more pizza, then said, "I have been thinking lately it might be time to get my own space. I mean, not that this isn't my own space, but it's still a little too close to home."

"Still, you're lucky to *want* to be this close to your parents. I can't imagine it. I'd kill myself inside of a week."

"Really? How come?"

Andrea set down her glass and wiped her mouth with a napkin. "I don't even know where to begin. My parents…they're not warm and fuzzy people. My dad comes first in life. He always has. Before his wife. Before his kids. He left my mom a couple years ago, after twenty-nine years of marriage."

"That's awful."

"I suppose, though he wasn't faithful…and I almost can't blame him because my mother can be unbearably cold. I'd have probably cheated, too." Andrea said it all with such a detached, unaffected tone, Kendall was a little taken aback. "He's on his… fourth? Fifth girlfriend since? I lose count."

"Wow."

"Yeah."

"Do you have siblings?"

"I have one older sister. Julia. We kept each other—we *keep* each other sane."

"So…not close to your parents, I take it."

"Um...no." Andrea smiled, gave a half-shrug, and reached for another slice of pizza. She seemed to study Kendall's face as she chewed. "Hard for you to imagine, isn't it?"

Kendall glanced down, inexplicably feeling like she should apologize. "It is."

"I can see how tight you are with your family just from the little bit of interaction I've witnessed." Andrea caught her eye. "You're lucky."

"I am. I know." Both true statements. Then a thought struck Kendall. "Is that why you started working so early?"

Andrea nodded. "Yep. I hated to be home, so between volleyball and Hagan's, I hardly ever was."

"Smart solution. Look where it's gotten you."

"Right. And look where else it's gotten me." Andrea made a show of looking around the apartment, then landing her gaze on Kendall, which made Kendall's blood warm.

"Well. We knew each other in school."

"We knew *of* each other. We didn't know each other. But how many years ago was that? And how weird is it that we haven't really noticed each other since until a day before that meeting?"

Kendall laughed. "It *is* weird."

"And here we are."

"And here we are," Kendall echoed as the delicious eye contact extended. And suddenly the air in the room was heavy with excited anticipation.

Andrea's voice was very quiet. "I think you should show me your bedroom."

It occurred to Kendall in the middle of it all that the second time being intimate with somebody was infinitely easier than the first. And less serious, more fun. And thank God for that. There was less trepidation; they were somewhat familiar with what the other liked, and because of that little extra bit of comfort, they were more relaxed. Kendall was less shy about being naked in front of Andrea and was almost brazen about undressing her, taking the steering wheel out of Andrea's hands more than once in order to bare more skin. Under the covers, they moved together, talking and directing. Pleas and moans gave way to encouraging and coaxing as they each wrung pleasure from the other more than once.

And when they were done, spent and breathless, they lay wrapped up in each other, gazing up out the skylight at the stars in the clear night sky. Andrea's head was pillowed on Kendall's shoulder, Kendall's fingers wrapped in her hair.

"Okay, so," Kendall said. "First time was *not* a fluke."

"Definitely not a fluke."

"Good to know."

"Mm-hmm."

"You know what would be really good right now?" Kendall asked as she let her fingers dig into Andrea's hair and lightly scratch her scalp.

"What?" Andrea asked, then gave a soft groan of pleasure.

"Pizza."

A beat passed before Andrea said. "You know what? You're right. Cold pizza. With anchovies."

"Exactly."

They looked at each other with tandem grins. Kendall kissed Andrea on the mouth, whispered, "I'll be right back," and jumped out of bed.

"I'll be right here," was the sleepy reply.

The lights were still on in the kitchen, but Kendall quickly turned them off and moved by moonlight, as she was stark naked. The apartment was far enough away from the other buildings on the property that it wasn't likely anybody would see her, but still. The last thing she needed was for her father to be wandering to the barn for some reason or another, glance up, and see his daughter, naked as the day she was born, parading around her apartment.

Plate in hand, she loaded it with the remaining four slices of pizza. She popped the tops on two bottles of beer and, foregoing glasses this time, scooped everything up and carried it to the bedroom—where she stopped for a moment to absorb the view.

Kendall's emerald green bedding could not have been more complementary to Andrea's coloring if she'd specifically tried to make it so. Andrea lay with her head on the pillow, auburn hair spilling off the side, her eyes closed peacefully. The comforter was pulled up only partway, and a bare breast was visible, the peek of pink nipple making Kendall's fingers ache to touch it. One leg was uncovered from the knee down, burgundy polish shining on the toes, shapely calf muscle prominent and gorgeous.

Kendall swallowed down a surge of desire before she cleared her throat and spoke, keeping her voice low so as not to startle Andrea. "Your post-coital meal is served, m'lady." She set the beers on the nightstand.

Andrea's eyes blinked open and she smiled softly. "Personal delivery, even. I may never leave this bed."

"I may never let you." Kendall kissed her tenderly as she crawled back under the covers and they made themselves comfortable in sitting positions.

"I guess this means you expect a tip now," Andrea said as she slid a piece of pizza off the plate and bumped Kendall with her shoulder.

"Duh," Kendall said as she took a bite.

With a weary sigh, Andrea replied, "I suppose I could come up with *something* that will suffice."

"Oh, I have no doubt. But just say the word if you need ideas. I've got plenty."

"Do you?"

Kendall leaned in close so their lips were not quite touching and whispered, "Oh, yes I do."

CHAPTER FOURTEEN

"You got laid, didn't you?"

Andrea spluttered with a mouthful of Diet Coke, which then shot out her nose. Shoving her chair back with her feet, she bent forward in a coughing fit, causing a couple of patrons at nearby tables to halt their conversations and look curiously her way.

Once she'd collected herself, she looked up at Julia, eyes wide in disbelief.

"Well, that answers that question," Julia said with a smirk, taking a bite of her salad. "Who was it?"

Andrea dabbed at her mouth with her napkin, waited for her eyes to stop watering. She'd spoken to Kylie on the phone the previous night and had deftly avoided anything on the subject of her dating life. But it had never been that easy with her sister. When she looked at Julia's sparkling eyes, she shrugged and with a shake of her head, said simply, "How do you do that?"

"I could tell by looking at your face. You can't hide anything from your big sister. Don't you know that by now? And stop avoiding my question. Who was it?"

Andrea knew better than to attempt to dodge an inquiry by Julia, who was even more relentless in her thirties than she'd been when they were teenagers. She'd chip at Andrea until Andrea couldn't take it anymore and told her whatever she wanted to know simply to get her to leave her alone.

Once she'd pulled herself together, she took a hesitant sip of her Diet Coke, pursed her lips for a moment, then looked at her sister. "It's Kendall Foster. The one I told you about? The one who was teaching me?"

Julia took a second or two to comprehend what Andrea said, but once she did, her eyes went wide. "Her? I thought you hated her. Or she hated you. Or something. Didn't you say that?"

"I did."

"And?"

"Apparently, I was wrong."

"Did you guys talk about it?"

"We haven't really talked about anything." Andrea lowered her voice and leaned a little bit across the table so Julia could hear her. "We've been too busy screwing like bunnies."

Julia burst into laughter. "Oh, little sister, that's good. That's really good. Lord knows you don't loosen up often enough. I think sometimes, it's a good thing to do. It's good for you."

"It is. It's...*very* good."

"Yeah? Do tell."

Andrea grinned. "I'm not going to go into detail, Julia. We're in public. Suffice it to say that I..." Her gaze drifted off as she shook her head and gave a dreamy sigh. "I can't get enough of her." She looked at Julia and shook her head again, at a loss to explain the sexual magnetic pull Kendall seemed to have.

Andrea looked down at her plate, picked up a fry. It was Wednesday afternoon. She hadn't seen Kendall since Sunday night when she'd somehow managed to get herself out of bed, away from Kendall's gloriously naked body and drive home, though not until after a serious make-out session at the front door. They both had work in the morning, and Andrea wasn't quite comfortable with leaving Zeke overnight alone yet. Not to mention, she wasn't nearly ready to deal with the implications of what another sleepover might mean. But they'd texted constantly since—last night had been a ridiculously hot half-hour of sexting —and were planning to see each other again this weekend. For now, she made an effort to change the subject with Julia. "In other news, I've got an interview on Friday."

Julia's eyebrows shot up. "With the big wigs?"

"Yup. I've shown them my interest. This will be a preliminary interview. Then I imagine they'll go through their openings, see what other qualified employees are interested and who would fit best where. Then they'll make offers."

"Wow. It's happening fast." Julia's gaze fell to her plate as she seemed to study her lunch a bit too closely.

"Jules? What's up?"

Julia shrugged. "Nothing. I'll just miss you if you go far away. That's all." Shaking off the melancholy, she added, "Not to mention, I'll have to deal with Mom on my own. Thanks for *that*."

"Well, I have no idea what they'll offer me. There are people higher up than me that will have first choice. I could end up in Fairport," she said with a laugh, referring to a suburb a mere five minutes from where they sat.

"Which would be fine."

"Which would be fine," Andrea echoed, though she knew she'd much prefer a store farther south, out of the harsh cold of winter, where she'd never have to lament another February again. And there were a few with openings. She knew this.

"How does Kendall feel about it?"

"About what?" Andrea popped a fry into her mouth.

Julia cocked her head. "Really?"

"It's very new, Jules. And honestly, I don't even know what *it* is. I'm not going to bog it all down with serious talk about a promotion."

"Okay. How about serious talk about you maybe moving away? Think she might like to know that?" Julia took a fry off Andrea's plate and put it in her mouth, staring Andrea down the whole time she chewed.

"Stop it," Andrea said quietly, looking away.

"You only say that when I do this and I'm right. Otherwise, you fight me." Andrea didn't look at her. "What's going on, Andrea?" She studied Andrea's face; Andrea could feel it as plainly as if Julia were touching her. "You like this girl, don't you? Is that it?"

The spark of anger Andrea had been holding down gave a small surge forward. "I don't have time, Jules. It doesn't matter if I like her or not because the timing could not be worse. I have worked too long and hard for this promotion and if they offer me a manager position in Maryland or Pennsylvania or North Carolina, you know what? I'm taking it."

Julia nodded slowly, chewed on the inside of her cheek, watched Andrea's face. "Okay. Okay. I hear you."

"Do you?"

"Yup. Do what you want. It's your life."

"But?"

"No buts."

Andrea snorted. "Oh, please. There's always a but with you."

Julia shook her head, but her green eyes snagged Andrea's and held them. "Just make sure you have your priorities lined up the way they should be. That's all I'm saying."

Back in her office later, Andrea had trouble concentrating. Julia's words kept coming back at her, which both irritated her and worried her. After all, her sister knew her better than any other person in the world, and her observations were usually pretty spot-on. But what she'd said to Julia had been accurate:

the timing with Kendall couldn't be worse. They seemed to have a lot in common. She was pretty sure they shared most of the same core values and wanted similar things out of life. These were facts gleaned from their time together, assumptions Andrea had made because she hadn't really asked anything outright, not about things that might affect a possible future together. Andrea already had her future mapped out. It was set. She knew exactly what she wanted to do and where she wanted to go and when. The truth of the matter was that a big part of her didn't really want to know if she and Kendall had anything at all beyond simple, amazing sexual chemistry because…

What if they did?

꩜

On Friday afternoon, Andrea flopped back into her desk chair and heaved out an enormous sigh of relief. Thank God she'd chosen to wear an actual suit with a jacket because she'd started to sweat the second she sat down for the interview and didn't stop until she returned to her office. The armpits of her blouse were uncomfortably damp, and she really wanted to take the jacket off now, but she didn't dare. Good thing the day was nearing its end.

She felt like her head was spinning as she tried to absorb everything that had been said. It didn't just go well. It went really, *really* well. Andrea basically had her pick of stores. Roger Hagan himself had popped into the meeting for a quick minute simply to shake Andrea's hand and to thank her for being such a valued employee for so long. That was surreal and even as Andrea thought back on it, thought back on Roger's salt-and-pepper hair, his infectious grin, his kind brown eyes, it seemed like it had been a dream. He was a bit of a legend in town and very few people ever dealt with him on a face-to-face basis. But the fact that he stopped in on her interview specifically to shake her hand and say thanks was mind-blowing to her.

She should be proud of herself.

And she was. Or at least she would be once the adrenaline rush let up and she could actually think straight.

"Your record is exemplary, Ms. Blake." That's what Connor Talbert had said to her. He was one of the big wigs Julia had mentioned. He was a tall, willowy man with a head of perfectly styled, snowy white hair and blue eyes so light in color they were almost eerie to look at. But his smile was handsome and inviting, and his voice low and soothing. Despite her nervousness, Andrea felt comfortable with him.

From that point on, the interview had been a blur.

Not so much of a blur that she didn't remember that they'd offered her a choice of three brand-new stores that were currently under construction and in need of managers in the next month or two. She was first in line, that the other qualified employees would get to pick only after she did.

Raleigh, North Carolina. Eleven hours away.

Philadelphia, Pennsylvania. Five and a half hours away.

Baltimore, Maryland. Also five and a half hours away.

Those were her options. All three up for grabs. She could have any of them, all she had to do was say the word. They were giving her four weeks and then they would have to start talking to the other candidates.

Four weeks.

Of course, she didn't have to make any moves for another two months, so there wasn't a huge hurry on that end of things. But she had to make up her mind, make a choice, decide where she wanted to live—essentially where she wanted to spend the rest of her working life—in the next month.

Despite the pressure, she was giddy. She'd expected it to go well—she was a good employee and she knew it—but she hadn't expected to have her pick.

She had no idea what to do.

Staring out the window was not the solution, but that's exactly what she did for the next twenty minutes until things began to settle in.

Remembering she'd silenced her cell phone, she pulled it out of her bag and checked the screen. Three texts awaited her. One from Julia, one from Kylie, and one from Kendall. She grinned and answered the first two—which both asked how things had gone—with quick *Fantastic! Tell you all about it this weekend!* messages. Kendall's simply asked how her day was, so she typed back, *Amazing. May need your help. Still on for dinner?*

Kendall's positive response came back within a couple minutes, complete with enormous smiley faces and even a heart. Andrea chose not to analyze what that might mean, if anything, but she let it warm her up just the same.

When she arrived at the restaurant at seven o'clock, Kendall was already there, sitting at the bar with a frosty glass of beer and chatting animatedly with the bartender. Andrea took a moment to just look at her before approaching. She wore black jeans that looked tailored just for her, the slight heel of her short boots hooked over the bottom rung on the barstool. The sleeves of her pink sweater were pulled halfway up her forearms, and her hair was down. As the bartender said something to make her laugh, Kendall reached up and tucked her hair behind her ear. For some inexplicable reason, Andrea found the move devastatingly sexy, and felt the now-familiar tightening in her belly that always seemed to happen when Kendall was around.

When Kendall turned her head and their eyes met, a strange sense of calm settled over Andrea.

"Hi," Kendall said with a huge smile. Andrea loved that she always seemed so happy to see her.

"Hey, you." She accepted the firm hug Kendall gave her, held her tight for an extra couple of seconds. "You smell good," she told her.

"Thanks. You look good." Kendall made a show of running her eyes down Andrea's body and back up, and even though it was done tongue-in-cheek, Andrea still felt a heated tingle run through her. "Here. I saved you a seat." Kendall removed her bag and jacket from the stool next to hers and gestured to it for Andrea. "I thought we could sit and have a cocktail or two before dinner. Okay with you?"

"That sounds perfect."

"What would you like?" Kendall asked as Andrea took off her coat and grabbed a seat. The bartender hovered, waiting. "Beer? Or is it a wine kind of evening?"

Andrea grinned. "It's a wine kind of evening. Red, please. Maybe a Pinot Noir if it's decent?" The bartender gave a nod and held up a bottle Andrea recognized as a brand she'd purchased in the past. "That would be great."

"On my tab, please," Kendall told him. When Andrea protested, Kendall held up a hand, traffic cop-style. "No. No arguing. We are celebrating your amazing interview, which you are now going to tell me all about. Buying you a glass of wine is the least I can do."

Andrea let it go with a smile and a nod.

"So? Tell me all about your day and what you need my help with." Kendall hunkered down, elbows on the bar, and propped her chin in her hands, giving Andrea all her rapt attention. It was adorable, and Andrea almost said so.

She told Kendall all about the interview, about what they'd said regarding her record, about how Roger Hagan himself had made an appearance. She then explained how rare that was.

"Wow. You're a big deal." Kendall held up her glass and Andrea touched her own to it.

"And then, they gave me my choice of three stores."

"Your choice?" Kendall's blue eyes widened. "Like, here are three stores that need a manager, which one do you want?"

"Exactly like that."

"Oh, my God, Andrea. That's *fantastic!*" She slid off her stool and wrapped her arms around Andrea, surprising her even more when she said quietly near her ear, "I'm so proud of you, baby." Rather than freak her out, the endearment brought a sheen of wetness to her eyes.

"Thanks," she said softly.

"Tell me about the stores. Which one will you pick?"

"I have no idea," Andrea said with a chuckle. She told Kendall her three options.

"Whenever I have a choice like that, I find that a list of pros and cons is the best way to narrow things down." She reached into her purse and pulled out a piece of paper and a pen. "Okay. Raleigh, Philly, Baltimore." She wrote down each name, underlined them, then broke them into columns. "First things first, let's start with the obvious: weather. Raleigh wins that one. I don't think you're going to get much less winter in Philly or Maryland than you get here. Second, distance from family." She stopped and looked up at Andrea. "Is that important to you? I know you said you're not very close with your parents."

"I'm not. But I do have my sister and my niece and nephew."

215

Kendall made marks on the paper. "Okay. Standard of living. I'm not sure which is more expensive, Raleigh or Philly, but Baltimore is probably off the charts being so close to D.C."

They went on like this for another twenty minutes, trying to come up with any important features that one city might have over another, Googling information on their phones. When they finally ended up at a loss for anything more to compare, Kendall set down her pen and they looked over the chart. Words and lines and cross-outs marred it, but overall, there was a pretty clear winner.

"Looks like Raleigh is the best choice," Kendall said. "But you'll have to decide which things are most important to you, you know? I mean, maybe being eleven hours away from your sister doesn't matter as much as warmer weather. Or maybe you're okay spending more for rent if the store is in a nicer part of town. That kind of thing. So, you'll need to sit down and roll that stuff around. You need to figure out your priorities."

Andrea nodded slowly as Kendall spoke, her eyes on the paper. It wasn't lost on her that Kendall had used the same phrase as Julia. "You're good at this."

"I'm good at logic. This is logical." Kendall shrugged and finished off her beer. "What do you say? Hungry?"

Dinner was delicious, and they took their time, even ordering a dessert of chocolate mousse with raspberry compote to share. And when they finished and Andrea asked Kendall if she wanted to follow her to her house, Kendall didn't hesitate with her affirmative reply. By the time they got inside Andrea's house, she felt like she might combust.

"I've waited long enough to touch you," she hissed as she pulled Kendall's coat off her shoulders.

"I was going to say the same thing about you," Kendall responded, and they ended up in a sensual dual of undressing each other while kissing deeply and moving toward the living room. A trail of clothing led to the couch where, in what seemed like mere minutes, Andrea found herself on her back in only her panties. And those were on their way off as Kendall's hand slid beneath the waistband just as her tongue pushed into Andrea's mouth.

How can it be this good?

It wasn't the first time the thought had crossed Andrea's mind, and she had no answer. She was no prude. She'd had plenty of sex in her life. Good sex. Even occasional great sex. But sex with Kendall went above and beyond and she had no explanation for it, no matter how hard she tried to come up with one.

Now was not the time that was going to happen, as Kendall had deftly removed her underwear and was now doing wonderfully erotic things with her fingers. Andrea was soaked already, and when Kendall's fingers pushed deliciously into her, all coherent thought was chased from Andrea's head as she let Kendall take her, have her, own her.

Later, they lay on the couch quietly spent, Kendall's naked body draped over Andrea's, an afghan the only thing covering them, the heat from their lovemaking still hanging in the air, their passion almost tangible. Andrea drew lazy patterns along Kendall's shoulder blades with her fingertips as they relaxed in the silence of the room, watching Zeke zip around the house, chasing some invisible nemesis.

"What do you think I should do?" Though Andrea barely whispered the question, it seemed loud in the peace they'd let settle, and she hadn't even realized she was going to ask it until it popped out of her mouth.

Kendall waited a long time to answer. Andrea was just about to peek at her face to see if she'd fallen asleep when she finally spoke. "It's not my decision, Andrea."

"I know that. But if you were in my shoes, what would you do?"

"I'd go over the lists we made, try to figure out where I could see myself."

"If you had to pick one. If you were me."

Kendall took a deep breath, Andrea's hand on her back raising with her lungs, then falling slowly back down. "I don't know…" Andrea felt her hesitation, but waited her out. "I guess…it seems like Raleigh would be your best bet. I mean, the weather's beautiful, it's not crazy expensive, I don't think. It's a thriving economy there." Her shoulders shifted with her shrug. "I guess I'd focus on that one."

"Yeah." Andrea let the words settle around her. "Yeah, I think you're probably right." Instead of feeling relief at that little bit of guidance, she felt sad. Let down. A little dejected. But she couldn't pinpoint why.

CHAPTER FIFTEEN

"It's really kind of ridiculous," Kendall said to Liz as she grabbed a beer out of one of six picnic coolers lined up against the wall. "I've never been like this before." A bottle opener attached to a string hung from the wall of the cabin above the coolers, and Kendall grabbed it, popped her top.

"In what way?" Liz asked.

They were in a large, open cabin in a park celebrating Maria Carter's thirtieth birthday. Maria was one of Liz's volleyball teammates and Kendall had known her for a few years now. About twenty-five people milled around the rented, park-owned cabin, which had a fire going in the pit to take the chill out of the mid-April air. Another dozen or so people—mostly lesbians —were outside playing an impromptu soccer game in the nearby field. It would end up a mudbath before long, as the snow banks had finally melted after a brutal winter, and the ground was soft, wet, and squishy. Kendall opted to stay far away from the mess. She hadn't wanted to come at all, but Liz had convinced her she was becoming a hermit and needed to get out more. Kendall pointing out that she'd spent St. Patrick's Day watching Liz get hammered not very long ago did nothing to help her case. With Andrea buried in work stuff, Kendall decided maybe a party was just what she needed.

Kendall took a swig of beer and looked around before lowering her voice and saying, "In that I can't stay away." She gave Liz a pointed look.

Liz squinted at her for a second before the meaning dawned on her. "Oh! You mean the sex is awesome."

"The sex is beyond awesome. It's earth-shattering. It's mind-blowing." She looked down at her feet. "It's really, really good."

Liz waved at Marcy, who stood at the other end of the cabin talking to some friends. Kendall watched the love on her face and felt simultaneously thrilled for her friend and painfully envious. Liz turned back to her. "So what's the problem? Why should you be staying away?"

Kendall sidestepped as two women reached toward the cooler. Hellos were said all around, small talk ensued for several moments. When they left, Liz looked at her expectantly.

Kendall shrugged. "I don't know, Liz. I just...I'm a little confused." She spilled the whole story about Andrea's job prospects, how they'd done a pros and cons list, how Raleigh seemed to make the most sense.

"Ah. I see." Liz nodded, swigged her beer.

"Yeah. She's been waiting for this for a long time. This has been her goal. She wants to get the hell out of here."

"But you want her to stay." It was a statement of fact, one Kendall tried hard to deny.

"No. Not necessarily. I want her to do what she wants, what's best for her. I want her to be happy. I am in no position to make demands on her."

"You sleep with her."

"I know. But that's all."

Liz turned to study her, eyebrows furrowed in concentration. "Okay, wait. Let me get this straight. No pun intended. You tried hard to resist sleeping with this woman because of the conflict of interest you two had at work."

"Yes."

"But once that passed, you pretty much jumped each other."

"Well, technically, she jumped me, but whatever."

Liz waved a hand. "Semantics. The sex is good."

"The sex is off the hook."

"Semantics again. What do you talk about when there isn't sex happening?"

Kendall made a thinking face. "Well...our cats. Work. Our families."

Liz nodded as Kendall spoke. "The future?"

Kendall shook her head. "Not really."

"Interesting. Why not?"

Kendall rolled her lips in, bit down on them for a second. "I can't answer for her, but for me...I think it scares me."

"Why?"

"Because I don't know what she'll say. This side of her, this... warmer side...it's new. I don't know if it's new in general, but it's new to me. I've always thought of her as a little cool, a control freak, somebody who keeps it all together by keeping people at arms' length."

"And now that you're having mind-blowing sex with her?"

Kendall blew out a frustrated breath. "I don't know. I'm afraid...I'm afraid..."

"That she's perfectly fine keeping you at arms' length?"

Liz could come across as many things. Flighty. Flaky. Not at all serious about life. But not nearly as obvious was the fact that she was shockingly astute when it came to feelings and this was not the first time she'd nailed exactly what had been in Kendall's head but she'd been hesitant to put into words. Mortification set in as Kendall felt her eyes well up.

"Yes," she said softly. "I was so good about the promotion. I helped her make the pros and cons list. I helped her research. I was happy for her. I told her I was proud of her. And I am. I did everything I was supposed to do so the decision wouldn't be hard for her."

"You didn't ask her to stay." Liz said it quietly.

Kendall shook her head. "I couldn't. I can't do that to her." Before she completely devolved into girly blubbering, she gave her entire body a shake and said, "You know what? Enough. This is stupid. I am thirty, not fifteen." Liz just looked at her, a small grin playing at the corners of her mouth. "Shut up, Liz."

Liz lifted her bottle to her lips and shrugged. "I just call 'em like I see 'em, Slick."

"Yeah, well, shut up."

Determined not to let Liz's observations ruin her enjoyment of the party, Kendall spent the rest of her time there mingling. She caught up with friends she hadn't seen in a while, watched some of the soccer game (and just barely managed not to get pulled into it), and stood around the fireplace chatting when the sun had gone down and she got a little chilly. If only April would warm up a bit, she'd feel much better about the change of seasons actually being on the way. She was so glad winter was over.

Later that night, at home in her apartment, all that outside air having made her chilly, she settled into a hot bubble bath. On the stand next to the tub, she'd placed her cell phone, a bottle of water, and her new iPad. Drying her hands, she picked up the iPad and checked her work e-mail. Not much there, as Sundays were slow, so she took the opportunity to visit some websites from different microbrewers she kept tabs on, then read several beer blogs. One blog in particular caught her eye, and when she realized why, she pulled herself back from it immediately.

But bookmarked it just the same.

Her cell phone pinged, saving her from any deeper thought on the subject of the blog, and she picked it up. A text from Andrea.

Sooo tired of work. Feels like my eyes have sandpaper for lids. Need a short break. How was your day?

Kendall grinned like a schoolgirl. She'd made a pact with herself that she wouldn't be the one to initiate contact today. She'd wanted to spend time with Andrea, but Andrea had insisted she would get no work done if Kendall was in the same room. Kendall had relented, but decided she wasn't going to be the one constantly poking at Andrea, making herself feel needy and desperate. Instead, she'd just occupy herself. It had *not* been easy. She'd started a text four different times before catching herself and putting the phone down. But it had paid off. Andrea had come to her. Now, she typed back.

It was good. Nice party. Got a little cold out, though. I'm in the tub trying to warm up.

Bubbles? came the response.

Duh, Kendall typed back with a wink.

So…if I was there, could I fit in the tub with you?

That familiar tingle shot through Kendall's body at the implication, and she shook her head at how easy she was with Andrea. *I'd make room*, she typed.

Fabulous. So I'd slip in behind you and settle you between my legs…

"Jesus Christ," Kendall muttered aloud as the visual Andrea presented solidified itself in her brain.

You could lean back against me, came the next text. *And I'd have easy access to all of you…*

The bath itself had successfully warmed Kendall up, but the idea of Andrea sitting behind her, her hands roaming Kendall's wet, naked body, caused almost too much heat to bear. She reached for the faucet and turned on some cold water, sweat beading on her upper lip.

You wouldn't get the rest of your work done, Kendall typed.

Very true, came Andrea's reply. *I should probably get back to it before I become completely lost in you.*

Though sad that it had only been a quick exchange, the line about getting lost in her did wonders for Kendall's head. *I'm in for the night, so give me a shout if you need another break.*

I will do that. Don't soak too long. You'll get pruney.

Yes, ma'am. Kendall set the phone down on the stand, her emotions mixed.

Was she being silly? In reality, she'd only been really seeing Andrea for what? Three, four weeks at the most? They'd spent the night together only a handful of times? "But there's all the sexting," she observed aloud. "Then it's a lot more than a handful." Seriously, what did people do before cell phones and computers?

But still. It had only been weeks. Why was she so worked up over…what? What was this? Were they dating? Were they exclusive? They'd never talked about it, and a large part of Kendall was afraid to—she hadn't been lying to Liz. She was afraid of what Andrea would say, even though she already knew what she'd say. She was leaving. That was the bottom line, plain and simple. She was going to move out of state sometime in the next eight weeks. So, analyzing this relationship, trying to make something more of it or put some kind of label on it was probably just stupid, and Kendall would be an idiot for trying. She'd only end up getting hurt. No, it was better if she left things as is, spent what time she could with Andrea, and take anything she was willing to give, because it wasn't going to last forever.

Hell, it wasn't even going to last until summer.

The bathwater was suddenly stiflingly uncomfortable. Kendall shook herself out of her head and sat up, pulled the drain plug, and let the water begin to empty. Grabbing a towel, she stood up and dried herself off, stepping carefully out of the tub as she did so.

She was cold again.

⤨

The next two weeks seemed to fly by. The end of April tended to bring much warmer temperatures and the lawns and fields everywhere were finally fully green. Crocuses had come and gone, and daffodils in various shades of yellow were on their last legs. Kendall could almost feel herself relaxing, the tension in her shoulders lessening, her steps becoming more leisurely. The days got longer, the sun became a more common sight, and people were happier in general. Such was the spring in upstate New York, especially after an unusually cruel winter.

Old Red Barn Brewcrafters was experiencing a boon. Business was crazy busy, which was a good thing, and at the same time, a very stressful thing. Orders were pouring in, and construction on both the addition on the back and the tasting room itself had begun. The plan was that by the end of May, Old Red Barn would be open to customers, to the public, but it was going to be close. Rick was beyond excited, stretched way too thin, and he and Adam snarked at each other constantly. Kendall had become the one to run interference, just like when they were kids and her big brothers were pummeling the snot out of each other. She'd step in, bodily, so in order to beat on each other, they'd have to hit her. Which neither of them would ever do under penalty of death from their father.

They were in the middle of one such snarkfest that Tuesday morning when Kendall stepped between her brothers, planting a hand in the middle of each chest and pushing them apart.

"Okay, okay. Knock it off, you guys. We should be thanking our lucky stars that business is so good rather than snipping at each other over stupid stuff." She looked from one brother to the other. Rick's reaction to an argument was to get silent and still, to show no emotion, and as Kendall looked at him now, she took his smooth brow and expressionless face to mean he was furious. Contrarily, Adam's way of dealing with anger was to flail and rend his clothing and gnash his teeth. His blond hair was more disheveled than usual (from running frustrated hands through it, Kendall guessed), his face was bright red, and he looked ready to punch somebody.

"Listen," she said to them now, understanding from years of experience that the best way to deal with a fight between her brothers was to change the subject. They'd get over it on their own. "I'm thinking of making a road trip."

Rick shifted his blank face from Adam to Kendall, and in doing so, his expression came back as if a mask had been yanked off. He met Kendall's gaze. "What do you mean?"

"Well, it's been a while since I visited some of the guys I chat with all the time and I thought maybe I'd map out a route, hit half a dozen on the way."

Rick nodded, warming to the idea. Since the inception of Old Red Barn Brewcrafters, the Fosters had made a pledge that they'd keep in touch with other small brewers, share ideas, visit each other. A handful of them had started out together and kept in touch via the Internet and it was important to all of them that they stay connected. Fellow brewmasters often visited Old Red Barn, spent a couple hours or even the whole day with Rick, touring the facility, sharing ideas and crafting methods. It wasn't that way with everybody. Some brewers refused to share anything about their craft, and that was okay. But it wasn't how Rick and Adam did business, and when they brought Kendall on board, they'd instilled the same values in her.

"What are you thinking?" he asked her now.

"Well, I've e-mailed most of them. I thought I could head out tomorrow, hit Erie and maybe get to Cleveland as well. Then down to Charleston, maybe Roanoke. Then come back via Richmond and maybe Baltimore." She'd fudged the route a bit, as she hadn't heard from every brewer she'd contacted, but she had a plan. "The whole trip shouldn't take me more than four days, give or take a few hours, depending on traffic."

Rick looked to Adam, their disagreement obviously shelved. "It's the right time of year for her to go, don't you think?" he asked.

Adam furrowed his sandy brow for moment, then gave a matching nod. "I think we can spare you for the rest of the week. You'll be back before Monday?"

"Oh, definitely. Hopefully by late Saturday."

"I think that'd be fine. It's been a while." Adam motioned for her to follow him to his office. "Let me get some notes together for a couple of the guys you'll be seeing. And let's make sure we load you up with some of the new brews so you can share them."

Kendall trailed behind her brother and spent the next hour going over notes of things he wanted her to share/tell/ask the different brewers she was planning to see. She loved this about her company. Many other businesses would scoff at the way Old Red Barn ran things. At the way many small brewcrafters ran things, really. Most of them were open, buddies with one another. Kendall was on a first-name basis with a very large percentage of the brewmasters along the east coast, all the way down to the northern parts of South Carolina. She counted many of them as friends. There were a good dozen or more that she messaged with on a regular basis, talking not only of beer and crafting processes, but of families and children and pets. Even sales. She had no qualms about sharing sales techniques with other brewers. In her ideal world, all brewers would be pals, there would be no such thing as competition. It might seem New Agey and unrealistic to some, but to Kendall, it was the only way she wanted to do business. She liked people; she was a people person. Being friends with people in the same line of work made her very happy.

Later that evening, she had just finished packing. Her plan was to head out by seven in the morning and get to Cleveland around eleven. That way, she'd have time to meet with her buddy there, take a tour, then take him to lunch so they could chat. She was filling her toiletry case when her phone rang and Andrea's name appeared on the screen.

"Hi there," she said, tucking the phone against her shoulder as she bagged the stuff she wouldn't need in the morning.

"Hey, sexy." Andrea's voice was smooth, low, and Kendall always felt a flutter when she heard it. "What are you up to on this fine evening?"

"Actually, I'm packing."

"Packing? For what? Are you taking a trip?" The hint of hurt in Andrea's voice was very slight, but Kendall picked up on it.

"Just a road trip for work. It was very last minute, which is why I didn't mention it. I wasn't even sure I was going until a couple hours ago."

"Road trip to where?" If anybody understood the demands of work, it was Andrea, and she apparently got this, too, as her voice was back to normal.

Kendall spent the next few minutes explaining the trip to her, how she tried to do it a couple times a year, how it helped to meet face-to-face with the guys she chatted with on a regular basis.

"How long will you be gone?"

"A few days," Kendall said, getting herself a beer out of the fridge and popping the top. She collapsed onto the couch as she said, "I'll be back some time on Saturday, but it could be late. Want to get together on Sunday?"

"What I want is for you to stuff me into your suitcase and take me with you."

Kendall smiled, her body and heart warmed by the sentiment. "I could do that. It'd be a tight squeeze, but we could make it work. You'd probably have to take all your clothes off. You wouldn't fit otherwise. I'm just saying."

Andrea chuckled. "Look at you, trying to get me naked any way you can."

"It is my goal in life."

"Well, you don't have to work very hard at it." As their laughter died down and they shared a beat of happy silence, Andrea said softly, "I think we'd travel well together."

"We totally would. You'd have every minute planned and I'd be the comic relief."

"I *am* rather organized."

"Truer words, hot stuff. Truer words. I love road trips."

"Do you?"

"Always have. Good tunes on the radio, open windows, some coffee in the middle console and munchies close at hand. What's not to love? You don't like to?"

"I honestly can't say I've ever done much road tripping," Andrea replied, her voice a little wistful. "My parents weren't big on family outings. We stayed home most of the time. Or went to my grandparents' place on the lake."

It never ceased to amaze Kendall how utterly different their childhoods were. Kendall's was happy, loving, warm. Her parents were not wealthy by any stretch of the imagination, but they did all right. And they managed to go on some kind of trip together at least once a year until both Rick and Adam were out of school. Most were road trips, as plane tickets for a family of five would be financially out of reach, and Kendall had very fond memories of driving to Washington, D.C.; Lake Placid; the Thousand Islands; Hershey, Pennsylvania; and Cleveland, Ohio, to see the Rock n Roll Hall of Fame. Dozens of wonderfully happy memories from her life that she couldn't imagine not having. When she understood that Andrea didn't have those, it just made her sad.

"We should plan a trip some time." Kendall blurted it out before she could stop and think, and now she wanted to snatch the words out of the air and stuff them back into her mouth. She tried to repair the damage by making light. "Just something simple. Wine touring around the Finger Lakes or something. Just a thought." She punctuated her fake nonchalance by shrugging, realizing belatedly that Andrea couldn't see it.

"We should," Andrea answered, and Kendall could tell she was keeping it just as light. A couple moments of awkward silence passed before Andrea asked, "You'll have your cell during your trip, I assume?"

"Of course. You'll call me? And I can call you?" Kendall wasn't sure why she suddenly felt uncertain and she didn't like the vulnerable tone that had seeped into her voice.

"Absolutely. I want to know you're getting around all right." Andrea lowered her voice to something huskier, deeper, more sensual. "And you'll be all alone in a hotel room. You might need some verbal…amusement."

Relief flooded Kendall, though she tried not to let it show. "I would *love* that," she said.

They chatted a little longer, flirted a bit more, and generally kept the conversation light and playful, as was their standard operating procedure. They finally hung up nearly half an hour later, with Andrea making Kendall promise to drive carefully, not to speed, and to let her know how things were going.

Kendall wasn't going to lie. She liked the concern.

CHAPTER SIXTEEN

The week had flown by for Andrea, as it seemed to do more and more often as she got older. It was weird to know her grandmother had been right with all her "time flies" speeches. Andrea wasn't old. Hell, she wasn't even middle-aged yet. But there were days when she looked at the clock—or worse, at the calendar—and wondered where the hell all the time had gone.

Another weird thing? She missed Kendall. That was weird for two reasons. One, she'd only been gone for three days, and it's not like they saw each other much during the week anyway. Two, she wasn't used to missing anybody. Ever. Andrea had been careful not to have that extra baggage around her neck. She didn't want to focus too much on somebody else. She had her career and she was steering it in the exact direction she'd planned on for the past fourteen years, like a giant ship at sea. It was cruising along exactly as she wanted it to be for exactly those reasons: planning, hard work, and nothing anchoring her.

She was still getting used to the fact that it was light long after she got home from work now. That span of winter when she left for the office in the dark and returned home in the dark was so depressingly smothering, and the change was so gradual. Now, spring was fully upon them. The snow was long gone. The days were warming up. She felt like she could breathe again. God, she despised winter.

That's what made going to Raleigh so tempting. Oh, Andrea knew that North Carolina got occasional snow, and that when they did, the entire state population flew into panic mode, swiping bread and milk from all the store shelves, hunkering down in their homes as if waiting for a blizzard of epic proportions, when chances were, they'd be lucky to get half an inch of actual snow. But those winters didn't happen all the time, and often, Raleigh got no snow. Sure, it could get cold, but according to her research, the average temperature for February in Raleigh was in the high 40s. She could get behind that. It sure would make her least favorite month that much more bearable.

She unlocked the side door and entered her house at not quite seven, a somewhat earlier night for her given the hours she'd put in recently. She set down her briefcase and keys and laughed as Zeke flew through the kitchen, entering on one side of the breakfast bar and leaving through the other.

"You're a goofball," she said in amusement.

She pulled her cell from her bag and thought about giving Kendall a call, but knew that the past two nights, she'd been at dinner with fellow brewers, so she didn't want to interrupt. She'd wait until a little later.

She headed upstairs and changed out of her suit, stepping into her comfiest yoga pants and a V-neck hoodie in heather purple. Pulling soft cotton socks onto her feet felt like heaven after a day spent in heels. Zeke peeked out from under the bed, and she snagged him up, burying her nose in his fur and giving him as many kisses as he could stand before he smacked her face with a paw.

Back downstairs, she pulled chicken pot pie from the freezer and set the oven. Normally, this was something she'd make from scratch on a Sunday afternoon, but with her recent schedule, she found it was a lot less stressful to have a few frozen things handy.

Maybe she'd make one for Kendall next time she came over for dinner...

She was smiling at the thought when her cell rang from its spot on the counter. A glance at the screen swiped the smile from her face. She groaned.

Steeling herself, she took a deep, calming breath, then hit the green button. "Hi, Mom."

"Well, hello there, stranger. Glad to know you're still alive and kicking."

"I am. Just been really busy at work. How are you?" Andrea rolled her eyes. Usually, if she could steer her mother toward talking about herself and her life, she could avoid the not-so-subtle guilt trip. Didn't work this time.

"What's this your sister tells me about you moving out of state?"

Goddamn it, Julia. Andrea made a mental note to kill her sister during their next visit. "It's not official, Mom. It's just a possibility. Nothing has been decided yet."

"Nice of you to let your mother know. I had to find out through the grapevine."

"Okay, Julia isn't exactly the grapevine, but I'm sorry I didn't tell you. I wanted to wait until I had some solid facts." Which was a lie, but she was going with it. "I'm up for a promotion and I have my choice of three stores."

"And they're all out of state." It wasn't a question.

"Yes." Andrea ground her teeth as she spoke. "But no decisions have been made."

"Well, of course you'll go. You want to be as far from your mother as possible. I know. Julia told me."

Andrea closed her eyes. Despite letting the general cat out of the bag, Julia would not say such a thing. This was totally her mother going off on one of her woe-is-me trails and Andrea was fully aware of it. "No, Mom, that's not true. You know it's not."

Her mother sighed heavily. "It's fine. Do what you want. You always have anyway." Andrea could almost see her waving a hand dismissively in the air. What she really should do is lay the back of her hand across her forehead and go all faint and weak like an actress in a silent film because that's the tone she had. "Julia will take care of me."

"Okay, enough. How are you? Aside from having a selfish and ungrateful second child?" Andrea went to the refrigerator and pulled out the bottle of Pinot Grigio she'd opened a couple days ago. She pulled a wineglass from the cupboard and filled it much higher than she normally would, figuring she deserved it after this conversation.

Another put-upon sigh and then her mother said, "Oh, I suppose I'm fine."

If Andrea rolled her eyes any more they were going to roll right out of her head and land on the kitchen floor, new toys for Zeke to chase around. But she listened dutifully while her fifty-five year old mother talked like she was eighty, lamenting her aching joints and sleepless nights and failing vision. "Maybe you should make an appointment with Dr. Robertson," she suggested.

"Oh, I don't think that's necessary. It's just regular getting-old-things, I'm sure."

Andrea shrugged, feeling like she'd played her part as expected. "Well, as long as you're okay."

"I'll live." Not quite the same, but good enough.

"I'm glad."

They chatted for a couple more minutes—and chatting actually meant Andrea listened and tried not to slug her wine in inappropriately large gulps while her mother complained about pretty much everything in her life. By the time they finally hung up, Andrea wanted to shoot herself in the head. She'd barely set the phone down when it rang again, and the idea that maybe her mother had forgotten to bore her with something else nearly caused her to launch the phone into the living room. Until she glanced at the screen.

Kendall Foster

The smile couldn't be helped, not that she tried. She hit the green button. "Your timing is perfect. I was just about to stick my head in the oven after talking to my mother for fifteen minutes. You saved my life."

"Well, I am incredibly happy to hear that. I happen to like your head very much and would miss it if it got cooked."

"Yeah?"

"Definitely."

"How's the trip? Where are you today?"

"I'm at Big Dog Little Dog Brewing and my buddy Kevin just took me to dinner. I was supposed to take him, but he wouldn't let me, the bastard." She giggled an adorable little sound, presumably at the swear word, and then added, "There may have been some beer."

"*Some* beer?" Andrea asked, grinning.

"Some beer, yes. Some more beer than I should have had, probably."

"I can tell."

"You can*not*."

"I can," Andrea said in amusement. "I'm not sure what it is."

"Well. You know me pretty well." Kendall cleared her throat.

"I do." The thought made Andrea smile. "So…you're heading back this way tomorrow?"

"Yup. I have one stop to make and then home."

"Driving's been okay?"

"Piece of cake. Easy traffic. And no construction yet, if you can believe that." They chuckled, then Kendall asked, "So, you talked to your mom?"

"Oh, God. More like listened to her complain about life for a year and a half that was actually only fifteen minutes. But not before she made me feel guilty about possibly moving out of state."

"You told her?" Kendall's surprise was apparent.

"Hell, no. I'm not an idiot. My sister told her. My sister to whom I am going to do grievous bodily harm next time I see her." She gave Kendall a brief rundown of the conversation, ending with, "And I am just about to finish my first glass of wine in record time."

"Let me know when you start glass number two," Kendall said, and Andrea could picture her arching one eyebrow suggestively. Her stomach did a little flip-flop as she slid the pot pie into the oven and set the timer.

"I will. In the meantime, tell me about Big Dog Little Dog Brewing."

That got Kendall talking and Andrea grinning. She loved the sound of Kendall's voice, something she didn't like to think about, though she wasn't sure why. A little too intimate, maybe? She'd expected a text tonight, but the fact that Kendall had called instead made her very happy. And had her maybe a tiny bit turned on. She listened with rapt attention as Kendall told her about the guys that owned the brewery, what they did the same as or differently than Old Red Barn, how she'd initially met Kevin at a trade show and he'd asked her out.

"You must have broken his heart when you turned him down," Andrea said, refilling her glass. "P.S.: glass number two."

"Oh, excellent. Go sit on the couch. And then tell me what you're wearing." Kendall's tone had changed in a split second and now it was as if Andrea could feel her voice travel down her spine, as soft and gentle as fingertips.

She sat. "You *did* have some beer, didn't you?" Andrea said playfully.

"Shh. Tell me."

"And beer makes you a little bossy."

"Don't pretend you don't like it."

"I won't."

"Good. Are you sitting on the couch?"

"I am."

"Tell me what you're wearing." Kendall's voice had gone soft, but still had an edge of authority to it that Andrea was shocked to realize she liked.

"Are you trying to have phone sex with me?"

"I might be. You never know. Tell me."

"Nothing fancy or sexy, really, so don't get too excited. I mean —"

"Andrea." Kendall cut her off, then spoke quietly, slowly. "Stop thinking so hard. Relax, let go, and tell me what you're wearing." It was a gentle command, but a command just the same. Andrea swallowed.

"Yoga pants."

"Uh-huh. Black?"

"Yes. And a purple hoodie."

"The V-neck one you got a couple weeks ago? The one that's kind of…snug?"

One corner of Andrea's mouth pulled up at the sexy vibe Kendall was giving off. "That's the one."

"I love that shirt."

"Yeah?"

"The way the V-neck shows just a peek of your collarbone? God, yes. I love it."

"I did not know that."

"Well, now you do."

"I am learning so much about you," Andrea said, amused.

"Yeah, well, if I was there with you right now, I'd have my mouth on your neck right where that V-neck opens up..."

Words died in Andrea's throat as a surge of arousal hit from the image Kendall handed her, surprising her much more than she expected. They had texted sexy things to each other, and that was a big turn-on for Andrea, but this? Kendall's sensual voice tickling her ear, painting an erotic picture that Andrea couldn't help but see? It was purely intoxicating; there was no other way to describe it. Finding her voice, she asked, "You would?"

"Oh, I would. I'd push you onto your back and kiss your neck while I slide my hand up under that shirt..."

Andrea's swallow this time was audible.

"I'd move my hand up your stomach to...are you wearing a bra?"

"I took it off when I got home," Andrea husked.

"Perfect. Then I would stroke your breasts, but just the undersides and around the outside. I would circle around and around your nipple until you start to move underneath me. I'd kiss you then, soft and slow, and just when I push my tongue into your mouth, I'd run my thumb over your nipple."

"Oh, God," Andrea whispered, shocked when she heard the words leave her mouth on a sigh.

"Makes for a really nice image, doesn't it?" Kendall asked. "I've been thinking about you all day."

"All day?"

"All day. And then I'd pull your shirt up so I could get my mouth on your breasts. I love your breasts."

"They're small," Andrea said with a light laugh.

"They're perfect, and I'd want to taste them. You'd have your hands in my hair."

Andrea grinned, as that had been exactly how her own vision had gone. "I would."

"Then I'd go back up—because I can't stay away from your mouth—and kiss you some more while I use my knee to push yours apart and settle my hips between your thighs..."

Andrea's eyes closed as she gave up any semblance of fighting off the arousal coursing through her and lay down on the couch. She was stunned Kendall was able to turn her on like this, from states away. This was new to her, as so many things regarding Kendall seemed to be.

"And then I'd start to move against you," Kendall said, her voice not quite a whisper, but close. "I'd kiss you, and I'd have your breast in my hand, and I'd move my hips against you... Andrea?"

"Hmm?" The world was hazy for Andrea as she answered.

"Are you wet?"

A small release of air escaped her lips at the bold rawness of the question. Andrea covered her eyes with one hand and told the truth. "Yes."

"Good. Now pretend your hand is my hand and slide it into your pants, because that's where I'd go next, and I want to hear you."

It was brazen. And blatantly erotic. And Andrea astonished herself by not questioning, not protesting, simply doing as she was asked. It helped that she was ridiculously turned on and craved her own release as much as Kendall did. She worked her hand under the waistband of her yoga pants and down the front of her panties where—she hadn't been lying—everything was hot, wet, and ready. She had very little work to do, as Kendall's voice and erogenous mental picture painting had pulled her so far along. With Kendall coaxing in her ear, it was only a couple minutes before she came hard on her own couch, against her own hand, and cried out Kendall's name as she did it.

For several long moments, the only sound was that of Andrea's ragged breathing as she recovered herself. Finally, Kendall spoke.

"Wow," she said simply. A beat passed, and then she repeated, "Wow," and laughed. "Andrea, that was…amazing."

"Yeah? You should've been *here*," Andrea said, her breathing almost back to normal.

"I wish I was."

"Me, too." They were quiet again for several seconds before Andrea said, "I feel a little weird now," and gave a nervous chuckle.

"What? Why?"

"I've never done that before."

"Never done what? Had phone sex?"

"Had phone sex." Her legs were weak and her center still throbbed lightly as Andrea lay on the couch, her own scent detectable on her fingers as she covered her eyes again.

"Oh, honey." She could picture the exact face Kendall was making, a perfect blend of reassurance and sensuality, probably with an arched eyebrow for punctuation. "You have nothing at all to feel weird about. That was incredible. You just…you just went with it. I honestly wasn't sure you would."

"No? How come?"

"Um…because you're kind of a control freak?"

241

Andrea barked a laugh at the statement, but knew better than to try to protest. "This is true."

"It is. And what we just did was about you letting me have control and *you* following *me*. Hard for somebody like you to do, I would imagine." Kendall's voice softened. "But you did."

Andrea nodded and said quietly, "I did." Was that a little note of pride in her voice? It might have been. She couldn't be sure.

"Well, that will certainly help me sleep better tonight in a strange hotel room all alone. I'll just replay the last twenty minutes. Over and over and over."

Andrea laughed. "Stop it."

"I will do no such thing."

They talked a while longer about superficial things, but it was comfortable and enjoyable, and it occurred to Andrea that she could listen to Kendall talk for hours. She was certain of it. She retrieved her dinner from the oven as they continued to converse. When Kendall yawned for the third time, Andrea smiled.

"You need to get some sleep if you're going to be driving all day tomorrow," she told her.

"I know," Kendall said on a sigh. "I just don't want to hang up."

"Me neither."

"Thanks for spending your Friday evening on the phone with me."

"Oh, I think the pleasure was all mine," Andrea said.

They both laughed and Kendall said quietly, "Sweet dreams, okay?"

"Definitely. Text me when you get home tomorrow night so I know you're safe." There were other things on her mind, other words lodged in her throat that she thought about saying, but kept them tamped down, shoved back in a corner. "Sleep tight, Kendall."

"You, too."

After hanging up, Andrea stared at the living room ceiling for a long time, thoughts and feelings bouncing around her head like so many pinballs. One idea that had been sitting in the back of her mind for over a week made itself known. She took it out, tipped it around to examine it from all angles.

It hadn't changed at all, but somehow had become just a little bit easier to look at.

CHAPTER SEVENTEEN

"I can't believe I let you talk me into this," Andrea muttered at her sister just as they made eye contact with their mother across the restaurant. Julia waved to get her attention.

"You promised to take up some of the slack, Andrea." Julia's teeth were gritted beneath her tight smile. And she was right. Andrea knew it. That didn't mean she had to like it, did it? She'd been pretty sure last night's phone call fulfilled her daughterly duties for a while, but apparently, she'd been mistaken, as Julia had called that morning and—not so much invited Andrea to lunch as demanded her presence. "I'm tired of doing this on my own," she'd snapped at Andrea's attempts to bail. "And if you're going to leave the state and stick me with her, the least you can do is put in some extra time while you're still here."

It was unlike her sister to get so angry. Julia was, in fact, a rather laid-back woman, and Andrea had often been jealous of her easy-going attitude. So the tight voice, the irritated tone, had struck a chord with Andrea, and for the first time, she realized what it was. Julia was panicking. The fact that she'd ordered wine at lunch only solidified that assumption.

Now, here they sat, in a nice, sunny restaurant with a classic layout, great food, and a sparkling reputation, waiting for the only person on the planet Andrea knew for a fact could level all three things in under five minutes, like a freshly sharpened scythe in a wheat field.

"My God, the parking around here is atrocious," Elaine Blake said with a scowl as she took the open chair at the table. "Why you girls picked this place is beyond me."

"We like this place," Andrea said, already over this whole event. "And hello to you, too, Mom."

Elaine shot her a look before allowing her expression to soften just a touch. "Hello, Andrea. Julia." She glanced pointedly at their wine glasses before flagging down the waitress and ordering herself a Sprite. With a lemon wedge.

"So, what's new, Mom?" Andrea asked, feeling the need to take control, give Julia the break that she apparently needed.

Elaine shook her head. "Oh, I had to call a plumber in. The damn toilet in the upstairs bathroom had a crack in it and was leaking into the foyer ceiling. Apparently, your father didn't put it in right and cracked it when he tightened the bolts. Thank God it was a very small crack and therefore a very small leak. Who knows how long that's been happening?" She nodded at the waitress, who dropped off the soda and took their orders.

It was always so weird to spend this kind of time with her mother, and Andrea often found herself almost watching from some "outer" location, as if she was floating nearby and observing from afar. Sound sort of faded out to a dull humming and she played along, either nodding at things her mother said or contributing tidbits that didn't rock any boats. Conversations with her mother were like minefields, and if she didn't step carefully, she'd get a limb blown off. So she and Julia had both learned to stay polite, and keep to safe topics like the weather or Julia's kids (strangely, their mother never had a bad thing to say about them) or television shows (even those could be dangerous, too, should they touch on a show Elaine despised).

They'd made it almost all the way through their meals before things took a turn.

"So, Andrea. Have you decided on the new job? When are you moving?" The questions weren't asked with a curious tone. They were accusatory. Elaine might as well have asked, "When are you moving twelve hours away from your mother, you ungrateful, selfish child?"

"Like I told you on the phone last night, I haven't made a decision yet." Andrea tried to keep her voice light and not speak through the frustrated clench of her teeth. She wasn't entirely successful.

"When do you have to give an answer?" This from Julia, who didn't look at her, just finished her wine and signaled the waitress for another.

"They gave me four weeks to think about it. I think that's up next Friday."

"Will they help pay for your move?" Elaine asked, ripping a piece of bread off and popping it into her mouth. "I would hope so. It's the least they can do, really, making you go so far away with all your things."

"Yes, they would."

"Mmm." Elaine chewed as she gazed out the window. "I will never understand why you chose working at a grocery store as your career." As always, she said it as though Andrea spent her life bagging groceries. Which there was nothing wrong with, certainly, but Andrea had a business degree and Hagan's was so much more than a grocery store; it was one of the most successful businesses in the state. Elaine just couldn't seem to wrap her brain around it and Andrea had never been able to understand the disconnect. "A *grocery store*."

This. This right here. This wildly uncomfortable situation was exactly the perfect reason to choose to move and Andrea had to bite her tongue to keep from saying so out loud. The idea of not having to do this, of not having to face the betrayed eyes or the accusatory tone or the blame or the guilt or the belittlement... The idea of having none of that in her daily life was exhilarating. Raleigh was just far enough away that a quick trip would be impossible. It was ideal, and part of her wanted to whip out her cell phone right that minute and make a call to Hagan's choosing the Raleigh store position, do it right in front of her mother.

"Have you spoken to your father lately?" Elaine asked. Terrific. A change of subject to a topic that was almost worse.

"I talked to him a couple weeks ago," Julia said, not looking up from her lunch. "He called me." Andrea looked at her in surprise. She couldn't remember the last time he'd called her.

"And how is he?" Elaine always asked it with a bucket of sarcasm, but Andrea knew she really wanted to know. She was still and always would be in love with Ed Blake, no matter how shitty a husband he had been. He took her for granted. He was unfaithful. He was a male chauvinist who sat around the house like a king while his wife doted on him. And then he decided he wanted a younger model and left. Yet Elaine still got that far-away, dreamy look in her eyes at the mention of his name, even as she pretended to despise him. Andrea would never understand it.

"Good." Julia had learned from experience not to go into detail about their father to their mother. It always ended badly.

Shockingly, Elaine didn't push for more and the lunch ended on a somewhat pleasant note. Elaine snapped up the check, something she always did, and which was so opposite of the rest of her personality that it baffled Andrea every time. "Thanks for lunch, Mom."

"You're welcome. And you be sure and let me know what kind of time frame you're looking at for your move. Don't leave your mother in the dark, as you so seem to enjoy doing."

Knowing better than to argue the point, Andrea simply nodded.

Outside the restaurant, the day was almost warm. No sunshine, as rain was in the forecast for later in the evening, but the lingering, impending spring chill was nearly gone and Andrea was glad she only had her light jacket with her. She and Julia each kissed their mother on the cheek and she headed off to her car, the opposite direction of the parking lot where the sisters' cars were. They strolled together.

"Well, that could have been worse," Julia said.

"Right? She was…almost agreeable."

"I was shocked."

"She didn't like that we were drinking wine," Andrea said with a chuckle.

"Yeah, well she obviously hasn't made the connection yet."

"The connection that we need it to get through a lunch with her?"

"Exactly." They were parked side by side, and Julia unlocked her car. "Hey." Andrea met her eyes and was astonished to see them well with tears.

"Julia? What? What is it?" Andrea laid a hand on her sister's arm. "Tell me."

Julia made a face, one that said it was obvious she was embarrassed by her emotions, but she managed to look directly at Andrea. "I will miss you terribly. But you should go. Get the hell out of here and away from her. I know I've been giving you a rough time about it, but..." She glanced down at the keys in her hands, toyed with them. "She's always been so hard on you. And if you don't take this, you may not get another shot at managing." Andrea was startled that her sister knew this fact. "It makes perfect sense for you to take the opportunity and get the hell away from her. I just want you to know that, no matter what I've said up until now, I love you and you have my blessing. Go."

Andrea didn't know what to say, so she wrapped her arms around her sister and held her tightly, hoping her grip and the love she was trying to radiate would make it clear to Julia just how important that blessing was to her.

They stood like that for a long while.

❧

Kendall was beyond irritated.

It was as if the Universe had decided to make her pay for the stress-free first leg of her four-day journey by making the very last leg absolutely miserable. She kicked herself for mentioning to Andrea last night that there had been no construction because she'd been brought to a dead stop by that very thing three times today. So far. Then there'd been the jackknifed semi that had completely blocked the thruway for close to an hour. And now? Rain. But not any rain. Torrential downpour rain, complete with thunder, lightning, and windshield wipers she should have replaced six months ago. Needless to say, her drive home was not smooth, it was not relaxing, and it was not quick.

The overall trip had been very successful. She'd stopped in on several breweries and was able to spend time with many people she talked to online almost daily. It was one of her very favorite things about the beer industry. Coming out of the bubble of brewing camaraderie, Kendall was pretty sure she'd be eaten alive in the cutthroat world of corporate business because she would trust everybody and she would share all her ideas. It'd be the kiss of death.

She'd given away all the beer Rick had crammed into her SUV, and yet she was returning home with just as much. Every place she'd stopped had insisted she take a complimentary six-pack of their signature brew or a sample growler of their newest blend. There was a lot of beer to taste and analyze. Rick and Adam would be pleased.

Kendall was tired. While she enjoyed a good road trip, doing all the driving herself was hell on her eyes, especially in the rain, and all she wanted to do was be done. Be home. Be with Andrea.

Be with Andrea.

It didn't surprise her, this thought. It had slowly wormed its way into her brain until there was no denying it. But no matter how hard she tried, she had to face facts: Andrea was leaving. Not tomorrow. Maybe not even next month. But she was leaving and that was that. Kendall rolled that around often. Even when she tried not to, it sat in the pit of her stomach like a rock, hard and unmoving.

The big green sign finally, *finally* indicated her exit. She'd be home in about twenty-five minutes. A glance at the clock told her it was after midnight and she blew out a frustrated breath. She'd texted with Andrea several times during her standstills, hoping to stop by and see her. But as it got later and later, that seemed less and less likely. The last text from Andrea had been an hour ago.

It's been a day and I've got to go to bed, but I'll leave the door unlocked, just in case. Your call. I won't be upset if you just want to go home and sleep. ☺

That was the last thing Kendall wanted to do, and it took less than a second for her to make up her mind and steer the car in the right direction.

Fifteen minutes later, she coasted into Andrea's driveway and killed the engine. That was when it occurred to her that this was kind of…a moment. She'd never randomly dropped by the house of a casual acquaintance at nearly one in the morning. That only happened if she was seriously dating somebody. *Seriously* dating somebody. She sat in the quiet car and looked up at the dark house as her thoughts whirled and churned like a pulsing food processor in her head.

"Screw it," she finally said, and pulled the door handle.

Inside was quiet and still. A small hurricane lamp on a side table was left burning, and Kendall smiled, knowing Andrea left it on for her. The house was ridiculously tidy, as it always was. Magazines and catalogs on the coffee table were stacked neatly, the remotes lined up like soldiers in formation on top of them. A small wicker basket in the corner held all of Zeke's toys, none of them left scattered across the floor. Even Andrea's boots and shoes were lined up on the boot tray in precise arrangement. Andrea was nothing if not neat and orderly. She liked things just so and was not somebody who appreciated surprise or unexpectedness. A grin came to Kendall's mouth as she shucked her coat and hung it up, removed her shoes, and locked the door behind her. It dawned on her in that very moment that one of her favorite things to do in all the world was to surprise Andrea, make her loosen up, let go of all that control and predictability, and just…*be.*

Like last night on the phone.

God, that was hot.

Quietly climbing the stairs, Kendall could smell Andrea now. A pleasing combination of her perfume, her shampoo, and her soap was obvious in the upstairs atmosphere, and she stood in the hallway for a moment just to breathe it in.

She took care in her steps once she reached Andrea's bedroom, remembering that the hardwood gave way to an area rug and she didn't want to trip and fall. *That'd ruin the surprise.* Walking carefully, she rounded the bed and stood until her eyes adjusted to the darkness.

Andrea's deep, even breathing was the only sound, and Kendall smiled as she watched and listened. Zeke was curled up at her shoulder, but lifted his head when he sensed Kendall's presence, and stood to walk across the bed and greet her.

"Hi, buddy," she whispered, bending to let him smell her face. Apparently satisfied she was allowed in the room, the kitten jumped off the bed and zipped into the hall. Kendall watched him go, then turned her focus back to the bed. Andrea was on her back, the covers pulled up to just below her breasts. It was hard to make out the color of her tank top in the dim light, but it didn't matter. All Kendall cared about was the way it pulled across her breasts and that it left her beautiful shoulders bare. She knew there would be adorable lightweight pants on under the covers, and suddenly Kendall's mouth watered and her stomach flipped and she couldn't get her own clothes off fast enough.

Naked, she lifted the blankets and slipped under them, then made her way to Andrea. Not wanting to startle her awake, she gently ran her fingertips along the exposed side of Andrea's neck, not lightly enough to tickle, but not firmly enough to frighten. She did this for several moments, reveling in the soft skin before moving slowly down along Andrea's collarbone. She retraced that path for a bit before moving lower and circling a nipple through the tank's fabric. Andrea began to stir then, just a little, not quite waking up, but no longer fully asleep. Kendall watched her face until she couldn't wait any longer and lightly ran her finger across Andrea's now-tightened nipple.

The intake of breath was powerfully erotic for Kendall, and Andrea had barely opened her eyes before Kendall was kissing her.

No words were needed. There was nothing to be said. There was only touch and taste and rhythm. Kendall made short work of Andrea's pajamas, and when they lay skin to skin, the elation she felt nearly overwhelmed her. She tried to take her time, but it was almost impossible. She wanted her hands, her mouth, everywhere at once, and when she finally settled herself between Andrea's thighs and touched her tongue to Andrea's center, they both moaned in unified relief. And when Andrea's orgasm ripped through her mere minutes later, Kendall's tongue pressed against her, her fingers buried deep inside, nothing in Kendall's world tasted, sounded, or felt quite as perfect.

"I missed you," Kendall whispered as she gathered Andrea into her arms and settled under the covers.

"I missed you, too," Andrea whispered back.

That was all Kendall needed. She placed a tender kiss on Andrea's forehead as she settled against Kendall's shoulder, tucked her head under Kendall's chin. It really was all she needed, and that realization made her happy and sad at the same time. Trying not to dwell on the future, she tightened her arms and closed her eyes. All the driving got the better of her, and she was asleep in minutes.

CHAPTER EIGHTEEN

The weather on Monday mirrored Kendall's mood. Sunny with blue skies and a pleasant breeze one minute would give way to clouds the next, and air movement would go from breeze to wind. Then the wind would ease and the sun would come back out. It was uncertain. A little bipolar. Somewhat muddled.

It wasn't a feeling she enjoyed. Kendall was a pretty confident, assured woman for the most part. And she was proud of that part of her personality. She credited her family. Her parents were never unsupportive; they cheered her on no matter what she did or set her sights on doing. Even her big brothers, obnoxious as they could be, helped lift her up and hold her high, convincing her she could do whatever she wanted and do it well.

Confidence was never a problem.

Until now.

Her thumb hovered over the green Send button for several long seconds before she backed out and ended her call to Liz before she even began it. She tossed her cell onto her desk with a frustrated sigh. That was the third time so far today and it was only—she picked the cell back up and squinted at the screen—twelve-thirty. She tossed it again. No, she couldn't call Liz. She couldn't talk to Adam. The idea of picking her mother's brain crossed her mind more than once, but she set it aside. No, this was all her. She knew what each of those three people would say to her, but this was all her. She needed to think, roll things around, come to a conclusion.

Yesterday had been amazing.

Kendall sat back in her desk chair, bit her fingertip, and grinned widely.

She and Andrea had slept soundly, wrapped around each other like vines entwining a trellis. In the morning, they'd made love. Twice. Then they'd showered together where Kendall had an orgasm pressed between the fiberglass wall and Andrea's wet and slippery body. A breakfast of poached eggs and hash browns had led to a warm and cozy day spent on the couch watching movies, again wrapped around each other. If Kendall hadn't had a suitcase full of dirty clothes and a cat she hadn't seen in five days, she probably would have stayed overnight again; leaving the warm softness of Andrea's body, of her mouth, of her hands had not been easy, and they ended up kissing goodbye at the front door for nearly twenty minutes before Kendall had finally extricated herself and made it all the way to her car.

This morning, Andrea had texted her a picture of the empty shower with a note that said, "Big. Empty. Lonely."

Kendall swallowed hard now as she was hit with a flashback. The sex with Andrea—good God, it was amazing. She'd never, ever been so physically compatible with anybody in her life. And she'd had good sex. She wasn't one of those women who just hadn't found a person who knew how to take care of her body. Kendall was familiar with good sex. But sex with Andrea? It was off-the-charts hot. Scorching. All Andrea had to do was look at her and Kendall's body started to ready itself for her. In fact, that's what it was doing right now; she could feel it as she sat there in her chair remembering.

It would be embarrassing if it wasn't such a damn turn-on.

They'd watched two movies. A romantic comedy (Kendall's favorite genre) and a thriller (Andrea's) and each of them had seemed to enjoy the other. Andrea laughed in all the right places during the rom-com, and Kendall caught her smiling happily not at the movie itself, but at Kendall laughing at the movie. During the thriller, she and Andrea had talked out the puzzle, trying to figure out the bad guy together. They'd been wrong, but it had been a fun process to work through as a team.

Buster sauntered into Kendall's office then, walked behind the desk and laid his big, square head on her thigh in greeting.

"Hey, buddy. Where've you been all morning? Hmm?"

His long, thick black tail wagged back and forth, smacking the desk on one side and the wall on the other. She grinned and scratched his head.

"So. What do you think, Buster? You seem like a smart guy. Great sex doesn't mean a relationship is—or should be—anything more than that, right? I mean, just because you're sleeping with a hot chick who rocks your world in the sack, that doesn't necessarily mean you should try to take things to the next level, does it? Or that there even is a next level. Right?"

Buster continued to wag his tail happily, his brown eyes soft with what Kendall decided was complete understanding and agreement.

"That's what I thought." Kendall nodded, but then stopped, cocked her head. "Although…what if there *is* a next level and if you don't shoot for it, you miss out on something spectacular? Then what?"

Buster's demeanor didn't change one iota. Kendall sighed.

Her desk phone rang then, which was a good distraction, and she ended up killing much of the rest of the day with work. Thank God.

It was going on four o'clock when Kendall made the decision. With a deep breath, she stood from her chair, left her office, and walked across the lushly green grass to the yellow house in which she'd grown up.

Cathy was making chocolate chip cookies when Kendall entered through the kitchen door, and it was actually kind of perfect. The blue flowered apron that was as old as Kendall's memories. The eighties music playing low on the ancient radio on the counter. The warm, inviting smell of melting chocolate and baking cookie dough. It all blended to create the feeling of safety and security Kendall had always had surrounding her whenever she was near her mother. As that love enveloped her now, she knew she was in exactly the right place.

"Mom?"

"Hi, sweetie." Cathy smiled as she cracked eggs into the mixing bowl for the next batch.

"Can I talk to you?" Kendall snagged a still-warm cookie off the wire cooling rack on the table and took a seat.

Cathy looked at her again, studying her face this time. "Of course." When she made a move to join her at the table, Kendall waved her off.

"No. Keep doing what you're doing. I can talk from here."

After a beat, Cathy nodded, went back to her mixer, and waited for her daughter to speak.

"I'm not sure what to do," Kendall finally said.

"About?"

"Andrea."

Cathy glanced at her. "Explain."

Even though she'd come to her mother to do that very thing —explain, talk about it—Kendall still balked. She broke eye contact, looked out the window, chewed on her bottom lip. Because saying it out loud, discussing it with somebody else, did the one thing Kendall had been trying her best to avoid.

It made it all real.

She swallowed down the lump in her throat and refused to let her eyes well up. Facing her mother, whose expression had grown concerned in the silence, Kendall told her the entire story of Andrea's career. When she'd begun with Hagan's—which Cathy already knew from their meeting in Kendall's apartment—to all the stops along the way, to the current offer on the table and the locations available to her.

"This is what she's been waiting for, what she's been working toward. Her own store. If she doesn't take it, she probably won't get another chance. There are too many other people in line."

"Okay," Cathy said. She'd stopped mid-cookie batter to focus on her daughter. "What's the problem?"

Kendall looked at her hands.

"You don't want her to go."

"Of course, I don't," Kendall said, exasperated. "But that's not for me to say. I can't do that to her. She doesn't owe me anything." She picked up another cookie, broke it in half, toyed with the pieces. "I think she's hesitating because of me."

Cathy furrowed her brow and sat down at the table across from Kendall. "How so?"

"They gave her a month to decide." With a shake of her head, Kendall said, "She doesn't need that long. She's been ready for this for years. She knows exactly what she wants. She can just point at a store and go."

"But she hasn't."

"No."

"Honey." Cathy took a bite of a cookie and chewed thoughtfully. "I'm not sure what you want me to say here."

Kendall's cheeks puffed as she blew out a breath. "I'm not either."

"I guess…just put yourself in her shoes, maybe? Think about what would help you if you were in her position. Then do that for her."

Kendall nodded slowly. That made sense. If she was in Andrea's place and having a rough time making the decision she knew she really wanted to make, what would Kendall want from her in order to make life easier, to make the decision not so tentative? An idea came to her then and she looked up at her mother, who was watching her carefully.

"You're right," Kendall said. "You're right. I think I know what to do."

Cathy searched her face for a long moment before giving her a small smile and saying simply, "Good."

CHAPTER NINETEEN

Curly's was quiet, which was exactly what Kendall had hoped when she chose it as a meeting spot. She waved to Paul, the bartender, and took one of the empty barstools on a corner. This way, she could see the door, and when Andrea arrived, they could sit at the bar and face each other rather than be side by side.

"How've you been, Kendall?" Paul asked as he approached her. He was tall and lanky, built like a cartoon drawing, complete with dark hair that pointed up in the front. Kendall had visited here many times to sell Old Red Barn products and she got along well with Paul.

"I've been great, Paul. What's new with you?"

"Not a whole lot. Business has picked up a bit with the weather getting nicer."

"Thank God for that, huh?"

"You know it. What can I get you?"

"Let me try the Down Boy red ale." She remembered Jeff O'Hanlon talking about their new red last time she'd run into him. "And I'm meeting somebody in a few minutes. What do you have for seasonal beer?"

Paul gave her the rundown as he pulled the tap and poured her ale. She knew which ones Andrea would like and made a mental note, thanked Paul, and asked him to run her a tab.

Curly's was nothing special, and that's what Kendall liked about it. It was your average, run-of-the-mill corner bar, complete with neon beer signs, classic rock playing over the speakers at a reasonable volume, and televisions mounted behind the bar tuned to poker, golf, and Quick Draw. Tuesday evening was not prime bar time, so customers were sporadic. Two men sat four stools down, their eyes glued to the poker game on the television. Kendall glanced at it and wondered, not for the first time, why the players were allowed to wear sunglasses during tournaments. Wasn't reading your opponents' faces and eyes part of being a good poker player?

Several other customers were scattered around, some at the bar, some at tables having dinner, but the overall atmosphere was fairly quiet. The smell of burgers was plain, and normally, Kendall would order something to eat. Not tonight, though. Her stomach felt like there was some kind of deep-sea battle going on, with the opponents swimming around and banging into each other. Not a pleasant feeling. Paul leaned on the opposite corner of the bar and talked to two women who sat there. Kendall's gaze was shifting from them to the door and back.

Andrea would be here soon. It was 6:15 and Kendall had suggested 6:30. She wanted to get here early, go over her thoughts, things she wanted to say. And honestly? She wanted to get a beer down, something to help steady her nerves.

She'd texted earlier, asking if Andrea would be interested in meeting her for a drink after work. She'd made no reference to the fact that she wanted to talk about something specific. She didn't think getting into it on the phone was a good idea. Face-to-face was better, no matter how nauseous the idea made her. Beer probably wasn't a terrific idea in her sour stomach, but she tried her best to focus.

Jeff's beer was good. She made note of it as she took a large gulp, then pulled out her cell and whipped off a text to him telling him so. She set her phone on the bar and looked up just in time to see Andrea pushing through the front door.

Despite its nervousness, Kendall's stomach tightened, then did its little flip-flop thing, just as it did every time she laid eyes on Andrea Blake. God, how could one woman have such an effect on another? How was it possible?

Andrea's eyes met hers and she smiled widely, so obviously happy to see her that Kendall felt herself blush. Andrea shed her light coat and headed toward her. Still dressed for work, she wore a crisp black pantsuit with a green top under the jacket that totally made her eyes pop. Her heels clicked as she crossed the room and took the stool next to Kendall. She touched Kendall's upper arm, squeezed it.

"Hi, you," she said. "This was a great idea. How was your day?"

"It was all right," Kendall replied, feeling like a schoolgirl with a silly, lovesick smile plastered on her face. She wanted nothing more than to lean over and kiss Andrea right on the mouth, but Curly's probably wasn't the place to do that. Another reason she'd picked it. She wanted to keep her wits about her, not get sidetracked by making out with a beautiful woman. She motioned to Paul. To Andrea, she said, "Are you up for a beer? Or would you rather have something else?"

"Is there a beer you think I'd like?"

"There are three."

With a tilt of her head and a half-grin, Andrea said, "I trust you. Order me a beer."

Turning to Paul, Kendall said, "Please pour an apricot ale for my lovely friend here, Paul."

"You got it." Paul was back in short order with a glass for Andrea. She held it up, looked at it in the light as Kendall had taught her.

"It's pretty," she said, causing Kendall to grin. Then she put the glass under her nose and sniffed. "You can definitely smell the apricot. And something else...coriander maybe?"

Kendall gave a proud nod. "Very good." She lifted her own glass and they cheered, then sipped.

"Oh, that's yummy," Andrea said, catching a dab of foam on her lip with her tongue. Kendall swallowed hard and Andrea gave her a knowing wink.

"You're a tease," Kendall said softly.

Andrea widened her eyes in feigned innocence, but her grin said she was fully aware of her effect on Kendall. She glanced around for several seconds, taking in the bar and its patrons. "This is kind of a neat place. Average and off the beaten path. I like it."

"Me, too."

"And I see they carry some of your beer." She gestured to the taps with her chin where logos for Stone Fence IPA and the new Yellow House Peach Wheat graced the handles.

"They do. Curly's was one of my very first bar customers."

"Really?"

"Yup. Pete and Madeline are the owners. They're this older couple and they've had this place for, like, a million years. Sweetest people you'd ever want to meet. I didn't even have to do much selling. Pete's just a nice guy who wanted to give my little microbrewery a chance, so he bought two kegs when we first started out. We sold well and he's ordered from me ever since."

"That is an incredibly sweet story," Andrea said, then sipped from her glass. "And I really like this beer."

"I thought you might. I'm getting to know you pretty well."

Andrea arched one eyebrow, catching the double meaning. "You are. It's true."

It's now or never. Kendall took a deep breath. "So." She cleared her throat and gazed into her glass as she spoke. "You pick a store yet?"

Andrea's smile tightened just a touch. If Kendall didn't know her, she might have missed it. "I have three more days."

Kendall nodded. "Yeah, but you don't need three more days. You know you want Raleigh. Just tell them."

Andrea took a small sip of her beer, and the smile pretty much disappeared.

Kendall seized the moment. "I mean, you don't have anything holding you back, right? No reason to stay here. You need to get away from your mom. Your sister has given you the okay. This winter was *horrendously* cold." She feigned a chuckle and could feel Andrea's eyes on her, but she pushed forward. "You and I, we've had a great time, we really have. It's been a lot of fun. *A lot* of fun. But let's be honest. We both knew you were going to be leaving, so…" She shrugged her shoulders and picked up her glass, not looking at Andrea even though she could feel her go completely still next to her. "You should just tell them. The sooner you do, the sooner you can be on your way and start your new life. No strings."

"No strings," Andrea said quietly after several excruciatingly long moments.

"Right."

"I see." Andrea set her beer down and Kendall noticed her throat moved as she swallowed. She took a deep breath and Kendall was stunned to see her entire demeanor shift. She went from comfortably familiar and warm to Businesswoman Andrea

Blake—calm, cool, and collected. And utterly removed. It was Andrea from the volleyball court. Andrea from the first meeting. Beautiful and cold. Kendall felt like a giant hand was squeezing her heart in her chest. "You know what?" Andrea took a cursory glance at her watch. "I just realized I've got things that need taking care of." She slipped off her stool and gathered her things. When she looked up at Kendall, her green eyes were as cold as marble. "You're right. It has been fun. I'm glad we had this talk, Kendall. It cleared up a lot for me. It helped me see things in much sharper focus. Thank you for that." With that, she turned and left.

Kendall watched her go and this time, she was powerless to stop the welling of tears in her eyes.

It cleared up a lot for me.

"Well, that was the intention, right, Kendall?" she quietly asked herself. She brought her fingertips to her lips, and stayed that way until she felt like she could get a full breath.

It was done.

Now Andrea would do what she needed to do, what she'd wanted to do for years, and there was no reason for her to hesitate. Nothing holding her back. Nothing standing in her way. Not family. Not work. And not love.

Certainly, not love.

CHAPTER TWENTY

Eight weeks went by in a flash. One thing that Andrea was sure of: North Carolina had a way more beautiful late spring/ early summer than upstate New York. And the temperatures were much more bearable and steady. None of the sixty degrees one day, eighty-five the next like back home. No sirree. It was stable and balanced here. Very enjoyable.

Not like Andrea had much time to enjoy the weather. Opening a new Hagan's was a ridiculously time-consuming job, and as the manager, Andrea oversaw just about everything. The first few weeks in Raleigh had been spent interviewing and hiring her staff. The store was one of the largest of all Hagan's locations, and she had nearly a hundred people to hire. More would follow in the first few weeks of being open. She was in the store bright and early, usually by six or seven. She stayed until eight or nine at night. Once it actually opened to the public, she'd be able to regulate her hours somewhat, but until then, she ate, slept, and breathed Hagan's. She was exhausted.

Exhaustion was good though. Exhaustion left no room for wallowing or reminiscing or regretting. No room for sadness or broken-heartedness. Being crazy busy left her no time to think about Kendall and that was good, because the last thing in the world she wanted to do was think about Kendall.

We've had a great time. It's been a lot of fun.

Wow, she had *not* seen that coming. At all.

No matter what she did to keep her brain occupied, those words replayed much too often for her liking, and she still had trouble accepting that Kendall had actually said them. Andrea was certain...*certain* they'd had something deeper. In fact, her plan that night had been to go home and call Julia, talk to her, pick her brain, ask her just how ridiculous Andrea would be if she'd asked Kendall to come with her to Raleigh. After all, she was the reason Andrea had been dragging her feet giving Hagan's a response. She didn't need an entire month to "think it over." She knew what she wanted. Once she and Kendall had made the pros and cons list, it was crystal clear where Andrea would go.

She hadn't counted on Kendall. Or the way she felt about her.

Hearing Kendall say that they'd just been a fun distraction for a while was like a knife in the gut, twisting against her insides until she wanted to cry out from the pain. How had Andrea been so naïve? What in the world had she been thinking? Had she really thought Kendall would jump at the chance to start this new adventure alongside her? That her beautiful blue eyes would light up at the thought? This was exactly why Andrea had kept herself at arms' length from most people. If you let them get too close, they'd only end up hurting you in the end.

Case in point: Kendall Foster.

Andrea took a deep breath of fresh North Carolina air as she unlocked her car. It was one of only four in the parking lot. It was going on ten o'clock at night and the only people left in the store were the guys working overnight on the floors. Andrea was heading home to eat something not nutritious, love her cat for ten minutes, and then hopefully grab a handful of hours of sleep before she'd be right back here again in the morning.

Traffic was light and it only took her twenty minutes to drive from the store to her townhouse. Down the line, she'd look into buying something, but for now, the townhouse was perfect. Hagan's had given her a few options and had paid for movers to bring her stuff down. Her house back home was still hers, but she knew there was a For Sale sign in front of it, and Julia and a realtor were taking care of potential buyers. There were still a few belongings left there. Andrea would make a drive back some time in the summer after the house sold and pick up the rest.

Her townhouse sat in a nicely landscaped, newly built complex and she was surprisingly comfortable here. The complex was shaped in a large horseshoe, with the office and community building centered in the bend. The building housed an impressively appointed gym, a locker room, and the maintenance office. Behind it was a large, gated in-ground pool. As a resident, Andrea was allowed access to all of it. Maybe by August, she'd be able to take an afternoon and just lounge by the water. Who knew? Anything was possible.

Her townhouse was in the third of five buildings on one side. She stopped at the bank of mailboxes to access hers, then pulled into her designated parking spot and let herself into the house. Zeke flew at her like a shot. This was his newest thing and Andrea wondered if it was because he never knew when she'd be home. She was actually considering a second cat, if for no other reason than to give him a playmate. He was alone for so much of the day, she worried about him.

She scooped him up in her arms and cooed at him as she dropped the mail on the small table in her tiny entryway and kicked off her heels. Business attire was certainly not expected of her as the manager of a grocery store still in its final stages of construction, but she felt better, more authoritative, more in control, if she looked the part of "person in charge." She might ease up on that as time went on, but for right now, this was good. That didn't mean she didn't want to get out of those clothes as soon as she was able, so she carried Zeke right up the steps and into the master suite of her two-bedroom place.

There hadn't been time for much decorating, but Andrea had done what she could to make the room feel like home. Her very first purchase for her move had been new bedding. She'd loved her old set, but something about it made her feel...weirdly tied to the past. She wanted all of it gone and she went with an entirely new set and color. Now, instead of all the shades of blue she'd favored previously, her room was purple. Eggplant, mostly, with small throw pillows of various shapes, all in shades of lavender. The valances on the two windows matched her pillow shams and she'd purchased an abstract painting in colors that perfectly complemented the bedding. She'd carried the colors into the attached bath and every time she came up to the bedroom, she was gently startled by how comfortable the room was.

I'm doing all right here.

The thought came to her often, so she was not surprised when it zoomed through her brain as she shed her suit and donned yoga pants and a white T-shirt with capped sleeves. Barefoot, she went back downstairs and fished through the freezer for a package of macaroni and cheese that would be delicious and would also horrify her if she actually read the nutritional information. Thus, she tossed the box quickly and put the plastic tray in the microwave, mentally vowing for the dozenth time to start cooking again when she had the energy. Even though cooking for one person was hard. The last person she'd cooked for...

"No."

She said it aloud. Zeke stopped what he was doing and looked up at her, obviously wondering if he'd done something wrong. She smiled a gentle smile at him. "Not you, buddy. You're fine."

No, she couldn't go there. Wouldn't go there. It was done. Kendall had made certain of that. Plus, it had been almost two months now and there'd been no word from her. Not a thing. Well, that wasn't entirely true. She'd gotten a text. Just one. It had been friendly. Light. A little bit of joking, like they were pals. Honestly, that was almost worse than getting nothing at all and Andrea had sent one text back: *Please don't text me again*. Kendall had obeyed her wishes. Which was disappointing.

Andrea shook her head as she poured herself a conservative glass of red wine. No, she was not going to dwell. She was going to take her macaroni and cheese, her wine, and her cat, and cozy up in her bed and watch Dateline on television. Maybe it would be a riveting episode, one about a mystery. Maybe it would be one filled with blood, betrayal, murder, something to hold her attention while she tried to figure it out.

Maybe then she wouldn't have time to stop and think about how much she still missed Kendall, to her own enormous irritation. Maybe then she wouldn't have a chance to dwell on just how very, very lonely she really was.

❧

Kendall's eyes burned. Hours in front of the computer at work plus hours on the tablet at home plus less than four hours of restless sleep a night were all combining to drive her insane with fatigue. A quick peek at the year-at-a-glance calendar on the wall told her it had been nearly nine weeks since she'd seen or even spoken to Andrea Blake. It didn't matter how often she told herself that she'd done the right thing for Andrea, that she'd done what she needed to do, it still crushed her chest. It still banged around inside her skull in the form of a migraine. It still churned her stomach so much she couldn't eat. She'd sent a text, but she'd taken the totally wrong tack, acting like they were best buds. Andrea had shut that down quickly. And then Kendall had made the mistake of driving by Andrea's house a couple weeks ago. The *For Sale* sign out front and the obvious empty feel of the place just about flattened her.

How was it that doing the right thing could feel so horrifically awful?

It was nearing seven when there was a rap on her doorjamb. Rick smiled from the doorway, then sauntered in, two open bottles in one hand and two glasses in the other. "You got a minute?" he asked.

"For my biggest brother? Always." She gestured to the chair across the desk from her and tried to hide how very tired she was. He handed over one of the bottles and a glass, and took a seat. She looked at the label, recognized it as a new red ale from the Cleveland brewery she'd hit in April, and poured. "Looks nice," she commented as Rick poured his. "Cheers." They touched glasses, then each sipped. Something heavy and bubbly was the last thing Kendall's empty stomach wanted, but she played the part for her brother.

Rick looked off into space as he obviously savored the flavors. With a slow nod, he said, "Not bad. Not bad at all."

"Not bad," Kendall agreed. "It's a little flat on the finish."

"I noticed that, too."

"It's got potential, though."

"Agreed." They sat in companionable silence for several beats before Rick spoke again. "So, how are you, Kendall. What's new?"

Kendall tried not to squint at him. It seemed like an out-of-the-blue question, though she suspected he'd noticed her less-than-enthusiastic attitude lately. While Rick wasn't a cold man, he was not one for intimate conversation, so this seemed…odd. But she went with it, pasted on a smile and gave him a casual shrug. "Not much. What's new with you? Still seeing Jennifer?"

He nodded, and his ruddy complexion showed adorable signs of pink. "Yes. I am."

"You like her."

"I do."

"Me, too. She's nice." Rick had been dating Jennifer for a few weeks now, and she could already see the change in him. He smiled more. His hair was neater. He smelled good.

"I'm glad you think so."

Kendall nodded, took another sip of beer for lack of something more to say.

"Kendall…" Rick's voice trailed off as he let his gaze wander the office while he obviously searched for the right words. Finally, his eyes came back to hers and he held her gaze steadily. "Talk to me," he said simply.

She furrowed her brow at him. "Talk to you about what?"

He wouldn't let go of her eyes. "You're here at all hours and you're obviously exhausted. You look like hell."

"Gee, thanks."

"Mom says you're not eating, and frankly, I see the way your clothes hang off you. You've got dark circles under your eyes and your skin looks gray."

Kendall chewed on the inside of her bottom lip, but wasn't sure what to say. She thought she'd hidden her depression well, but isn't that what all depressed people say?

"It's Andrea." Rick didn't ask. He stated it.

To her own mortification, Kendall felt her eyes fill with tears.

"She's been gone for, what? A month and a half?" Rick asked. His voice was gentle, kind, his eyes soft with tenderness.

"Two," Kendall croaked out.

"Have you talked to her?"

Kendall shook her head.

"How come?"

She gazed off toward the door, her eyes focused on nothing as she said, "It's complicated."

Rick sat back in his chair, made a show of getting comfortable. He'd gotten a fresh haircut, and the lines around his ears were neat and precise. He sipped his beer, then said, "Uncomplicate it for me."

She sat there for what felt like a long time. Buster had wandered in and curled up on his dog bed, and she stared at him while she tried to organize her thoughts. Rick was an easy guy to talk to. He didn't offer up a lot of unsolicited advice, but he was a stellar listener and a very smart man. She'd gone to him with many issues. Sometimes, it had been college classes. Other times it had been about dealing with a client. Occasionally, she needed guidance regarding an employee. But she'd never talked to him about dating or her love life. She hesitated.

"Kendall." Rick sat forward in his chair. He set his beer on her desk, and braced his forearms on his knees. "It's okay. Talk to me."

He looked so much like their father then, his blue eyes soft and gentle, his face open, and Kendall suddenly felt completely safe. A deep breath in, she wet her lips, and spoke. "I told her to go. She needed to go. She was hesitating and I was worried she'd lose out on something very important to her if she didn't act. So...I told her to go."

Rick nodded once, waited for her to continue.

"I told her that we'd had fun, but basically that it didn't really mean anything, so she shouldn't be worried about how her move would affect us. Not in so many words, but that's kind of what I said." Listening to her own retelling now made her stomach roll uncomfortably.

"And now you're miserable."

Kendall nodded. "Yeah."

"Because she did what you told her to instead of arguing with you about it."

Kendall opened her mouth to speak, but snapped it closed again as the meaning of Rick's words hit her. Is that what she'd hoped? Did she think Andrea would argue with her? Tell her she was wrong, that they were more than just fun? That Kendall meant more to her than a hot lay?

Rick leaned forward even farther, ducked his head until he caught Kendall's eyes. Then, so softly Kendall barely heard him, he asked, "Do you love her?"

She lost the battle with the tears at that moment. She couldn't get any words out as her throat closed up around the lump of grief that had been sitting there for the better part of eight weeks, so she simply nodded as tears streamed down her face.

Rick sat back. "I thought so. Does she love you?"

Collecting herself enough to find her voice, Kendall answered honestly. "I don't know. I thought so."

They sat in silence for long moments. Finally, Rick's eyes on Buster as he snored away in the corner, he said nonchalantly, "Joe Benjamin from Benbeer in Raleigh, North Carolina, called me this morning."

"Yeah?"

"Yeah. He's got a new summer ale they're working on and just lost one of their best salespeople. So he's actively looking for somebody who knows what they're doing."

Kendall watched him as he finished his beer, set the empty glass down, then met her gaze. He said nothing more.

"Huh," Kendall said.

"You know, you've been doing this for awhile now and you've got a great handle on the whole sales and marketing aspect of it all." He lifted his hips, dug a piece of paper out of the back pocket of his jeans, and handed it across the desk to Kendall. "Here's his number. Maybe you should give him a call."

"Rick, I..." Kendall's voice caught. She cleared her throat as she stared at the paper in her hand.

Rick gave her time to collect herself before he asked simply, "Don't you think maybe you should talk to that girl you love?"

She nodded, not trusting her voice to work.

"Look at me." She did as she was told and met his blue eyes across the desk. They were wet, much to Kendall's surprise, and soft with love. His voice was kind, but determined. "The boss doesn't want to lose you. That's a given. But your big brother just wants you to do what makes you happy. That's all he's ever wanted. That's what big brothers want for their little sisters. For them to be happy. Whatever you decide, we'll figure it out. Okay?" That shimmering wetness in his eyes made hers spill over yet again. He stood up and came around the desk, arms open wide. "Come here, Ken-Doll." She stood and stepped into his embrace, did her best not to sob into his chest. She was unsuccessful.

For a guy who was not overly emotional, Rick gave the best hugs in the world. She always felt undeniably safe when he wrapped his big bear arms around her. Nothing could get to her.

Nothing could hurt her. She was completely protected when her brother held her. She stayed that way for a while, her face buried against his solid form. She felt him press his lips to the top of her head. As he finally loosened his grip, he said quietly, "Do yourself a favor. Talk to that girl."

Kendall nodded and swiped at her eyes. "I will."

Rick picked up his glass and the two empty bottles and strolled toward the door.

"Rick?"

He turned to look at her, his sandy eyebrows raised expectantly.

"Thanks."

"Anytime." And he left, Buster following him out.

Kendall flopped back into her chair, suddenly exhausted. The beer was good and she took another swallow, but knew she'd need food ASAP or she was going to bring that beer right back up. Her stomach hated her lately.

Using her feet, she slowly turned her chair one way, then the other, eyes on the ceiling, fear like a giant pit sitting in her belly. What if it was too late? After all, nearly two months had gone by and she hadn't even called Andrea. She thought she was doing the right thing, but now she realized her lack of contact may have been seen as cruel. As heartless. As uncaring.

Kendall was none of those things.

Kendall was terrified.

But Rick was right. There was no other solution to this. Kendall would never be able to get her head straight and figure out her next step if she didn't first take this one. She was a big girl. Andrea was a big girl.

Maybe it was time for the big girls to have a talk.

CHAPTER TWENTY-ONE

Andrea rubbed roughly at her eye, not caring that she was probably smearing whatever mascara and eyeliner she had left into her skin. Her eyes itched. Her feet hurt. The subtle pounding in the back of her skull was the sure sign of an impending headache. She was exhausted. In the Good News Department, though, it was almost over. The grand opening was in two weeks and after they settled into a routine, she could start working fairly normal hours. Not that, as manager, her hours would ever be what was considered normal, but they'd be a bit more regular and a bit less grueling than they had been for the past two months.

She was packing up her things, draping the jacket she didn't need over her arm, when her cell phone rang. She'd gotten used to getting dozens of calls a day and since she needed to talk to just about everybody who called, she had begun simply pressing the green button and answering without checking to see who it was first.

"Andrea Blake," she said into the mouthpiece, pulling her office door shut behind her.

"Hi."

The voice made her knees go weak, forced her to stop in her tracks. She pulled the phone away from her ear to look at the screen, already knowing what it would say, but needing to be sure.

Kendall Foster.

"Andrea? Don't hang up. Please."

She could hear Kendall's voice saying her name, but she continued to stare at the phone in her hand wondering if she had actually fallen asleep at her desk and was now dreaming. Slowly, she brought the phone back up to her ear. "I'm here."

Kendall cleared her throat, and when she spoke, her voice tremored a bit. Nerves? Andrea didn't allow herself to wonder. "How are you?"

A hundred snotty responses flew through Andrea's head. Too many to choose from, so she opted to be cautiously, coolly polite. "I'm fine."

"Good. That's good. That's great." There was a pause, but Andrea would be damned if she was going to fill the silence. *Really? Now you call? Now you want to know how I'm doing?* She shook her head at the angry words, wondering how long she'd last before spitting them at Kendall. Her heels clicked loudly through the quiet of the enormous building during her trek to the back door. There were still people working, but only a handful at this hour. She gave a quick nod or a wave to people as she passed them, still waiting out Kendall.

"Listen, Andrea, um…can we talk?"

"I'm sorry?"

Andrea could actually hear Kendall swallow, and part of her was perversely satisfied at the thought of her being uncomfortable. Ashamed, maybe. She certainly should be. "I have some things I want to say," Kendall told her. "Things I need to say. Things I should have said two months ago, but…I was too much of a coward."

Well. Self-flagellation was good. Andrea would take that. But it was going to take a lot more before she'd even consider an actual conversation. "Look, Kendall. It's late. I've been working my ass off and I don't have the energy to get into this with you."

"Does that mean you won't talk to me? You won't hear me out?" Kendall's voice was small, and though Andrea had never seen her cry, she suspected tears were close to the surface. Her heart squeezed a bit, which annoyed her. She was not an easily swayed person, but this was Kendall…

Andrea sighed. "It means that I'm tired. And I'm cranky. And you hurt me, Kendall. I'm not in a big hurry to relive that, no." She reached the big, steel swinging fire door at the back of the building, and she turned to hit the horizontal bar with her ass, backing her way out.

"Even if I'm already here?"

Andrea's steps faltered and she stumbled to a complete stop, the door slamming loudly behind her. There, leaning against her car, was Kendall. Actual Kendall. In the flesh Kendall. Dressed in denim capris, flip flops, and a peach V-neck top and looking absolutely beautiful. Phone to her ear. Uncertain half-smile on her face. Terror in her eyes.

In tandem, they each lowered their phones, but neither made a move.

"What are you doing here?" Andrea asked quietly, her emotions a jumble of anger, happiness, relief, irritation, utter joy, and back to anger.

Kendall straightened her stance, but didn't take any steps forward, as if she was uncertain she should. "I had to see you." Andrea just blinked at her. Kendall went on. "There's so much to say, so many things I should have said before you left. So many things I should *not* have said before you left." She punctuated that last line with a gentle scoff.

Still keeping her feet glued in place, Andrea said, "Really." She was determined to hold onto her anger…and there was a lot of it. But Kendall's face was etched with sadness and regret. She'd lost weight; it was obvious that her clothes were hanging off her frame. Andrea couldn't do what she'd initially wanted to do, which was push Kendall away from her car, hop in, and drive away. That desire was immediately followed by the desire to throw her arms around Kendall and hold her like she was never going to let go, but she couldn't do that either. Instead, she stayed rooted to her spot. Screw it. If Kendall wanted to talk, she could talk. Right here in this parking lot. "Like what?"

Kendall shifted her weight from one foot to the other, studied the ground, cleared her throat again. "Like I was an idiot. A really, really big idiot."

Andrea tilted her head to the side, raised an eyebrow.

Kendall went on. "I meant well, Andrea. I know it doesn't seem that way, but I did. I didn't want you to not take this job because of me. And I didn't think that was the case, but you kept waiting, you kept hesitating. And I got worried."

Andrea pulled her bottom lip into her mouth and bit down on it. She had things she wanted to say as well, but she waited. Her silence paid off in that Kendall felt the need to fill it.

"When I said we were just fun? Just a good time?" Those blue eyes welled up now and Andrea had to concentrate hard to keep from going to her, from wrapping Kendall up in her arms. "That was such a lie. *Such* a lie. It's just...I thought it was what you needed to hear to go. It was dumb and hurtful, I know that now, but at the time, I thought it was the right thing to do. I swear."

"It was dumb," Andrea finally said, her voice gravelly with emotion. "And it was incredibly hurtful."

Kendall nodded, swiping at the tears rolling down her cheeks with the back of a hand. "I know."

"Didn't it occur to you that maybe there was another option? A couple other options, in fact?"

Kendall shook her head as she stared at her shoes. Her voice was quiet. "I didn't really think it through."

"Well, that's a fucking understatement."

Kendall's head snapped up at the profanity, but she didn't move.

Andrea glanced off into the distance. The night was peaceful, the sounds of cicadas chirping tapped at the air, and a gentle breeze rearranged her hair around her head. She blew out a breath and turned to Kendall. "I was going to ask you to come with me." It was very nearly a whisper, but she could tell by the widening of Kendall's eyes that she'd heard. Andrea nodded the clarification. "Yeah. I was. That night, in fact. The night you told me we'd been lots of fun." She made air quotes around the last word.

"Oh, God," Kendall said, and more tears spilled over. "I'm such an idiot." She sniffed hard and wiped her face. "I'm so sorry, Andrea. I'm so sorry. The second you walked out of that bar, everything felt wrong, but I thought that was just a side effect of my doing the right thing. I know now that I was just stupid. I miss you so much. Nothing is right since you've been gone. I can't eat. I can't sleep. I think about you all the time." A sob pushed from her lungs. "I miss you so much, Andrea. I miss you so much." She stood there, softly crying, as Andrea looked on, mentally forcing herself to stay put until she heard the right words.

"I miss you, too," she said, her voice gentle.

Kendall looked up at her, blue eyes sad, wet, pleading. "You do?"

"Of course, I do."

A slow nod began as Kendall held her gaze. "I love you, Andrea. I miss you so much because I love you. I tried not to, I swear I tried. But I can't help it. I love you."

There they were. The right words.

Andrea let herself move then. She crossed the asphalt to her car, dropped her crap on the ground, and pulled Kendall into her arms. "I love you, too, baby. I love you, too."

And then they were kissing and it was the most wonderful kiss in the entire world to Andrea, who had come so close to giving up on ever imagining the way Kendall made her feel could happen again—or last. They kissed slowly, softly, tenderly, murmurs of love and emotion between small sobs.

Finally, Kendall pulled herself away enough to speak clearly. "I have a lot to tell you."

Andrea cocked her head, still holding tightly to Kendall, afraid that if she didn't, her form would evaporate like fog and this would all have been a dream. "Yeah? More than what you just did?"

Kendall laughed. "Yes. More. I've been putting possible plans in place."

"Plans for?"

"Plans for being here with you." Andrea's eyebrows raised, but before she could say anything, Kendall rushed forward. "No pressure. No pressure. Really. But…maybe we can go to your place and talk and I can tell you all about it. And then…we can make some decisions."

"Make some decisions *together*, you mean."

"Yes. Exactly that." Kendall's smile was radiant, and Andrea felt that familiar flip-flopping in her stomach. God, how she'd missed that feeling.

"Come with me. Leave your car here. I don't want to let go of you." She punctuated the statement by lifting Kendall's hand in hers and kissing it. They picked up her stuff and hopped into Andrea's car. Andrea started the engine, but didn't shift the vehicle into drive. She gazed straight out the windshield as her eyes filled with tears. Kendall squeezed her hand tightly, but said nothing, gave her time and space to collect herself. After a long moment, Andrea turned to Kendall, eyes shimmering. "I'm so glad you're here," she said softly.

"Well, that's excellent news because I'm not leaving." At Andrea's widened eyes, she pointed out the window. "Drive. We've got a lot to talk about."

EPILOGUE

The day was hot, which was a little weird for September in upstate New York, baking the earth in ninety-degree heat, complete with way too much humidity. Andrea's hair was pulled back into a ponytail, the only defense she had against the moisture in the air if she didn't want to look like a giant mop of auburn frizz.

She steered her car toward Old Red Barn, amused by how a mere five months ago, she'd had to use the GPS on her phone to get there, but now it felt almost like a second home, even though she wasn't there often. It had nothing to do with proximity and everything to do with how special the entire Foster clan had become to her. It was hard for Jim and Cathy when Kendall told them she was moving to Raleigh to be with Andrea, but to their credit, they'd worked through their sadness at seeing their last child leave the nest in a fairly short span of time, and just two months ago, helped Kendall move the furniture and belongings she wanted with her to Andrea's.

It was a new experience for both Andrea and Kendall, as neither of them had lived with a girlfriend in the past, and in the grand scheme of things, they'd moved pretty fast. Kendall getting her own place just seemed like a colossal waste of money, though, so she'd moved into Andrea's townhouse. Adjustments were necessary, some they were still making, but almost nine weeks later, Andrea was shocked to find herself *not* freaking out. They each still worked long hours, too long sometimes. Kendall was putting in extra time to get herself up to speed at Benbeer, to learn and meet the list of clients that was a good five times larger than Old Red Barn's. Andrea's schedule had smoothed out some now that the store was open and business was in full swing, but she still worked late sometimes. Luckily, it was the idea of coming home to Kendall or being home when Kendall returned from work that bolstered Andrea during the day. Made her smile. Made her look forward to the end of the afternoon.

And now she had somebody to cook for.

Kendall was already complaining about putting on weight, but Andrea just laughed. Kendall loved her cooking and Andrea loved feeding her. It was the perfect situation.

Now, she turned her car down the driveway, past the Fosters' yellow house, and into the parking lot near the barn. They'd come back to New York to finalize the sale of Andrea's house and to see the Fosters while doing so. She'd dropped Kendall off that morning, stopped in on Julia and the kids, gone to see the real estate lawyer, and was now back to the Fosters'. Kendall had a "big surprise" for her, as she'd been calling it all week, and Andrea was slightly leery. As somebody who liked control, surprises were not high on her list of things she enjoyed.

Her trepidation slid away as soon as she saw Kendall's face. She stood in the parking lot, grinning like a fool, obviously awaiting Andrea's arrival. Coming around the car as Andrea opened her door, Kendall grabbed her up in a big hug.

"Hi, baby," she said, and gave Andrea a quick kiss on the mouth.

"What is the big surprise?" Andrea asked.

"Close your eyes," was Kendall's reply.

With an exaggerated sigh, Andrea did as ordered. Apparently, Kendall didn't trust her because she clamped one of her own hands over Andrea's eyes. The other closed tightly around Andrea's upper arm as she led her through the parking lot, out of the hot August sunshine, and into a building. Andrea was a good sport and she kept her eyes closed even as she paid close attention to their path and tried to figure out where she was being directed. She wasn't a hundred percent certain, but if her sense of direction was right, they had come to a stop in the tasting room of Old Red Barn.

"Okay. Don't move," Kendall said, her voice as excited as a child's on Christmas morning. "And keep your eyes closed." She slowly removed her hand and Andrea obediently kept her eyes squeezed shut. "Stay right there."

"I am staying right here," Andrea said unnecessarily. "But I am growing impatient. Show me the surprise already." She grinned, her tone playful.

"One more second..." Kendall said, her voice farther away now. After a beat, she said, "Okay, ready?"

"I've been ready since I got here, what, a year and a half ago?"

"Ha ha," Kendall said. "Okay. Open your eyes."

Andrea obeyed, and had to blink several times to let her eyes adjust. They were indeed in the tasting room of Old Red Barn, as were Kendall, Rick, Adam, Denny, Mr. and Mrs. Foster, and several other employees of the brewery, as well as Kylie and Gretchen, Liz and Marcy, Julia and Phil.

"Ta-da!" Kendall said with a huge smile and stretched her arms out, a la Vanna White, toward a stack of boxes on the bar.

Andrea blinked at them, at the logo. It was a painted picture of two rather familiar-looking green eyes. Underneath in fancy red lettering were the words "Green-Eyed Beauty Wheat Beer." Below that, in smaller type, it read, "an autumn wheat beer brewed with cinnamon, cloves, and other fall spices." Andrea stared at it, blinked again, and stared some more. "What…what is this?"

"It's your birthday present," Kendall said proudly. "We made you your very own beer."

Andrea looked at her, then at Rick, then at Adam, then at Kendall's parents. She opened her mouth to speak, closed it again, and felt her eyes fill with tears.

"Oh, honey," Kendall came to her and wrapped an arm around her shoulders. "Don't cry."

"There's no crying in brewing," Adam said, making Andrea laugh.

"I'm sorry, I just…" She pulled herself together and looked at Kendall. "I can't believe you did this for me," she said quietly.

Kendall grinned. "Well, maybe you should taste it." And there was Rick, with a glass already poured. "We talked it through, picked some stuff we know you like. Rick helped. Denny added the spices."

Andrea took a long sniff. "Oh, it smells so warm and yummy." One sip and Andrea was in love. "Oh, my God, this is good. This is *good*."

"Yeah?" Kendall asked.

"Yes. It's fabulous." She took a larger mouthful this time, held it, then swallowed. "Wow. That's wonderful. It's warm, but complex. Refreshing, but in a holiday kind of way. Just enough cinnamon to not overwhelm it." She looked at Rick and Adam, at Denny, then at Kendall. "It's delicious. I love it. Thank you."

"Happy birthday, baby," Kendall said, and gave her a quick kiss on the mouth. The crowd burst into spontaneous applause and then each person came up to hug her or shake her hand.

Andrea had never felt so loved.

"When you're ready, grab a case and come to the house," Cathy Foster said, raising her voice to be heard. "There are hot dogs and hamburgers, potato salad, lots of other food, and a cake for the birthday girl. Let's celebrate." With a quick kiss to Andrea's cheek, she and Kendall's father took their leave and others followed, Denny swooping up a box and hauling it out of the room. Soon, there was only Andrea and Kendall left.

"Do you really like it?" Kendall asked. "You can tell me the truth. It's just us now." She winked.

"I don't like it. I love it. It's delicious. And I can't believe you guys did this." Andrea stepped up to the bar and picked up one of the bottles, studied the label. "The logo?" She held the bottle up for Kendall to see.

"My buddy Eric designed it from a picture of you I gave him."

"So those really are my eyes."

"They really are."

Andrea looked back at her and grinned. "I have my own beer."

Kendall laughed then, a sound Andrea had grown to love more than any other. "You absolutely do."

"I don't know anybody else who can say that."

"Me neither."

They stood there for a beat, looking at one another before Andrea cocked an eyebrow. "You know this is totally going to get you laid tonight."

Kendall snorted. "Duh. Why do you think I did it?"

Andrea laughed, grasped Kendall's chin in her hand, and kissed her hard. When they finally broke apart, Kendall was breathing raggedly and Andrea was smiling with satisfaction. "Just a little preview."

Kendall used a finger to swipe the corner of her mouth. "And now I must go have dinner with that in my head. At my parents' house. Thanks for that." She gave Andrea a look.

Andrea kissed her on the forehead and headed for the door, beer in hand. Over her shoulder, she gave Kendall her sexiest half-grin and said simply, "Eat fast."

THE END

By Georgia Beers

Novels

Finding Home
Mine
Fresh Tracks
Too Close to Touch
Thy Neighbor's Wife
Turning the Page
Starting From Scratch
96 Hours
Slices of Life
Snow Globe
Olive Oil and White Bread
Zero Visibility
A Little Bit of Spice

Anthologies

Outsiders

Georgia Beers
www.georgiabeers.com